Brit Babes – British E
Sexy Just Walked

With stories from
Lexie Bay
Victoria Blisse
Harlem Dae
Natalie Dae
Lucy Felthouse
K D Grace
Lily Harlem
Kay Jaybee
Ruby Madsen
Sarah Masters
Tabitha Rayne

To Amy,
Enjoy the Brit Babes!
L Felthouse

Text Copyright 2014 © Lexie Bay, Victoria Blisse, Harlem Dae, Natalie Dae, Lucy Felthouse, K D Grace, Lily Harlem, Kay Jaybee, Ruby Madsen, Sarah Masters, Tabitha Rayne.

All Rights Reserved.

With the exception of quotes used in reviews, this book may not be reproduced or used in whole or in part by any means existing without written permission from the aforementioned authors.

Warning: The unauthorized reproduction or distribution of this copyrighted work is illegal.

No part of this book may be scanned, uploaded or distributed via the Internet or any other means, electronic or print, without the author's written permission.

This book is a work of fiction and any resemblance to persons, living or dead is purely coincidental. The characters are productions of the author's imagination and used fictitiously.

Cover Art by Posh Gosh.

Publishing Credits

Caught Naked by Sarah Masters - Especially for you, dear reader.

Corporate Punishment by Ruby Madsen - Especially for you, dear reader.

The Doll by Harlem Dae - Especially for you, dear reader.

End Result by Lily Harlem and Lucy Felthouse - Especially for you, dear reader.

Figment by Natalie Dae - Especially for you, dear reader.

Flesh for Fantasy by Lexie Bay - Coming Together with Curves, Coming Together, 2013.

Francesca's Mother by Tabitha Rayne - Oysters & Chocolate, 2012.

Red Rag to a Bull by Victoria Blisse - Coming Together with Curves, Coming Together, 2013.

The Scribe by Tabitha Rayne - Sudden Sex, Cleis Press, 2013.

Secret Servicing by Lily Harlem - Especially for you, dear reader.

Stones by K D Grace - Seducing The Myth, Lucy Felthouse (ed), 2011.

Topiary by K D Grace - Obsessed, Cleis Press, 2011.

The Wife by Kay Jaybee - Twice the Pleasure, Cleis Press, 2013.

The Wrong End of the Stick by Lucy Felthouse - Coming Together with Curves, Coming Together, 2013.

Underwear by Kay Jaybee - Sweet Confessions, Cleis Press, 2011.

Thank you for adding a copy of the Brit Babes Anthology to your book collection. We hope you enjoy the variety of the sexy stories nestled within these pages, each one a sample of the individual Babes' voices and styles. You'll find contemporary, BDSM, same-sex loving, ménage a trois, paranormal, sporty, military, Rubenesque and more. There's something to suit everyone here including a few Brit Babe collaborations to add extra spice to the collection.

So who are the Brit Babes? We are eight UK based authors who spend our days writing steamy tales of love and lust. Ranging from sweetly vanilla to so-hot-it-will-blow-your-mind we aim to please in every literary fantasy department. Our heroes are strong, determined and soul-achingly divine and our heroines sassy, sexy and not afraid to grab what they want. Passion and pleasure is the name of the game, romance and raunch a top priority and it all comes with a delightful sprinkle of kink.

With a whole host of awards, best-sellers and accolades between us we just know you'll find something in The Brit Babes Anthology that will keep you turning the pages and squirming on your seat. Then, if you like what you read here, check out the individual authors' websites to investigate their collection of published works. Also visit the Brit Babes' home on the web which acts as a library for the hundreds of books published by us. Tell your friends, spread the word, because one thing you can be sure of, is when the Brit Babes arrive, sexy has just walked into town!

Happy Reading!

Love,

The Brit Babes xx

Contents

- Flesh for Fantasy by Lexie Bay
- Red Rag to a Bull by Victoria Blisse
- The Doll by Harlem Dae
- Figment by Natalie Dae
- The Wrong End of the Stick by Lucy Felthouse
- Stones by K D Grace
- Topiary by K D Grace
- Secret Servicing by Lily Harlem
- End Result by Lily Harlem and Lucy Felthouse
- The Wife by Kay Jaybee
- Underwear by Kay Jaybee
- Corporate Punishment by Ruby Madsen
- Caught Naked by Sarah Masters
- Francesca's Mother by Tabitha Rayne
- The Scribe by Tabitha Rayne

Flesh for Fantasy

By Lexie Bay

I can't concentrate today because I am seeing her tonight. The thought makes my pussy wet. I crave her flesh, the smooth pale curves of her body. She is my obsession, my carefully guarded secret and she is filling my head with filthy thoughts about what I will do to her later.

My boyfriend thinks we are just friends. He doesn't know how much I yearn to be in her arms, how I ache for the contrast of her soft body as he holds me against his hard muscle. She isn't his type; he likes his women like me, boyish and skinny with no bum and tits that are only just a handful. Sophia is the opposite of me. My hands glide over her curves, fingers disappearing into the folds of her flesh, always a different place to explore as she moves beneath my touch.

My phone heralds the arrival of a text and I grab it. Please let it be from her. My need to be with her is bordering on insanity and I want to know that she is thinking about our evening together as much as I am.

Hey beautiful, I'm counting the minutes until you get here. I've got a treat for you later; I'm going to give you a makeover.

I smile because she wants me as much as I want her. I know this deep down but I hunger for the reassurance her words give me. No one has ever taken the time to woo me with words like she does, no one has taken the time to find out what I like and then turn my fantasies into reality. I am desperate for the evening to come.

I've dressed up for her tonight; my prettiest bra which tries valiantly to give me some semblance of cleavage and a tiny thong. Sophia wears beautiful French knickers, with frills and lace and satin. A thong would be lost in the abundant sweep of her sexy buttocks but she likes to tug mine to one side, the floss of lace the only thing between my lips and hers. She answers the door and I'm lost in her embrace as she holds me. I breathe in her warm, musky smell and she pulls me into the living room.

"God I've missed you Zoe," she says pushing a large glass of white wine into my hands. "I've been thinking about you all day. I'm totally behind in my new routine, the rest of the girls were getting completely fed up with me by the end of rehearsal."

Sophia is a Burlesque dancer. This means I get to see her milky white curves spilling out of divine corsets, her creamy thighs adorned with stockings and suspender belts on a regular basis. Her home is a cornucopia of vintage prints, feathers and pictures of beautiful women. She is Hollywood glamour and retro beauty made real, living and breathing in front of me. She must have just got back from practice because she is still wearing a dusky pink corset with matching knickers and fishnet stockings underneath a frilly tutu. She is taller than usual in a pair of sky high heels that accentuate the turn of her ankles and make her legs look very sexy. I pick up a feather boa that she has discarded on the sofa, wrap it behind her neck and pull her towards me, her full lips too irresistible not to cover in kisses.

Sophia moves away and takes both my hands. I want her lips on mine again but she is smiling. "Come into the bedroom; your treat's all set up. I'm going to pamper you before I fuck you."

My pussy clenches at her words, the harshness at odds with her beautiful, innocent face. I like to hear her talk dirty when we fuck, like to hear her tell me how I turn her on, what she wants me to do to her. I watch her pretty mouth as the words tumble out, *fuck me, lick my pussy, I want your fingers inside me*; and it makes me so wet for her.

I let her lead me into the bedroom and she sits me down on a chair that she has positioned in the middle of the room. Her makeup is spread out on the bed, bright colours in pretty packaging. Sophia is always trying to get me to be more adventurous with my makeup and tonight she is obviously excited to see me all dolled up.

She kneels in front of me and slowly removes my t-shirt. I'm embarrassed by my flat chest and try to cover myself but she shakes her head, her laughter infectious as she tickles me to keep my hands away from my body.

"Let me look at you, Zoe. You know how much I love your body."

"Not as much as I love yours," I reply, my fingers skimming over the smooth flesh spilling out of her corset. She is warm and soft and I cup my hands over her ample curves. I am torn between looking at her in her beautiful underwear and an overwhelming desire to see her naked, to suck a rosy nipple into my mouth as my hands wander amongst the folds of her body.

"Ah-ah, not yet baby. I have plans for you tonight." She undoes my jeans and motions for me to stand up so that she can remove them. "That is a very sexy thong," she says, stroking her finger over the scrap of material and I feel my pussy tighten again, a gush of warm liquid soaking it. Sophia smiles as she smells my desire.

"Sit back and relax. I'm going to make you even more beautiful than you already are."

I give in to her request and let her do what she wants with me. I watch her as she rubs something cool and wet into my face. It smells like rose and I breathe in, letting the soft fragrance relax me. Sophia's face is only centimetres from mine and it is so hard to stop myself kissing her. Her lips are full and pouty, a soft sheen of dark pink lip gloss making them look wet. They remind me of her pussy and again mine responds as I picture kissing it, my tongue sliding across her wet slit. I love to hear her moan when I go down on her; watch her face as she gives in to my tongue.

I can smell her face powder, a hint of rose, of moisturising cream and Chanel No 5. She smells how I imagine the Hollywood starlets would have smelled back in the days of Marilyn Monroe. Her red hair frames her beautiful face, the retro curls in stark contrast to her pale skin. I marvel again at how someone as beautiful as Sophia could be interested in plain old me. She makes me feel like a teenage boy, my body so different to hers. I covet her Rubenesque figure and her ability to make all the boys drool with her tits and arse.

She smoothes foundation over my nose and my cheeks, her cool fingers trailing over my lips. I kiss the tips of them. "Keep still," she laughs, stroking my face to blend the ivory liquid into my skin. She takes a step back to admire her handiwork and I see her eyes travel down my almost naked body. I can see the lust in her gaze and it gives me a thrill to know that she is thinking about fucking me, just as I am thinking about fucking her. This makeover is exquisite foreplay, her body so close, her breasts in my face, her legs between my thighs as she fusses around my face, touching up the base with concealer until she is happy with what she has done.

"It's no wonder I don't bother with all this," I mutter. "It takes forever." Sophia shakes her head. "But it's fun Zoe, it's like creating a piece of art. Your face is your canvas. You can be whoever you want to be."

"Don't you like who I am normally?" I ask, a little bit of self-doubt creeping in.

She tuts at me as she reaches for her brushes. "Zoe, you know I love you just as you are. I'm simply enhancing your natural beauty."

She stands back again. "And from where I'm looking, your natural beauty is outstanding." She's looking hungrily at me and my pussy floods again. I wonder if I will make a damp patch on the beautiful lilac velvet seat of the chair.

Sophia brings the little pots of coloured powder closer to the edge of the bed as she kneels between my thighs, pushing my legs further apart so that she can get as close as possible to me. She arranges everything just so, and I feel like it's a ceremony and I am the willing sacrifice. Unrolling a velvet pouch, she reveals an array of brushes. They are jet black in all different sizes and I watch as she peruses the collection, deciding on which one to use to inflict colour onto my face. I could watch her for hours, the gentle jiggle of her breasts against the satin of her corset.

She pulls out one of the largest of the brushes and swirls it through a pot of pink powder then deposits it on my cheek with a flourish. The brush tickles my skin and the scent of the powder fills my nostrils making me want to sneeze. Sophia repeats the process on my other cheek and grins as she looks at me. "You suit a pretty flushed cheek," she says. "It reminds me of how you look when you're turned on."

"I am turned on," I say, smiling back at her. "It would be hard not to be with your sexy curves so close to me."

"Am I making your pussy wet?" she asks, walking her fingers up my inner thighs towards my damp crotch. I spread my legs a little wider, bucking my hips in a desperate attempt to get her to stroke my throbbing pussy. She is teasing me, the mischievous glint in her eye telling me that I am not about to get relief anytime soon. Sophia purses her lips and blows on the brush, letting a fine dusting of pink powder rain down onto my thighs. She leans towards me again and trails the fluffy end of the brush over my cleavage. I gasp at the sensation of the brush on my skin, my nipples hardening instantly beneath my lacy bra so that they rub tantalisingly against the fabric.

Sophia runs her tongue over her bottom lip as she watches my reaction. Then she leans forward and runs it over the small curve of my left breast. Before I can react she blows gently on the wet patch, watching my skin pucker into goosebumps, sending darts of pleasure through my body. My breasts feel heavy and swollen, the nipples aching to feel her tongue, lips, fingers, anything.

She has something else in mind though and goes back to her pots of colour, biting her lip as she thinks about which colours to use to paint my eyes. I love how she gets all serious as she works on me. She trained at beauty school before she became a dancer and she knows her stuff.

She picks a small brush and dips it into a pale pinky colour. "Close your eyes," she murmurs and I do as I am told. The loss of my sight makes my other senses go into overdrive. I can smell the musk of her pussy and the hot scent of my own need. I can still taste the sweetness of her lip gloss and the smooth slide of her skin against my thighs is driving me crazy. She sweeps the brush over my eyelid. She is so close, her ample breasts rub against mine. I keep my eyes closed even when she removes the brush, waiting for her to continue. Letting her lips press against mine briefly, her free hand is on my leg before she moves to the other eye. Her breath is warm against my cheek as she concentrates on getting the colour even. I stay perfectly still, my eyes closed, waiting to see what she will do next, the thrill of the unknown making me wetter than I have ever been.

Sophia blows briefly over my eyelids to remove the excess and then I feel the soft bristles of a tiny brush stroke over my cheeks and linger on the bow of my lips. She teases me with the sensations, stroking and dabbing against my skin. I giggle as she tickles me, trying to squirm away but she holds my hand to keep me still.

"Stop wriggling," she chides, giving me a playful spank on the thigh. I am so desperate for her touch that I wriggle again, trying to get another slap.

"I know what you're doing," she says, "but if you can't sit still I'll have to make you." With that she grabs a silk scarf and binds my wrists together behind the chair. I moan softly as the material holds me tightly against the chair. I spread my legs a little wider, knowing that my thong is barely covering my pussy and that the sight of it will be making Sophia hungry for me.

I keep my eyes closed, wondering if she will continue with the makeup. I find out soon enough. She tells me to open my eyes, and I feel the cool of the mascara wand as she delicately flicks my eyelashes with jet black, defining and highlighting my features with her miracle touch. In that moment I adore her, the way she fusses over me like I am her living doll.

"So beautiful," she says, standing back to admire me, "but I think we need a little more work elsewhere. With that she slides her scarlet-painted fingernails into my thong and in one swift motion pulls it down my legs, flinging it unceremoniously across the bedroom. The sudden cool of the air on my pussy makes me moan and I look at her, watching as she studies the dark pink slit she has exposed. She kneels before me again and with a flourish, takes two more scarves and ties each ankle to a chair leg.

"Such a pretty little pout," she murmurs, "so pink and juicy. Did I do that to you?" She grins as she speaks, knowing full well the effect she has on me. I almost forget to breathe as I wait for her to continue. Slipping her hands into my bra, she pushes it beneath my tits, exposing my nipples. My mouth drops open and she kisses my lower lip, pinching each rock hard tip and eliciting a desperate gasp from me. "I love the contrast against your skin," she whispers, "like ripe berries dipped in cream." Again she picks up her brush but this time she wastes no time on my face, instead heading directly for the rosy buds of my arousal and surrounding them in the tantalising prickle of the brush tip.

Sophia flicks and twirls, painting my breasts with every colour she has laid out. I see her open her glitter and watch as she rains the sparkling particles over my small mounds. I am a rainbow, a colourful bird and she kneels to take a photograph of her handiwork.

As she puts the camera down she turns her attention to my glistening pussy. I can feel the liquid desire dripping onto my thighs, between the cheeks of my arse and I know, am sure, that I have left my mark on the pastel velvet beneath me. She slides a finger under me and presses the chair. "So wet," she marvels, "you've left a little imprint of your pussy for me. I should draw the shape and frame it. Better yet I should make you sit on coloured paper and mark that with your lust, you naughty girl. I would keep it by my bed to remind you of how wet I make your pussy."

I sigh as she reaches for me, the cool of her fingertip meeting the aching heat of my clit. She circles it gently and I arch towards her, a pathetic mewl the only sound I can make. I want her fingers inside me, her mouth on me. I want to be enveloped by her creamy flesh, to breathe in the perfume of her skin and lick the salty taste of her arousal from every nook and cranny of her body. I stretch out my leg and wrap it around the softness of her thigh, pulling her until she squashes against me. I could lose myself in her sexy, soft, curvy body for the rest of my life and I am almost shaking with the need to feel her hands on me. She knows what she is doing though and I know that she is not done with me yet. I am right.

Sophia stands and moves around the room. "These make up brushes are all very well," she says, "but I think we could get some interesting results with other kinds." As she speaks she is opening drawers and gathering items from around her bedroom. When she has finished she deposits them on the bed. I can see a large hairbrush, a toothbrush and a small comb amongst her haul. I gaze up at her adoringly, and she rewards me with a kiss, soft and tender and full of the promise of what we will do when she has finished with me. I wonder how long she has had me tied here, but it doesn't really matter. The rest of the world can go fuck itself when I'm here with Sophia.

She nestles back between my thighs and strokes her fingers up and down, getting teasingly close to my aching cunt before sliding back down to my knees. Leaning towards me, she slowly parts my lips until I am completely exposed. My clit hums with anticipation. "Please," I murmur and she smiles.

Picking up the makeup brush again, she slowly, delicately trails it over my clit. The sensation is incredible and I feel my pussy contract, sweet-scented liquid dribbling out of me. Sophia dips the brush into it and paints a heart over my shaven mound. Then she shakes glitter over it, watching it land on the sticky shape. When she blows away the excess I almost come just from her breath. She takes another picture and I feel myself open for her. I love being watched, exposed for her private view, knowing that every slick contour of my body is turning her on as much as I am turned on by her looking.

"Your clit looks like it needs some attention," she says and I nod, hardly daring to speak, my mouth dry with longing. She reaches out her hand and circles thoughtfully over the array of brushes. Then with a decisive nod she takes a toothbrush in her hand and slowly, gently applies it to my aching pearl. The bristles are sharp, much harder than the others and I squirm on the seat. Sophia rotates the head, barely touching me yet it feels as though she is running her fingernails over me. I pant, my body flexing and bucking beneath her touch. I long to have her press it hard against me, to rub me, the pressure that I crave to make me come so close and yet I don't want this exquisite torture to end.

She teases me some more, circling, pressing lightly then harder, then taking away the brush and blowing on my abused flesh. I can see how much the skin has darkened, the rush of blood to the surface, the swollen puff of my lips in contrast to the paleness of my thighs. She picks up the hairbrush, the thick handle taunting me as I picture it delving into my pussy, the smooth bulb of its length plundering my hole. I beg her to push it inside me but she shakes her head, tapping my slit gently with it, the solid wood slapping against my heated skin. It feels so good and yet it is not enough. I slide towards her on the chair, my thighs so far apart they ache and I know they will be a constant reminder of our evening; tomorrow when I am back in the office they will serve to give me exquisite flashbacks of the attention she is lavishing on me right now.

Tap, tap, tap; she is tormenting me, her fingers gliding across my stomach, edging ever closer to my swollen breasts. Finally she takes a nipple between her thumb and forefinger and twists, drawing a hiss of breath from me and as she does she slowly eases the bulbous end of the hairbrush inside me. I almost scream but her ruby lips find mine and she silences me with her kiss, sliding the length of the handle deeper. I can hear the sticky wetness of my pussy as it clutches at the intrusion. The sharp bristles mark my inner thigh and the pain only serves to heighten my desire. I am soaked, my honey running freely down the handle and over her fingers. I drop my head back and give in to the sensation of her fingers, the thick wood of the brush. She nibbles from my jaw line to my earlobe and then down to my neck, licking, biting and nipping at my skin. I look down, the sight of my rainbow chest against the milky white of hers making me shiver. She pulls back and we watch the dark wood of the hairbrush as it parts my swollen lips, the slurp and slip of its entry and exit turning me on even more. Kissing me again, Sophia's lips then travel over my breasts, down my stomach and as I open my legs wider for her she fastens them over my clit. Lips suckle; fingers pinch and the relentless thrusting of the thick handle leaves me in a melted pool of desire. She has ensnared me, has me captive and I am at her whim. I watch her flame red hair, the curls bouncing and bobbing around her face as she licks and sucks, her tongue laving the little bead nestled between my folds.

I feel my orgasm building, a wave of desperate longing which she is about to release. I can no longer think about anything except the feel of her, the scent of her and my complete submission to her ministrations. I exist only for her pleasure and she is determined to take every last drop of mine.

My legs are stiff, my body crying out as she laps and tongues at my pussy. The hairbrush has been discarded, replaced by her fingers and she has her hand in her knickers, frigging herself as she drags me ever closer to climax. I can hear the wet mess of her lust as her fingers glide in and out and as I breathe deeply I can smell her, mixed with my own desire.

I wriggle free of my bonds and let my hands wander through her hair, over the creamy skin of her back, her arms and around to the pillowy softness of her tits still encased in the dusky satin of her corset. I pop one out, then both, heavy in my palms as I tweak her nipples.

Her moan of pleasure sends me over the edge and with a low wail I feel my pussy contract around her fingers, the intense pulse of my orgasm leaving me incoherent as wave after wave of sensation hits me. There is nothing but her mouth and fingers, my world goes black as my eyelids flicker and I am whispering her name as my cunt twitches and jumps, creamy liquid spilling from me. I feel her breathe hot on me as she stiffens and I know she is coming too. The knowledge that I have done this to her grips my heart and makes me dizzy.

She slumps forward against me, her chest heaving, her fingers still inside both of us and I stroke her pretty skin, then smoothing her tangle of fiery curls. I shiver. Now that the heat of our lust has dispersed the room feels cold and she smiles up at me.

Sophia unties the scarves at my ankles and we slip under the feather duvet of her sumptuous bed. I am enfolded by the mattress, the duvet and her beautiful soft curves, a suffocating whiteness that I could sink into forever and never come back from.

I close my eyes and we sleep.

*****

More about Lexie Bay

Lexie lives with her two daughters on the south coast of England, and spends her days working as an accounts director. She loves the adrenaline rush of the unexpected, craves peace to write every day, likes to lose herself in the realms of fantasy and has a thing for smells that take her back to her childhood. She started writing to immerse herself in a fantasy world where women are adored and men fall at their feet but it didn't take long before she realised that sometimes men do that so you can stomp all over them in your sexy stiletto boots. Ever since then she's been creating stories that stay true to her original romantic dream while exploring the erotic, the kinky and the downright filthy.

Her style is contemporary naughtiness often with a twist of humour, because life is funny and she likes her characters to be as real as possible. So far she has had eleven short stories published and is currently working on her first full length novel.

Lexie is published by House of Erotica, Sweetmeats Press and Ravenous Romance.

Links

Website: http://www.lexiebay.co.uk
Twitter: http://www.twitter.com/lexie_bay
Facebook: http://www.facebook.com/LexieBayAuthor
Goodreads: http://www.goodreads.com/author/show/4475587.Lexie_Bay
Pinterest: http://pinterest.com/lexiebay/

Praise for Lexie Bay

Inside Looking Out **from** *Immoral Views*

"The story is hot, no doubt about it." **Amazon Review**

"Inside Looking Out is wonderfully written…. The sex scenes in this short novella are pretty steamy. The scenes themselves are dispersed throughout the lead-up to a final scene where Ms. Isabella Delaney's deepest sexual desire is sated in the middle of a room full of people at a very exclusive orgy. The little sex scenes sprinkled throughout do a good job of keeping one interested until big thrill at the end, and even serve to build up more for said thrill. This story features some dogging (a British sexual trend where a couple goes out and has sex with others watching, usually in a secluded place), some man on man action (surprisingly well written), and pegging that I wish could have been described more viscerally." **Mr Will's House of Thrills**

Taking Care of Business **from** *Smut In The City*

"What a wonderful read this was. I felt like I was reading one of those old mobster stories. Lexie Bay managed to convey the lust and heated love that the main character felt with exquisite detail. Great job!" **Amazon Review**

Best Supporting Actress **from** *Sex Toy Stories 2*

"Wow, I mean just wow! This is book of 12 stories by 12 seriously talented authors. Lexie Bay sure knows how to grab your interests with her story Best Supporting Actress. Holy cow she just shocked me with her toy of choice. I would have never thought of it being used for that purpose. Just goes to show you what a talented writer she is." **Amazon Review**

Red Rag to a Bull

By Victoria Blisse

I've not had sex in four years. I was miserable for one of them and I've taken Zumba classes for the past three. You're probably thinking that doesn't make sense, but believe you me, it does. I will be forever thankful for the day that Sharon, my workmate, told me about her dance class.

I laughed her down at first. I am not terribly well co-ordinated and I'm a big woman, I love my curves and I didn't want to lose them. But she explained it was just exercise, it wasn't a serious dance class and I could eat extra chocolate and cake to maintain my luscious body if I wanted to. The extra chocolate tipped the balance so I decided to try it out with her one night. It was fun. The first lesson I spent most of the time trying to not trip over my own feet or stand on anybody else's, but I enjoyed it. The upbeat music, the laughter and the sociability of it all.

I also loved the ache, the dull pain that told me my muscles had been used, the twinges that reminded me so much of the after effects of really good sex. I got into a routine, a routine I still follow. I'd go to my Zumba class, dance around like a fool, get sweaty, laugh, sing and work my big sexy butt off then I'd go home and masturbate.

I'd never stop to eat, drink or wash, I'd just get onto my bed and wank whilst the sweat was still beading on my skin and my muscles were on fire with exertion and I'd come. I'd come so hard it was just like having sex but without the messy bit. The other person and the emotional attachment you form to them. Perfection.

So Zumba and sex became one and the same to me. I shimmied and shook each week and wiggled my hips and imagined I was writhing against a man. A hot, sexy man with just enough muscle and a smile to melt my heart. In fact, when I saw him there a few weeks ago I thought I was having a really vivid daydream. It wasn't until we took a break that I realised he was a real true life man.

"Hi," I gasped between gulps of my water, "you're new."
"Yes," he replied. "I am."
"Enjoying it?" I asked.
"Not sure yet." He gripped a sports bottle in his huge, tanned

hand. I wanted those fingers to grip me. "I'll tell you when I'm capable of thought again."

"Fair enough," I smiled. "It does get easier, I promise. I've been at it for three years now."

"That's why you look so confident up the front then."

"No, that's just because you're viewing me from behind, you can't see the funny faces I'm pulling."

He chuckled. The velvet force of the sound rumbled in my chest, arousing my nipples and making me think of my post-Zumba session a little earlier than usual.

"I'm Dean, nice to meet you." He held out his hand and I grasped it, hoping my palm wasn't too sweaty.

"Grace," I replied. "Lovely to meet you too."

His fingers enfolded mine, exerted pressure but didn't crush me. I imagined it would be the same if we had sex, a bit rough but nothing I couldn't handle and give back in equal measure. I let his hand go reluctantly as the instructor's words pulled us back into positions for the next dance.

I was energised. I swung my hips powerfully, followed the steps with a precision that I didn't normally achieve, all because I knew his eyes were on me. We didn't get to speak again until the end because every woman in the class wanted to talk to him. That was clearly the bonus of being the only man in the room.

I changed my shoes and picked up my bag and slipped in beside him as he left the hall.

"So, will you be back next week, Dean?" I asked, much to the chagrin of the woman who I'd just slipped in next to, though she had a wedding ring on so she shouldn't have been flirting in the first place.

"Oh, definitely," he nodded. "Great work out, great company and I really would like to get some of the steps right eventually."

I put my hand on his bicep, noting its pleasant bulge, nothing fancy, just strongly sprung male muscle. I wanted to test it to its limits but in a much more private setting.

"You'll manage that next week," I said confidently, even though my stomach was churning with lust and nerves. "See you then?"

"Sure," he replied, "you couldn't keep me away."

I wouldn't want to.

There's no big cash prize for guessing who was on my mind

when I jumped into bed that night. I imagined us dancing alone, no instructor and face-to-face. I could see the sweat on his brow, the flex of his muscles, the sweep of his hips. He devoured me visually too, taking in my bouncing breasts, which even in a sports bra wobbled impressively with each movement. He dropped his gaze to my ample hips and long, curved legs as I cucaracha-ed side-to-side.

When the music stopped the fantasy continued. We hurried towards one another, crushed together in a mass of passion, lip-to-lip, crotch-to-crotch, burning with need and ripping off clothes.

I gripped my naked breast, plucked the nipple as I imagined him doing it. I ran my finger up and down my slit, gathering and spreading moisture and caressing my clit, bringing myself closer to the brink. I hurried my mental masturbation material on. We were completely naked and my back and buttocks were chilled by the wooden floor beneath me. He pressed his hard cock between my plump wet lips and I wrapped my legs around his long, lithe body, feeling the bounce of his taut buttocks with every thrust.

I came with a loud grunt, the visual dissipating as the orgasm bloomed and soon after withered away. I was left hungry, sweaty and wanting more. Zumba and masturbation were no longer enough, I needed a man between my thighs. I needed Dean.

I got to know him more with each session. We'd talk in the breaks. He'd put his water bottle down next to mine and we'd swig back the precious, cool elixir we needed, then we'd chit chat. I found out he was a mature student at the local University. He'd worked as a shelf stacker for some time and decided enough was enough. He joined the Zumba class to keep up the exercise that he was lacking because of the time his studies took up.

I also found out he enjoyed Italian food, James Bond films and was really rather ticklish. The last fact was the most fun to find out. We were bantering as usual after learning a new dance.

"I just can't get that move right, you know, where you have to put your arms together in front of you and pull down."

"That'll be your boobs getting in the way," he responded, straight faced. Then he cackled with laughter when my mouth and eyes went wide with shock.

"You cheeky bugger," I exclaimed, shooting out my hand to grab at him but he'd moved out of the way. My fingers landed just beside his nipple, almost under his arm and when I scrabbled to slap him he giggled almost girlishly and pulled away. We laughed hysterically together then. Tina, our instructor, had to yell at us to get us back to dancing.

I should have asked him out when I saw him at that second lesson, but I couldn't. I might not be backwards at coming forwards as my Gran likes to say but I was scared half to death he'd say no. Zumba was so much more fun with him to chat to. I didn't want to lose that. So I continued with my usual plan of action but instead of looking forward to my post-exercise wank I found it increasingly frustrating. I just wasn't satisfied, I needed more.

I'd always worn the same tracksuit bottoms and the same red, baggy top for the exercise class but as time passed and I felt more and more frustrated I came up with a plan to get Dean to proposition me. Other members of the dance class had sexy workout-wear down pat. I was sure I could find something to show off my ample roundness and as Dean always stood directly behind me, I could let my shapely arse do the seducing.

I bought shorts. Not teeny-tiny ones--dear God no, they'd ride up into my bum crack and me tugging the disappearing material back out would not be the way to seduce anyone. No, they were long enough to cover almost to my knee but tight enough to show off my butt when I bent down. I even invested in a slightly tighter t-shirt, one with a v-neck that I hoped Dean might look into when we had our dance interval chats.

I was all ready for him that night. I shaved my legs, since so much of them would be on show and I washed my hair before I went so at least it would start off looking sleek and sexy, held up high on the back of my head in a ponytail to keep it off the back of my neck. I slipped into red, seductive lace knickers and I was all ready for Operation Seduction.

"New workout clothes?" Dean asked when he arrived. He sat next to me and put his water bottle on the windowsill next to mine.

"Yeah, now the summer's coming I thought I'd go for something a bit lighter, you know."

Dean nodded. He always wore shorts and a vest t-shirt, no matter the weather, although he would come in with a hooded top on and strip it off before the lesson started. It was the Diet Coke moment of the night, you could hear a pin drop when he did it.

"And you'll give all the blokes on the bus a thrill by showing off your sexy legs, so everyone wins."

"Yeah," I replied, "though to be honest, I might wear some pants over them next week, some of the men leering were old enough to be my granddad."

"Ew." He made sympathetic faces to go along with the noises. "Well as long as you get them out for Zumba, it's all good."

I didn't know if he just meant that from a me not overheating perspective or for his own voyeuristic pleasure, but I took it as a good sign. Dean whipped off his dark blue hoodie and I watched intently, getting a sneak peek at the fuzz of dark hair around his navel as his t-shirt raised up too. I wanted to feel those hairs tickling against my stomach but before my thoughts could become any more lewd the call to Zumba was announced.

"Are you ready ladies?" Tina shouted.

"And Dean." We all echoed together. It was a long standing joke after the first week when Tina had to apologise half way through for calling him a lady. Every Monday, every class, Dean took it with an affable smile. What a gentleman.

I was sure he wasn't so gentlemanly in bed, though.

It was strange dancing in my new clothes, they pulled in when I least expected them to. I was far more aware of my breasts as my t-shirt stretched with my movements and when I reached up a little band of flesh was revealed to the cool air, chilling me. I wondered if Dean had noticed and my cheeks glowed red after far fewer songs than usual.

It was in one of the fast numbers where things started to feel weird. One of the moves involved squatting. Now squatting wasn't bad if I did it slowly, I could hitch the material at the front of my shorts to loosen things off. But the squats in a particular song were rapid and between other moves so I didn't have time to alter myself. My buttocks were cupped firmly, the crotch dug into parts I rather they didn't and by the midpoint I had sworn never to wear the bastard things again. I didn't care that Dean was getting a good eyeful of my bum, there was too much chafing for me to feel sexy.

Then it happened, that moment that all of us dread. I squatted, maybe I pushed it a bit lower than the rest or maybe the poor stitching just couldn't take any more but either way I heard a disconcerting rip followed by gasps and giggles from all around me. The damn shorts had split showing off the bright red knickers I had on beneath.

I quickly straightened and stood still. I reached round behind myself and surreptitiously checked out the damage. Yep, the seam had blown from top to bottom, I was completely undone. I had nothing with me to cover up with either. The hot day meant I hadn't thought to put on a coat before leaving. How the hell was I going to make it home with a big rip down the back of my pants? I wish I'd thought of that earlier, my mum always said I should plan and prepare for all eventualities.

Dean sprinted past me and I wondered what was going on, as the song hadn't finished. I smiled at Tina who flashed me a sympathetic look, although I had heard her laugh into the microphone a minute earlier, so maybe she was feeling a bit sheepish. There was a low murmur of conversation around me as the song continued and the class moved in unison, but many of them whispered to their friends about the tragedy of the poor woman on the front row.

I was seconds away from running out in sheer panic when Dean ran past me again. He came up close behind me and draped something over my backside. I moved my hands away and he embraced me from behind to push the arms of his hoodie around me.

"This will cover your blushes," he whispered. His breath tickled my ear.

I pulled the arms of the top around my waist and tied them in a knot. He stepped back and I looked over my shoulder. I smiled and mouthed a thank you. He grinned back before resuming the dance.

I continued too. It felt a little funny. The split material rubbed against me as I danced and the hole extended further. I just hoped it wouldn't run all the way round to the front. Then I would be in trouble.

"Thanks for that," I said to Dean after I swigged back my water. "You're a life saver."

"No worries," he responded with a smile. "As much as I appreciated the view, I knew it must have been mortifying for you. I'm glad I could help."

"Will I be okay to take this home with me, I mean, I don't want to get on the bus with split shorts."

"No." He took a sip from his water bottle and my stomach churned. Was he really telling me I'd have to go home displaying my knickers to the world?

"You're not going home on the bus, you don't know what kind of perv might be on there. I'll give you a lift."

"Are you sure?" I let out a sigh of relief and tried to hold in my excitement. He was only giving me a lift home, it didn't mean he'd want to come in and help me take care of business afterwards.

"Positive." He pushed the top down on his bottle and slammed it down on the sill beside me.

"Thanks." I took one last calming suck of water from my bottle then joined him back on the dance floor. I was definitely distracted for the last few routines. It was a combination of feeling the gap in my shorts as I moved and the anticipation of getting a lift home with Dean. The crotch of my knickers chafed against me, the damp cotton clung to my flesh as the stitching of my useless shorts rubbed up between my pussy lips. By the last song, the rip had extended right down the cleft of my buttocks, I could feel where the split stopped just at the bottom of my pussy. When I bent forward to stretch out my legs I imagined Dean behind me, clasping my waist and driving his cock into me. He'd only have to rip my knickers and he could do it.

"Are you ready?" he said afterwards.

I picked up my bag and my water bottle after slipping out of my dance shoes and into my trainers with as little movement as was possible. I didn't want to rip the shorts any further.

"Yep," I replied. "Thanks again for helping me out."

"No worries." He flashed me that heart melting smile once more. "I couldn't resist saving the damsel in distress."

"My hero." I clasped my hands before me and fluttered my eyelashes dramatically. We laughed together and I almost forgot about the mortifying embarrassment of what had happened earlier. That was until I overheard a stinging comment.

"Well, that's what you get for stuffing so much arse into such small shorts."

The words were followed by a gale of titters and I felt tears prick at my eyes. I love my curves, I'm not ashamed of them but it still upsets me when someone makes fun of me because of my shape. I am only human.

Dean put his arm around my shoulder and squeezed me. I looked up and smiled, I knew he'd be able to see the tears glistening in my eyes.

"At least you've got some arse," he said to me in a very loud stage whisper. "Some of the girls here just talk out of theirs."

I chuckled and looked across at the gaggle of women who'd

been so cruelly discussing my misfortune. Each one looked mortified.

"You should be ashamed." He looked directly at the woman in the middle, the clear ring leader. She at least had the decency to look down at the tips of her expensive trainers.

"And the rest of you too." None of them could meet his gaze. One lady stepped away from the others and looked at me.

"I'm sorry," she said. "I hope you're all right."

I nodded, I couldn't say anything. I was very grateful for her stand on the matter. She grabbed her workout stuff and walked out of the door, not hesitating to look back on the group who still huddled together, looking to the woman in the middle to see what they should do next.

Dean kept his arm around me and we walked away, out of the hall and down the corridor.

"Some people are just plain nasty," he said, squeezing me.

I shrugged gently, not wanting him to let go. I loved the feel of him so close to me. "I'm kinda used to it," I sighed. "And I did kinda bring this down on myself."

"No," he said forcefully. "It's not your fault, shoddy workmanship in the shorts and downright bitchiness from that woman, neither of them are your concern."

"Thanks," I smiled. "From me *and* my bum."

"You're welcome," he squeezed me again. "Now let's get you home."

It was quite a challenge getting into his car without further embarrassing myself. I held the sweatshirt in place with one hand and balanced myself with the other. When I sat down I felt fairly comfortable and just hoped I was covered.

I gave Dean my address and we set off. It was strange, we chatted so freely in the lesson but in the car I didn't know what to say. The silence was heavy, like an old itchy blanket, I wanted to remove it but I wasn't sure how to manage it.

"You know, red is my favourite colour." Dean grinned.

"Really?" I chuckled. "Well, you had a treat tonight then."

"Were they red? I hadn't noticed; I was too busy ogling your arse."

"Cheeky!" I spluttered, my cheeks warming with embarrassment.

"Oh, yeah," he moaned. I squealed and slapped his arm.

"My poor butt is feeling completely abused now."

"Oh, I've not even started abusing it…yet." He purred, keeping his eye firmly on the road ahead.

"Is that a threat or a promise?" I enquired.

"Both."

We pulled up outside my house and I turned to face him properly.

"I'm ever so grateful to you for saving my blushes, do you want your top back now?"

"Nah, it's okay, keep it until I next see you."

"Are you sure?"

Dean nodded but at the same time his stomach growled loudly enough so I could hear it.

"Look, I've got some delicious Moroccan lamb soup ready to be heated up for my dinner in the house and there's loads. Please come in and share a meal with me, it's the least I can do to thank you."

He paused for just a moment then replied with a hearty yes. I climbed out of the car without thinking about my arse. The split shorts became exposed at one point as I was scrabbling in my sports bag for the door keys, but I didn't do anything about it.

I slotted my key in the door at the second attempt and took a deep calming breath before I turned it. Not a single man had crossed the threshold into my house in years, it was quite a significant moment, even if the guy was only coming in for something to eat.

"So," I announced when I was sure he had followed me in. "I'll just go and get changed, then I can give your hoodie back and heat up the food—"

"Grace," Dean interrupted me mid flow. I turned to look at him and found him just centimetres away. I didn't get to answer him because before I could he forced his lips against mine and the rest of his body followed. I was stiff with shock at first then I blazed with arousal and pushed my curves against him wanting to feel all of him all at once.

I didn't let a logical thought enter my mind, I just let the pent up sexual frustration go wild. I gripped his shoulders and pulled him tightly to me.

He slipped his big, strong hands around my waist then lower to squeeze at my hips. His fingers dipped under the heavy material of his own top to squeeze my buttocks. I could feel the heat of his fingers through my lace knickers. He ran his hands appreciatively over the ample curve of my butt and I moaned directly into his mouth. He darted his tongue between my lips and I engaged it with my own, twisting and turning and caressing in time with the throb and ache of my needs.

I was pliant, completely and utterly enthralled by him and each new movement. I was floating around in a sea of endorphins and hungrily eating up the heat of his body, the weight of it against mine. I only just registered Dean fumbling with the jumper around my waist. It was only when it fell around my feet and left my split shorts exposed that I really paid any attention.

"Turn around," he said, levering his lips from mine. "Put your hands against the wall."

I pulled back and let him move away from me even though I ached with the lack of his hard muscles pressing into my softly giving places. I stepped forward and pressed my hands out in surrender against the wall. It was hard and flat but not as hot and exciting as Dean's body. I leant my breasts against its cool, unforgiving surface and waited.

My skin tingled, the blood that pumped around my body after the exertion of Zumba rushed all the quicker, excited by his kisses and caresses. My body was alive with need and it seemed to echo around me. I shifted uncomfortably. The mad rush of attraction wearing off a little as I stood exposed on my own. Just when the silence became too heavy to bear, I heard him moan deeply.

"Grace, you have the tastiest looking arse I've ever seen." Dean growled from behind me. He took a few steps and suddenly I was aware of his substantial body, the tickle of his breath on my neck. "I love watching it every week as you dance. I imagine such dirty things Grace, and today, my wishes came true. I nearly came when your pants split and I saw the flash of red, racy lingerie beneath. I covered you up quickly only because I was jealous, I didn't want anyone else to see. I want to see, to play with and feel your curves. Will you let me?"

I nodded silently, unable to force words from my dry throat. I felt objectified and I didn't mind. I liked being the centre of his fantasies. Knowing that every week I ogled his sweat soaked pecs he was appreciating my gluteus maximus made me glow with excitement.

Dean skimmed his hands down my back to my hips and I felt

the displacement of air as he dipped down behind me. I wondered what he was doing then his hands settled once again on my arse, massaging, making me very aware of how damp I was between my thighs. A second later I was exposed because he gathered up the lace of my knickers and ripped violently down. The delicate threads burst asunder and revealed my flesh to him. He held the sides of my ruined shorts apart along with the lace he'd just busted open. He stared at my buttocks. I couldn't move. I felt I could hardly breathe, locked under the weight of his gaze and shocked by what he'd done.

When his lips touched my left buttock I jumped slightly. They'd cooled after our hot kiss but soon warmed against the heat of my flesh. He peppered kisses all over my exposed curves, slow and soft, longer and harder. He had me whimpering and pressing my bottom out for more and when he bit me I thought I was going to explode with joy.

As he kissed he let go of one side of the ratty material and moved the attention of his fingers to between my thighs. He traced the split in my shorts which ran around the front. It was just the enforced crotch of my underwear that preserved what little modesty I had left.

I was both shocked and thrilled when I felt his tongue slip between my buttocks. I worried for all of a split second about how sweaty I might be after such an intense workout session, but when his searching tongue sunk deeper and caught the bottom of my puffed up lips I forgot to worry. Dean moved swiftly, prodding and poking while his fingers slipped to the bottom of my pants and with a sudden show of strength he ripped. The material gave and I felt cool air on my split, then his fingers and his mouth, vying to find purchase between my slippery lips.

I spread my thighs wide and pressed hard against the wall, holding on the best I could under his pleasurable assault. He pulled back for a moment and I re-grounded myself. I was about to suggest we moved somewhere more comfortable but before I could he was between my thighs again, sliding beneath me like a mechanic under a car. He grabbed my buttocks and buried his face into my wet cunt once again. His nose pushed against my clit as his tongue plunged deep inside me, scooping up my juice. He slurped and moaned rudely and my own yelps and groans of surprise blended beautifully with his muffled noise. I was shuddering and shaking, desperate for release. My nipples scraped against the confines of my sports bra and my cheek rubbed hard against the wall. None of these little irritations distracted me from the pleasure building where Dean's mouth attached to my body. He was concentrating his efforts on my clit, his tongue wiggled from one side to the other, then up and down, tickling me in an most erotic way.

My orgasm boiled within me, it coalesced and pulled together under his ministrations, different to all those self-aroused climaxes brought on by my own fingers or my vibrator. I was bent to his will, I was taking the pleasure he gave me and I wanted so much more but I couldn't hold on a second longer.

I know that exploding at point of orgasm is clichéd by I did indeed feel as if I was completely blown apart. My legs turned to jelly and I pushed even harder against the wall, struggling for grip, holding myself together any way I could, not wanting to collapse onto him. Dean lapped gently for a little longer, extending the vibrations of lust that shook me, then he pulled back and looked up at me. When I opened my eyes he was wiping my juices from his mouth and smiling.

He extracted himself from beneath me and I pushed myself away from the wall.

"You can go and get changed now," he said with a cheeky wink.

I laughed and held out my hand, "want to come upstairs and join me?"

He wrapped his fingers around mine and I pulled him upstairs after me and into my bedroom. I shut the door and turned around to find him directly behind me and once again he surged forward and kissed me. He helped me out of my t-shirt and I pulled off his, he unbuttoned my shorts –what was left of them –and they fell to the floor. We moved closer and closer to my bed and once I untangled him from his tracksuit bottoms we fell on to it, entwined in each other's arms.

It all seemed so natural, his skin was sheened with sweat and I could taste the salt as I nibbled his chin and neck and lower. He tasted good. I wanted to devour him, all of him and I slipped lower down the bed to come face-to-face with his erection, straining against black cotton boxer briefs. As I pulled them down, he lifted to help me.

I studied him, my mouth open slightly, taken by the beauty of having a real phallus right in front of me. I took in the texture, the dark pink colour, how it curved and strained, the moisture pooled at the tip that just called to be sucked. No matter how realistic my plastic cock was it just paled in comparison to the real thing.

I glanced up at Dean and he smiled with gentle amusement.

"I've not seen a real one of these in a long time," I explained with a blush. "I'm just reacquainting myself."

"I hear the best way to do that is to put it in your mouth." He kept his face solemn for a moment then winked.

"Oh it is, is it," I replied with a chuckle. "Well I suppose I'd better give that a go then."

The banter made it easier for me to lean over and taste him. Whereas a moment before I'd felt overwhelmed and very aware of my years of celibacy, after he broke the ice I just concentrated on enjoying the moment. He felt good between my lips and I loved his musky, masculine flavour. I sucked with vigour, taking more of him with each dip of my head. I stroked his balls and enjoyed the way they rippled beneath my touch. I remembered the joy of lapping at that little spot just beneath the head, the spot that makes men writhe and grunt. I loved Dean's noises, the desperation in his voice.

I popped him from my mouth, took a deep breath and asked him the big question.

"Can I fuck you?"

"Yes," he replied. "Oh God yes, of course you can."

I scrambled up and over him to reach into the drawer beside my bed. I prayed that the condoms would still be in date, I couldn't remember the last time I'd optimistically brought them. I had a sneaky look at the date before slipping it into Dean's hand and the year on it confirmed we were good to go. I lifted up from him just enough so he could reach between us and cover himself. My large breasts dangled over his chest and with their swaying tickled against his thatch of chest hairs. I wiggled with purpose, enjoying the sparks of lust that ignited on the tips of my nipples and spread down through my flesh to suffuse me with a sexual glow of anticipation.

"Ready," he growled, and I shuffled a little lower, my knees against his hips, my inner thighs against the outside of his. I lowered myself down, hit the tip of him and he manoeuvred his dick until it hit the right spot. I sank down and he removed his hand from around his erection but left it to sit between us in the sweet slit of my wetness.

I was consumed by the warm stretch of his girth and amazed

by the way I gave so easily to his invasion, his way eased by my juices. I squeezed around him once I was fully seated, enjoying the slight give compared to the plastic rigidity of my vibrator. He throbbed in time to my squeezes and his heat matched mine. I was lost in glorious sensation.

I eventually moved. As good as it felt to be fully filled, there was a gap of need and to satisfy that, it was essential that I lifted and lost some of that completeness. It was the yo-yo from full to almost empty that felt close to perfection. It was when I found my rhythm, steady and fast but not quite a salsa, that I became aware of the hand between me and the soft give of his pelvis. His knuckle was raised and hit my clit when I dipped down, his fingers were spread around his cock so that they pressed against my soft folds when I was fully immersed in him.

I felt my orgasm approaching. I couldn't open my eyes even though I wanted to see his face, I couldn't do anything but hold on to his upper arms and power myself up and down. I wondered for a moment if he was watching me, my eyes screwed up, cheeks flushed, boobs bouncing wildly. I knew he was enjoying himself, his groans and the grip of his free hand on my fleshy hip told me that.

I shook and stumbled in my dance as intensity got the better of me. I held him deep inside as I came. I loved the rigidity of him inside me that did not budge while I throbbed and vibrated and screamed out the second orgasm gifted to me that day. Somewhere in amongst my rocking, yelling and revelling he came too, just as loudly.

I slid with little grace and much gravity to the bed beside him. He rolled over and rested an arm across my waist. I looked at him, took in his flushed face, his sparkling eyes.

"I'll have to split my pants every week if this is what comes of it." I gasped as I struggled to control my breathing.

"Well, if you promise to flash me your knickers each week I promise you I won't be able to help myself from ravishing you."

"Red rag to a bull?" I laughed.

"Exactly." He nodded and kissed me. I could see a new post-Zumba workout routine on my horizon and I liked it.

*****

More about Victoria Blisse

Victoria Blisse is a mother, wife, Christian, Manchester United fan and award winning erotica author. She is also the editor of several Bigger Briefs collections, and the co-editor of the fabulous Smut Alfresco and Smut in the City and Smut by the Sea Anthologies.

She is equally at home behind a laptop or a cooker and she loves to create stories, poems, cakes and biscuits that make people happy. She was born near Manchester, England and her northern English quirkiness shows through in all of her stories.

Passion, love and laughter fill her works, just as they fill her busy life.

Links

Website: http://victoriablisse.co.uk
Twitter: http://twitter.com/victoriablisse
Facebook: http://facebook.com/victoriablisse
Goodreads: https://www.goodreads.com/author/show/1941449.Victoria_Blisse
Pinterest: http://pinterest.com/victoriablisse

Praise for Victoria Blisse

"When I want an uplifting erotic read one of my favourite go-to writers is Victoria Blisse. There's a real feel-good factor about her erotic writing and it comes from the combination of her inimitable saucy approach to the subject matter and the down to earth good lovin' she conveys so well. It tickles me in more ways than one and makes me happy." **Saskia Walker**

"You cannot go wrong with a story by Victoria Blisse. Her characters are believable and their conflicts lead to the most delicious resolutions." **Kristina Wright**

The Doll: Spin-off Story From the Sexy as Hell Trilogy

By Harlem Dae

It was nearly midnight, midnight on St. Valentine's Day. It would have been traditional to be arriving home from a romantic candlelit meal with a lover, but all that mush wasn't for me. For three years now I'd kept my heart well out of harm's way; it was the way I rolled, the way I stayed sane.

I reached for a big, soft brush and my Frankly Scarlet rouge. I overly made up my cheeks, centring the colour into round apple shapes. My base layer of foundation was porcelain-white so it was a shocking contrast with the blush, almost geisha-like. My blue eyes were set off with golden glitter on the lids and lashings of kohl, and my lips were slick with sticky candy-pink gloss that tasted of sugar.

It was an artificial, stage-show look because that's exactly what I was about to do—go on stage.

Midnight was my time as Vicky the Domme Doll—she always had that slot. But would *he* be here tonight, waiting, on the edge of his seat—my silver fox?

Lately I hadn't been able to stop thinking about him. Mr Kennett was his name, or at least that's who he'd registered as when he'd joined Sexy as Hell. Goodness knows if it was an alias or not. Many of Zara's clients used fake names. The reception girls called him Mr Dresden, which was a little unkind, I thought. They understood kinks—they were all as kinky as fuck. So what if he liked tossing off to a bossy, whip-wielding doll and appreciated a short blue polka-dot dress teamed with red and white thigh-length socks. That was up to him, that's what this place was all about.

Catering to needs.

Of guests *and* employees.

I stood, straightened the frills around my low neckline, and fluffed the puff-ball sleeves. It really was the sweetest of my dresses this one, and probably my favourite.

Turning a full three-sixty, I admired myself in the mirror. I was edging thirty but I still had it. Could still get it, if I wanted to. Thing was, nobody really got me going anymore.

Except him.

Damn, where had that thought come from? I knew I'd been thinking of Mr Kennett a lot but I hadn't actually realised up until this point that he'd affected me physically.

I stilled and stared in the mirror, ran my hands over my pert breasts and slim waist. Did I want him to touch me? Did I want to touch him? I guessed the answer was yes. Yes, finally I was ready, again, for more than just a scene. For something that had meaning, that made me excited to see how another individual—not just a body or body part—could make me feel.

And on Valentine's Night, too. What a sap I was after all.

I laughed, my reflection outrageous, over-the-top and slightly manic.

Perhaps I'd shake things up tonight, if I could. I was surfing a crest of excitement; I should hang on for the ride.

* * * * *

The showroom was set as usual with a small striped podium that I stood my subs on—to start with, at least. Tonight it was Carlos in place and he stood, head bowed, wearing tight leather trousers that had gaps at his buttocks, giving me great access to his super-sweet arse.

Carlos belonged to someone else, but he was a complete pain-whore and his Mistress didn't have any objections to him finding satisfaction with me. I enjoyed using him because when we were in a scene he was never anything but wholly submissive, which suited me well.

Strutting in, I let my hands sweep over the row of whips and floggers, agitating them as I eyed the semi-circle of windows that led to the private viewing rooms. It was quiet tonight—no, make that dead. Each window was empty. I had no audience.

What the fuck?

I shoved my hands on my hips and scowled, feeling the thick makeup on my forehead creasing.

"There's no one here," I said.

"No, Mistress, no one waiting in reception, either," Carlos replied. "I guess they're all out being romantic."

I tutted. "Waste of time all of this, then." I gestured to my face and down my body. It had taken me nearly an hour to organise my get-up.

"Doesn't have to be," Carlos said. He caught my gaze and then quickly looked away as a rise of colour stained his cheeks.

Insolent sod; he knew damn well that in here he wasn't allowed to look me in the eye without permission. For that I *wouldn't* whip his bare arse.

There was a noise to my right. I turned and spotted a man entering viewing room six, the end one.

It was Mr Kennett.

My heart gave a ridiculous little flip as I watched him pause and take a deep breath. He appeared to have been rushing. He pushed his fingers through his peppery grey hair and then straightened his dark tie. He wore a pristine black suit jacket, as usual, and a crisp white shirt. I presumed his lower half was just as well tailored but I'd never seen that; he'd always been in room six when I arrived and the window stopped my view at his waist.

"I'm going to do something different tonight," I said to Carlos. "So just stand there and shut the fuck up."

"Yes, Mistress."

I wasn't sure if Zara would agree to my plan, but I was going to give it a shot—while I was feeling brave and while I had a slick of damp in my knickers that had arrived at the same time Mr Kennett had.

Walking up to the window, crossing my footsteps over each other in an exaggerated way, I set my sights on my one viewer. When I reached the glass, I stopped and curled my right index finger at him in a come-hither action.

He tilted his chin and swallowed, his Adam's apple dipping just below the fastened collar of his shirt.

I cocked my head and raised my eyebrows.

He stepped up to the window.

This was the closest we'd ever been despite his visiting my show twice a week for nearly three months.

"It seems you are the only member of my audience," I said.

He nodded. His eyes were a pale shade of blue, almost lilac, and his lips, though thin, were very sensuous. He had a small scar on the rise of his right cheek, shaped like a fat, rolling tear, and I noticed a few crows' feet, but up close he appeared younger than I'd first thought, perhaps early forties, nothing more.

"So I think we'll do something a bit special," I said. "Get to know each other better."

"Works for me," he said, his voice journeying through the speaker next to the glass.

It had been surprisingly steady considering the connotations beneath my words. He knew what I was capable of. Had witnessed me driving Carlos and others wild with severe thrashings. Doling out erotic torture was my specialty.

I might look as though I would melt with sweetness, but that was just a ruse. My dolly smile was designed to put subs at ease and lull them into a false sense of security.

"Do you know what I like the sound of?" I asked.

"Tell me." He twitched his eyebrows.

His expression was almost defiant, and if he'd been mine I'd have given him a nipple pinch for that.

Oh, my breasts got heavy at the thought of a sharp squeeze. Sometimes I wore my clamps when I took to the stage and let the sting zap around my body as I lashed out whatever punishment my co-performer had agreed to. The discomfort gave me a euphoric headiness that hit my spot and reminded me why my subs enjoyed taking their beatings the way they did. It made them high as kites.

Tonight I hadn't worn my clamps. But maybe…

I came back to the moment, to the question I'd put to him. "I love this sound," I said, pacing up to Carlos and thwacking him as hard as I could on his left buttock.

He didn't even flinch despite the bite of pain that shot from my palm up to my shoulder and into my teeth.

Damn, I should have grabbed a whip.

As I frowned and rubbed my hands together, Carlos' round globe of flesh bloomed and I knew he'd have at least a semi from that, if he hadn't had one already, that was.

"I get off on that sound," I said, "the sound of flesh on flesh, a flogger on flesh, a whip on flesh." I smiled angelically and twisted one of my long blonde plaits over and under my fingers in a distracted manner. "I'd like to hear the sound your flesh makes when I hit it, Mr Kennett. Are you up for that?"

He walked nearer to the glass, his breath creating a tiny round fog. "I'm up, that's for sure."

His mouth pressed into such a flat line that his lips damn near disappeared, and I had no doubt in my mind exactly what was standing to attention.

I swiped my tongue over my sweet lip-gloss and fluttered my eyelashes. "Well, in that case, I'm coming to get you. Wait there."

Bugger, I hoped Zara *would* go along with this. I was sure

she would—after all, what did she have to lose? I'd pay for the hire of one of the privacy lounges if that's what she wanted. I just needed to have Mr Kennett alone for a while. Find out why he came to see me so often. What it was that sometimes compelled him to wank while I performed, other occasions hardly even moving or blinking as I tortured some lucky sod into a state of orgasmic frenzy.

I slipped from the show room. Carlos was close behind me, his breaths loud and his footsteps heavy.

"Vicky," he said. "Pardon me for asking, but what the fuck are you doing?"

"Don't speak to me like that." I turned and waggled my finger at him. "I'll tell your Mistress you've been impertinent."

He huffed. "And then I'll get punished, which is a bad thing?" He pulled a face and his eyes sparkled.

I knew damn well his punishments always ended in him coming magnificently, so it was hardly a threat on my part.

I tsked. "Okay, but I'm not performing when there is only one member of the audience, it's pointless."

"My arse doesn't see it that way, if you don't mind me saying, that is."

"Well, your arse will just have to remember that getting beaten is a perk of the job, not a guarantee."

"I guess."

"Where's Zara?"

"She's out, with her Virgin."

"Oh, yes, I forgot." Damn, now what should I do? Just go ahead with my plan?

"With all due respect, Vicky, you hardly know him."

"We all have to start somewhere. And I want to *get* to know him."

"You do?" He raised his thick eyebrows. "Mr Dresden, really?"

"That's not his name." I scowled. "And, yes, I like him, and clearly he likes me—"

"But—"

"Shut the fuck up, Carlos." I was losing patience. "You have no idea what I've been through and how many years I've waited for someone to come along who yanks my chain." I calmed my voice. "And he does, so just forget the protective big brother routine."

He shrugged. "Just letting you know I care."

I sighed. "I'm sorry." I glanced away. "Perhaps it wouldn't do any harm for *you* to escort him to one of the lounges and then tell him you'll be outside and if he tries any funny business you'll rip his limbs from his body."

Carlos flinched, as though he didn't like the violent image. Odd when erotic thrashings got him off so spectacularly.

"I'll certainly give him a warning," he said, "though I've never doubted you being able to handle a bloke, Vicky."

"You've never seen me with one."

"Exactly." He grimaced and shoved his hand down the front of his tight leather trousers, appearing to adjust himself.

"Sorry about that," I said, nodding at his impressive bulge.

"No worries, you were right, it's a perk of the job getting a whipping from you. I can't complain, I get enough of them."

"I'm sure your Mistress will see to your needs."

"If she thinks to."

"She will." I rested my hand on his thickly muscled bicep.

Carlos was a hunk of power, all hard and coiled and ready to explode. He didn't, though, he kept himself calm and was always graceful in his movements. He also adored his Mistress and was undemanding and grateful for anything she gave him.

Carlos turned and headed towards reception. "You wait in lounge two and I'll get him," he called over his shoulder.

"Can you grab my bag, too, the red one, from my dressing room…please?"

"Sure."

I darted as fast as I could on my heels to lounge two. Opened and shut the door, leaned back against it, and stole a couple of rapid breaths.

The air smelled of polish, and the room was warm and dimly lit by two table lamps and an artificial fire. In the centre was a couch, double-bed sized and made of white leather—easy to clean. Above the fire was a plasma TV linked to porn channels and to the show room, but it was off, the screen black and still.

I stooped and straightened a stash of erotic magazines that were set on the low table. I lined them up and stared at the buxom topless lady on the front. She had enormous chocolate-drop areolae and pouty red lips.

After a minute or two a knock at the door had me catching my breath.

I straightened, turned, and pulled my plaits over my ears so they hung down to my tits. I'd tied little blue ribbons on the end to match my dress.

I blew out a breath and tried to settle a tumble of nerves in my stomach. This was it, the moment I'd been subconsciously wanting for weeks.

My silver fox was here.

But was he just a cunning predator, wily and clever and out to see what he could get from me? Or did he have something to offer in return for my Dominatrix services? Could we be more than a symbiotic BDSM relationship?

I hoped so, and finally, I'd plucked up the courage to find out.

* * * * *

This woman would be the death of me.

I stood outside the room with Carlos, the man I'd watched Vicky the Domme Doll spank on more than one occasion. Of course, I wished she'd been doing that to me—or that she'd let me smack her pert arse instead. Either way I'd be happy. The fact that she'd asked me to this room… What did it mean? Jesus Christ, I was nervous—more nervous than I'd ever been—but it wouldn't stop me from seeing what she was like in a one-to-one situation. Unless Carlos was going to join in?

I wasn't sure how I felt about that. Another man sharing her with me?

Fuck, no. No.

Carlos lifted his hand to knock on the door but must have changed his mind. He lowered it, giving me a look that said so many things at once. A sub he might be, but if I made one wrong move, I had a feeling he'd kick the shit out of me. Brawny as he was, he'd knock me down no trouble. Not to say I was weedy—lithe and compact was more like it—but still, I didn't fancy finding out just how far this man would go if pushed.

"You're to go in alone," he said, his voice gravelly. "But I'll be outside—right here. You follow the same rules as the ones you signed for when you first joined. You deviate, you'll have me to deal with. Understand?"

"Yes," I said, bristling a bit. "Why would I choose to break them and risk not seeing—coming here again?" I'd nearly revealed my true feelings for Vicky, and that wouldn't do.

No getting romantically involved with the staff—rule number one.

I was fucked there. She invaded my dreams most nights, appearing as the delicious little doll she was. I'd wondered, too many times to count, what she'd look like without those dresses of hers on, without the makeup. Just as pretty, just as hard-on inducing I was sure, but I wanted to know, I wanted to see *her*, inside and out.

"I didn't think you would," Carlos said. "I was just making sure." He frowned at me, cocking his head. "Vicky's one of my friends."

There had been no need to tell me that. I'd got what he was saying way before then. Mess with her, he'd mess with me. Did I look the deviant type, was that it? Or had another customer treated her badly in the past? If they had and I knew who it was, I'd string the bastard up.

I nodded, wishing he'd just open the door so I could get inside to see her. I imagined her there alone, waiting for me, hoping for more than she was probably willing to give. But who the hell shacked up with their customers? She must have a boyfriend or husband tucked away somewhere, I was sure of it. How could she not, a beautiful, dainty little thing like her?

Carlos rapped on the door then turned the handle.

My guts rolled over. This was it, my time with her, no one else present—no sharing. He pushed the door—it appeared to be stuck—then abruptly it flowed wide, bringing the whole of the room into view.

Vicky wasn't there.

My excitement sank, and I immediately thought she'd had a change of heart. She'd been rash, hadn't she, inviting me in here. Or had Mistress Zara put a stop to it?

I looked at Carlos, who gestured for me to enter, and he handed me a red bag.

"Give this to your dolly," he said.

That was trust, right there—then again, this place was crammed with cameras. I wouldn't dare to root about inside Vicky's property—unless it was her cunt, arse, or mouth, and only then with her permission.

I stepped inside, and the door was closed. I didn't know what to do with myself so took in my surroundings. Very nice. Very comfortable.

"Do you like what you see?" Vicky asked from behind me.

I turned around, heart leaping, to see her standing beside the door. There she was, my dolly, cute as a fucking button and pressing all mine just by being in the same room as me. I swallowed, smiled, and nodded—the only things I could manage.

"Are you Dom or sub?" she asked, pushing off the wall and holding her hand out.

I wished she'd been doing that to wrap her fingers around mine, but it was clear she wanted her bag. I lifted it up and she took it, delving inside as soon as she'd got it open.

"Only it makes a difference to what I pull out of here," she said.

"Both," I said. "It depends."

"I see. So you come here to watch me, a Domme, yet you have Dom tendencies yourself. This should be interesting."

It would be—depending on how far she was prepared to go. I wanted all the way—*all the damn fucking way*—but did she? Vicky had only mentioned the sound of spanking...

I'll take that. I'll take anything.

"Remove your clothes," she said nonchalantly, as if she said that kind of thing to men all the time.

I was startled but refused to let it show on my face. I'd proclaimed to be a Dom sometimes, and Doms didn't falter. They got on with it. As did subs. They obeyed without question. I stripped off my suit and shirt, going for casual as I fiddled with my tie and the buttons, acting as if *I* did *this* all the time. I wanted to be a match for her, not some weird freak she might think me to be. Some bloke who stared at dolls through windows and wanked while the doll smacked some other man's arse. Maybe I was weird, but she catered to my fantasies, and...weird or not, I'd enjoyed myself every time I'd watched her. She had grace, nothing brash about her when she put on a show. When she struck with a paddle or whip, it wasn't hurried, it was as though she was born to do it.

Her calling.

I want her to call me. After tonight. And while we're in here? Call my name as she comes.

I threw my clothing onto the coffee table. The smut mags fell off, landing on the floor with a *thwap*. I stared at them, a fan shape, where only sections of women's bodies on the covers were displayed. A seductively placed leg, one half of an exposed breast, and the mag on the bottom, a woman's cunt spread wide for all to see. I didn't mind porn, but I'd prefer to see the pie as a package rather than the contents spilling out.

Vicky's contents, though, they were another matter, and I had many fantasies that I'd like her to be the star of. Starting as soon as possible.

"My, my," she said, coming towards me then circling around me until she stood right in front. "That's an impressive sight."

What, my body as a whole or my rock-hard dick? Was I a Dom or a sub here? The rules hadn't been made clear, so I wasn't sure whether to thank her as my Mistress or come out with something a Master would say. I had to know the boundaries, had to ask.

"What am I?" I said, staring into her eyes.

"Whatever you want to be. I'll play switch if you will."

She batted her eyelashes, and shit, I'd do anything she asked. I reached out to place my fingertips on the swells of her tits, letting them linger before drawing my touch down towards the low neckline of her dress. She didn't flinch, didn't shy away, and I took that as a positive. Did she find me attractive? There was no question I found *her* attractive, my cock showed her that.

"This is you," I said, taking my cock in free hand. It was weighty, throbbing, and thick with my need for her. "Because of you. No one else makes me this hard." There, I'd given a confession of sorts, my way of letting her know how I felt about her. Either it would put her off or make her step back—or she might well think I'd just said it for something to say.

She widened her eyes a little, as if what I'd said had surprised her, yet at the same time she looked pleased. A small smile lifted the corners of her mouth, and she closed her eyes briefly. I imagined that's what she'd look like when coming, and my dick ached—fucking hell, it *ached*.

Instead of answering, she pulled her hand out of her bag and handed me something. I couldn't see what it was until they were nestled in my palm. Nipple clamps, diamante with a small ring on their tops. I stared at them a moment longer then raised my head to look at her. She'd asked me to put them on.

On her or me?

I hesitated, then, "Do you have any more of these?"

She lifted her eyebrows, delving back into her bag, maintaining eye contact all the while. Out came another set—ruby-encrusted this time—and held them out. I took them, my fingertips skimming hers, and a rush of lust—ball-busting, heady lust—went through me.

I released my cock, took the diamante clips and attached them to my nipples. The pinch far exceeded anything I'd experienced before, and I let out a long groan. She licked her lips at that, the pinkness of her tongue compared to the white of her face a deep contrast. She lightly bit the tip of her tongue, breathing unsteady, the pulse in her neck fluttering.

I stepped forward and, ruby clips in one hand, I used my other to drag down her neckline. She was braless and her tits popped out, heavy and begging for me to touch them, suck them, slip my dick between them. Her nipples were hard, rigid points that I longed to roll my tongue around. I glanced up at her face to check she was okay with what I was about to do. She sighed, thrust her chest out, and closed her eyes.

I hovered one clamp over a nipple, wanting her anticipation level to skyrocket. I counted silently to thirty, knowing how slow it went when you were on the receiving end, when you wanted something so bad and it was there, right there, just not there enough.

I counted another ten seconds.

Then let the clamp snap onto her nipple.

She bucked her hips, sucked in her bottom lip. I stared at how her flesh was squashed between the sharp little teeth biting it, at how she fought against the pain. Her hands were by her sides, one clenched into a fist, the other clutching her bag, and she kept her eyes closed. Irregular pants came out of her, as if she were frantic not to divulge any more emotion. *My* breathing was erratic, and I coached myself to bring it under control. Difficult, when all I wanted to do was crush the woman to me and touch her all over. Kiss her, show her with my mouth that I was full of passion. Whisper dirty words that would send her towards an orgasm that was more explosive than any she'd had before.

I held the second one over her other breast. Counted again. She must have known what I was doing, how I was playing this, yet she didn't protest. I waited a few beats then let the teeth do their thing, gnawing at her tit and hopefully giving her the same steely pleasure-pain as I was getting from mine. My areolae throbbed, the surrounding skin burned, and my bollocks drew up as I imagined jerking at her clamps and giving her a fresh burst of cunt-soaking agony.

"God," she whispered. "Oh, my God…" She opened her eyes, staring directly into mine. "Take my bag," she said breathlessly. "Look in the…in the side pocket. The one with the…zip. Little chains."

I did as she'd asked, dropped her bag to the floor then tested the links by giving them a sturdy tug. They had attachments on the ends, and I looked from my chest to hers. She nodded. I raised my eyebrows. My initial thoughts as to what these toys were for was clearly correct.

Fuck, she likes the same damn thing I do.

I clipped the ends to the rings on my diamantes, letting the slim metal ropes dangle to just above my navel. The added weight, although not *that* much, drew the clamps down. A fresh wave of pain radiated outwards. I watched her watching me, then, after she'd nodded again, I secured the attachments to her ruby-studded rings. We were joined by thin silver threads that bowed—any jerky movements from either of us could rip the clamps clean off or have them gripping harder. Whatever happened, the pain would be unique, mind-blowing.

"What do you want me to do now?" I asked.

"Step away," she said. "Until the links are straight."

It meant moving away from her, erasing the close proximity where her body heat reached me and I could imagine what she'd feel like flush against my body. But if it meant doing something she wanted or needed, I'd forego the pleasure I'd so far gained from being near her.

I stepped back once, gauging how many more paces it would take before the chains were how she wanted them. One more would do it. I moved again. Her tits rose with the pull, nipples slightly elongated, and she sucked in a breath. If her tits were being tortured as much as mine and she loved pain, she'd be in seventh heaven now.

A guttural sound came out of her, maybe a garbled word that hadn't quite formed properly, and she tipped her head to look at the ceiling, exposing the arch of her slender neck. I was torn between so many actions. Stepping forward to kiss her throat, licking up the column until my tongue reached her jawline then her mouth, where I could take her lips in a savage kiss; staying put; or easing away just a bit more to increase the pressure.

"Tell me what you want," I said.

She swallowed, lifted her head, and stared at me. "Hold the chains and tug them."

I obeyed, pulling carefully, flicking my gaze from her tits to her face to check she was okay. She sighed, a flush appearing on her chest and neck, and her doll-like appearance suddenly didn't belong, didn't matter. I'd spotted her in the reception area, the beautiful Vicky, before she'd got dressed in her frilly gear. Mistress Zara had told me who Vicky was, and I'd booked room six immediately, waiting patiently inside for her show to start. That she was a painted doll when she appeared had made me think I had a kink I'd never discovered, but now? No, it was Vicky herself.

I brought the chains together in the middle so I could hold them in one hand. With the other, I smeared away her rouge, her lipstick, swiping the makeup from my thumb onto the side of my thigh. I kept going until it was almost gone and the real woman was displayed. She didn't complain, didn't do anything but stand there as I denuded her face, letting out more sighs every time the links were jerked. Her skin was soft, her lips softer, the bottom one fleshier than the top. I stepped forward, pulled again, dragging her closer. With a final, nipple-wrenching jerk, she cried out and her knees gave way.

I caught her in my arms, dragging her small body up to mine. My cock became folded within the material of her dress, and the steely coolness of the metal attached to her tits pressed into my chest, a delightful sensation of hot and cold.

"Vicky," I gasped, looking down into her face.

A smear of mascara swept from the corner of her eye to her temple, and now I could see a true rise of colour on her cheeks, not one created by powder.

"Yes, Master?" she said, moving her body against mine as she hitched in rapid breaths.

"I want to take you to the places you take others. It's your turn tonight, to give it up." Damn, I hoped she went along with my suggestion.

She was silent, staring into my eyes as though searching the absolute depths of my soul. She licked her lips and her jaw slackened. I could almost feel the tension leaving her body, from her face to her shoulders to her back and legs. She became heavier leaning onto me, and I knew I had her.

* * * * *

My silver fox had a dominant streak and it wasn't a feeble thread, either. By the look on his face, it was a goddamn thick wedge that ran right through to his core.

"I need to go there," I said. "But…" It had been a long time since I'd subbed, and then it had been to someone who I knew more about than just their fake name and their penchant for dolls—not that that had given me any advantage.

He swept his lips over mine. Not a true kiss, just a breeze of mouths passing.

"Tell me?" he whispered. "What are you afraid of? I can see that there is something in your pretty eyes."

I'd rested my hands on his shoulders as he'd pulled me close with the chain, and now I curled my fingers over them, letting the heat from his skin penetrate my palms.

"So much," I said. "But at the same time, nothing at all. I'm not afraid with you." I let out a small giggle that turned into a groan as my nipples were tortured by the clamps being shifted over his chest.

A frown line on his brow softened. "You have nothing to be afraid of with me," he said. "I know we're not exactly your average couple, but I can assure you that you are my world. In here…" He paused and glanced around the room. "Here and now, you are my everything. Your happiness, pleasure, and safety are all that I'm thinking about." He took one of my plaits in his hand and rolled the end, where the hair was loose, between his thumb and index finger. "And if someone, from your past, didn't make all of those things his priority, I'm truly sorry."

Fuck! How could he know that? Had he guessed? Was I such an open book? Jeremy had been a total shit. His idea of being a Dom was to be a bully.

"Shh…" Mr Kennett said. "It's okay."

I hadn't realised that a tremble had run up my spine. I must have shaken within his arms.

He smiled as he stroked his hand down my back, soothing that shake away. "Shh…" he said again. "I've got you. Don't think of bad times, only now, because this is good times, Vicky, good times."

Oh, the way he spoke, posh-like, with vowels all round and full, and he'd said my name in a slow, unhurried fashion, like savouring the syllables.

I pushed thoughts of Jeremy from my mind. He didn't belong in this room. He'd done his damage, it was time to heal.

Mr Kennett pulled back, and I missed his warmth and his hard body slotted alongside mine.

"The safeword is London, okay?" he said.

"Okay."

"Now, please, take off your clothes so I can start worshipping your delectable body." He removed the chains from his clamps so that they hung heavy and long from mine.

I hurried to do as he'd asked, shimmying out of my dress and tossing it aside. I then rolled down my knickers and kicked them beneath the table.

"No," he said. "Not the socks."

I paused and looked at him, the discomfort in my nipples simmering nicely in my half-stooped position.

"Allow me one reminder of the doll," he said, reaching for my bag. "I like the socks, a lot."

He held my bag up. The open zip gaped, and his bicep tensed under the weight. I had a lot of stuff in there.

"May I?" he asked.

"Be my guest." I paused. "Sir."

His mouth twitched at that, then he delved into the bag, staring upwards while he fumbled inside. "What's that?" he asked, his attention settling on something above us.

I knew without looking what he'd referred to. A metal bar, about a metre long, was pulled close to the ceiling, secured there by thick chains either end. A rope pulley was attached to the wall, coiled round a black holder to keep the bar up high while not in use.

"Want me to show you?" I asked.

He nodded, hand still inside my bag, and I walked to the wall and unwound the rope. I lowered the device to my belly height then secured the rope around the holder again. I pushed on the bar to make sure it was safe.

"You hold it like this," I said, gripping the bar. "Making sure to hold it steady because it can swing. And you stick your arse out so…well, it's obvious, isn't it?"

"So you can be spanked or taken from behind." He stared into my bag. "Are you willing?"

I was—yes, I fucking well was. I got myself into position—bent over, arse out, legs spread wide—and waited for him to find what he needed. A condom. My stomach clenched with my excitement. He dropped my bag onto the sofa then rolled the rubber onto his impressive dick, coming to stand behind me.

"I can see your cunt lips opening," he said.

What he'd said had startled me a bit. I hadn't expected him to say such a thing. His words excited me further, along with the idea that there was more to him than I'd first thought. Did he like to talk dirty in that posh voice of his? It was one of my favourite things, and to find a man who also enjoyed it…

Oh, God, I've hit the sodding jackpot.

"Talk to me," I said. "Say whatever you want."

He placed his hands on my waist, drew closer, his body heat warming my behind. I resisted shoving back into him. The image of his cock sprang to mind, and from the width of it I knew I'd be stretched so much I might have to clench my teeth.

"I'm going to fuck that cunt of yours so hard," he said.

Oh… "So do it. Do it now, Sir. Please, just do it."

The thought of what I looked like, makeup wrecked, had me feeling all kinds of slut—and I loved that. No more pretty little dolly tonight. My layers had been peeled back. I'd removed my mask. He was seeing me, and for the first time in a while I was happy with that.

He surged in quickly. His speed had me sucking in a sharp breath.

I revelled in the heat of ecstasy spreading through my cunt. "Oh, oh, oh, that's so—"

"—fucking hot. Yes, so hot…wet…"

He moved one hand to take hold of my plaits, yanking my head back so he could kiss my cheek. God, my scalp burned—burned so much my eyes watered. I eased my head forward a bit so it hurt even more while he continued to pull. As he withdrew, leaving only his tip inside, he reached beneath me with his other hand, gathered the dangling clamp chains and drew them down. I tightened my grip on the bar, clenched my teeth, and groaned so loud my throat swelled.

"You're a dirty dolly," he said, shunting in and out of me. "*My* dirty dolly. Oh, yes. You're so damn tight. So fucking wet."

I closed my eyes. All the parts of my body that were feeling the strain—my tits, my hole, my head—seemed to radiate with pleasure-pain. If I didn't have to hold onto the bar with both hands to stop if from swinging wildly I would have slapped my thigh, whacking myself so hard that my knees gave way. The thought of that had my clit bobbing.

"Put the chains in my mouth, Sir," I said. "Then you can touch my clit. I need you to frig me off."

He did as he'd been told, and I held the chains between my teeth. As he pulled my head back again, my tits were lifted. And oh, God, the pain on my already abused nipples was sublime. I keened, staring at the ceiling. With him ramming into me the bar jostled, and then he cupped my needy pussy. Just that alone started my orgasm off.

"More," I mumbled around the chains.

"Oh, I'll give you more, you sexy little bitch."

"Bitch…yes, your bitch…"

"I want you as mine—just mine, do you understand?"

"Yes!"

"Leave this place and come with me. Then you'll be treated to more of this…"

He rubbed my clit almost savagely, using what felt like four fingers flattened against the area. Bliss uncoiled further at a speed I hadn't anticipated, shocking me with its intensity. Everything seemed to explode at once, sensations flooding my body from all the points pain was being applied. I let out a whine of what sounded like frustration, but it wasn't that. No, I was overwhelmed with everything going on and needed to sink into it, to just let it happen.

"Mr Kennett," I shouted. "Mr Kennett…Mr Kennett…ah…"

I relaxed, and there it was, that massive rush of pleasure ripping through me. I went lightheaded and almost let go of the bar, wanting to drop to my knees so he could fuck me into oblivion.

"Christ," he ground out. "Christ, this is intense."

His cock thickened, pulsed, then he released a succession of feral grunts. The sound of them added to the rawness of what we were doing, and a new swathe of bliss arced through my body. I was a mass of pinging nerves, panting, seeing us in my head, the visual sexy as hell. The heat of his cum penetrated the condom. He sped up, his in-and-outs so quick. The pressure he was applying to my clit sent me from this external orgasm into another, while the internal one still raged. I whimpered, wrung out yet wanting so much more. My nipples numbed, so I let the chains fall from my mouth. He relaxed his hold on my plaits, eased off on my clit, slowing so the aftershocks weren't severe.

He stopped fucking me, sliding his hands up my belly to my tits. Without warning, he removed the clamps then pressed is palms to my breasts, suffocating the pain and whispering, "I've got this. Got you. Breathe. That's it, breathe."

I sagged against him, his cock still pulsing inside me, and wondered how I'd managed to get this far in life without ever fucking like that before. I turned to face him, suddenly in need of intimacy, and realised I wanted a hug, a kiss. He took me in his arms, enfolding me in an embrace that felt so *right* I could have cried.

"There, my beautiful woman," he said, stroking my back. "I've got you, it's okay."

I lifted my face, looked at his, and leaned forward.

That kiss…that kiss sealed my fate.

No getting romantically involved with the customers—staff rule number one.

If Mr Kennett wanted me as his personal doll, then that's what he'd get. The way he looked at me now, the way he held me…I didn't doubt his sincerity for a second.

And I didn't doubt that this would be one of my last nights as a public Domme. A new time had dawned. My awareness of how I could be loved, adored, and treated to such fine fucks by this man had reached high levels.

"Rule number one?" I said.

"Can go to hell," he answered. "It doesn't apply to us anymore."

*****

More about Harlem Dae

Harlem Dae is the pen name of two authors—Lily Harlem and Natalie Dae. They have been writing together for several years on top of their individual author projects and enjoy being represented by traditional houses including HarperCollins and Totally Bound as well as self-publishing their sexy stories on Amazon.

The Novice, **Anything for Him** and **Good Cop, Bad Cop** have all recently claimed the #1 spot on the Amazon Erotica chart and with the popularity of the newly released **Sexy as Hell Trilogy** it looks like the future is going to be another wild ride of success for Harlem Dae.

Both live in the UK and gain great satisfaction from bouncing characters and their raunchy antics back and forth, growing, nurturing and stoking plot lines until they steam off the page. They consider themselves to be solitary, whacky, spontaneous and desirous for many things including perfection and are frequently caught sending messages back and forth referring to each other as Rodney and Delboy.

Links

Website: http://www.harlemdae.com
Facebook: https://www.facebook.com/NatalieDaeandLilyHarlem
Magazine: http://www.harlemdae.com/p/sexy-as-hell-newsletter.html

Praise for Harlem Dae

Sexy as Hell – "The best erotic trilogy I have ever read! FSOG and Crossfire series have nothing on these books. If you like your books a bit edgier then you should read these. Lots and lots of hot sex but also a love story. Read and enjoy!"

Good Cop, Bad Cop – "OMG! This book by Lily Harlem and Natalie Dae was amazingly hot! I do love a good ménage story and this had everything I liked in it. Oh my, the three of them together in the villa - hot off the charts. I highly recommend this book for the little ménage freak in you."

That Filthy Book – "I recommend that every woman read this book, because unless you experience it for yourself, I am not sure I can convey the emotion this book evokes. Read the book. You won't be disappointed."

Figment

By Natalie Dae

I need a woman who wants me to fuck her until she thinks she's going to fall apart. I need a woman who wants me as much as I want her. I need...her.

In the murk of his bedroom—just a small nightlight glowing on his bedside cabinet—Will stared at the grey, shimmering shape in front of him. He shivered, anticipating its manifestation into the woman who'd visited him nightly for God knew how long. Time was a blur. She had remained a shape at first, then, over the nights that followed, showed herself more and more. He knew why he hadn't been able to see all of her—she wasn't real, wasn't firm enough in his mind for him to bring her into proper focus. In short, he didn't know what he wanted, wasn't sure who his perfect partner would be, and he needed to know in order for her to exist. He was nearly there, though. The previous evening she'd almost revealed her whole self, from her naked, hour-glass figure to her long, blue-tinted black hair, but her face was still a mystery.

Nude beneath the sheets, he let out a laboured breath, staring at the foot of his bed and willing her to change. To speak. If she did he'd be lucky. No woman had spoken to him in *that* way for months. And that was what he wanted—a woman to encourage him out of his shell with filthy words that inspired his cock to harden, had him reciprocating, getting her wet and wanting. Yet he didn't have the courage to return those words—he knew he wouldn't, that if a woman approached him and whispered the things he imagined she might, he'd stall, become more introverted. She was a figment of his imagination, nothing more, borne of loneliness and the need to share his life with someone.

How had it come to this...this woman of his dreams plaguing his nights?

He knew only too well. Leading a solitary life was a killer.

There, a sparkle of her outline, an aura that lit her up, then she filled herself in, much like the hour glass she was, the sand growing from the bottom up until she became full. At last, her face was clear, one of staggering beauty that had him realising he'd known her all along in his subconscious. A breeze through his open window fluttered her hair, streaming it out to one side, showcasing a dainty chin and a smattering of freckles across the bridge of her nose. Startling green eyes seemed to light for a moment before dousing—*I imagined that; no one's eyes glow like that*—and she curved her full, rose-pink lips into a slightly parted smile.

Christ, she's so fucking beautiful...

That was the problem. He'd created a woman who didn't exist. He'd made her ideal, while he was far from that. He needed to have his hair cut—it had grown long and unkempt since...well, since the other *her* had been in his life—and he'd allowed his stubble to grow into something more than a speckle of five o'clock shadow.

He wondered if he was going crazy, holed up as he was each evening after work and only going out every so often at weekends. Whether he'd created his perfect woman so he could feel less alone, less of a... failure. Since his last relationship had withered, he'd lacked the self-confidence to go out and find a new lover, someone to laugh with, be with. Someone to sit beside and not have to say a word to. A woman who just knew him. Instead, he'd concentrated on working out, his muscles so defined now, the skin covering them untouched by feminine hands.

"What do you want?" she asked, her voice reedy, as though she hadn't quite been able to completely arrive.

I should be asking her that question.

"I—" If he spoke to her, it would mean acknowledging her existence, acknowledging that he saw her or, frighteningly, admitting he thought she was real—or that he was so stuck in this dream, this... whatever-the-hell it was, that having a conversation with her was *normal*. It wasn't, damned well wasn't, but he knew he'd speak to her all the same.

"You... what?" she whispered, moving closer to the bed and placing her hands on the mattress, leaning forward to show off her cleavage.

"I... What do *you* want?" Turning the question around would buy him time and, perhaps, give him information about her that would solve it once and for all—either she was here or he was mad.

I know the answer to that one...

"I want whatever you want," she said. "I know what that is, but you have to tell me, otherwise it won't..." She glanced to her right at the window, narrowing her eyes at something he couldn't see.

The breeze had picked up, lifting the heavy drapes as if they weighed nothing. The air chilled, reminding him of winter mornings with sparkling frost on the ground and skeletal tree branches stretching to touch the lower belly of the gloomy sky. He rubbed his arms and chuckled at the absurdity of what was going on—full-on mental, that's what he was, believing this kind of thing happened.

His breath misted as it left his mouth. *That* sobered him.

"Won't what?" he asked, staring at her profile.

Her skin, creamy and so soft. Her hair, so long, so silky. Her lips...

He imagined them as a perfect "O" circling his cock and gasped at the realness of the image in his mind. He felt, goddamn *felt* the heat of her tongue, his tip touching the back of her throat, his cum barrelling out of him, her cheeks hollowing as she sucked him hard and swallowed everything he gave her.

What the hell?

"It won't work, won't happen unless you tell me what you want," she said. "It won't do any good showing me images like that, as erotic as they are." She looked at him again, all bright green eyes and wafting hair, nipples perking.

"I see." He didn't know what else he could say, what she *expected* him to say. He'd been out of the dating game too long. Had lost the ability to be relaxed, charming, and do whatever he needed to make a woman like him, want to be with him. He'd lost the driving urge to try, too, although not completely. No, it was still there, inside him; otherwise, how was this figment here?

"So tell me," she said, gliding over and climbing onto the bed, resting beside him, propping her face into the cup of one hand, "exactly what you want."

He *knew* exactly what he wanted—a woman to share his life with—but he wasn't about to get it anytime soon. He couldn't look at her so fixed his gaze on the wall behind her, focusing on the billowing curtains then the cats'-cream moon hanging in the lead-grey sky. Clouds shunted in front of it, fast-moving. A storm was brewing.

"I don't want to know what you need for the long-term," she said, her voice clearer, "but what you need right now, this minute."

Will shifted his gaze to take stock of her again, snatching in a breath at her closeness, one breast touching the top of his arm. Although she was on top of the sheet and he beneath, her body heat seeped through, warming those chills racing over his skin. So she was real, then.

Or a bloody good imitation of reality.

"This minute?" he asked, unsure whether he ought to nurture the nugget of thought threatening to grow in his mind. It didn't seem right to do so, not with where the thought was heading—images of them on this bed, him commanding her to do as he asked without question. No, he couldn't tell her that.

"Yes, right this minute. I know you're thinking something, I can *see* it, see what you want, but you have to *say*..." She sighed, but not unkindly—more of an exhalation of regret that he didn't have the balls to do as she'd requested.

Embarrassment unfurled inside him, weaving a path right up to his cheeks. Damn it. He wasn't usually so... so bloody schoolboyish, but something about her made him feel young and stupid. Unsure. And *her*—the one he'd loved before—she'd had him feeling all kinds of fool, pretending she loved him when all along he'd just been a dalliance, someone to play with until a better option had appeared. He'd fallen for that one—hard—and it still stung to think about it.

"I can't tell you that. It isn't right."

I can't let you know what I want, give you a part of me, because you'll take it, throw it on the floor, and trample all over it.

He stared into her eyes, purposely avoiding those beautiful swells of her tits in his lower vision, wanting to raise an arm from under the sheet and place his hand on one of them, to see how it would feel against his skin. His cock twitched—*please, not now, not when she's so close*—and he fought back the erection that would come if he indulged in the carnal images his mind prodded him to entertain.

"Of course you can."

She stared back, willing him, he was sure, to express every sordid thought he'd ever had. And how was it she knew what he'd been thinking? How was it she could *see* what he wanted? She was from his mind, that was it, yet... here she was, appearing as real as any woman he'd ever seen.

"No, I can't." He shuffled across a little, away from her, already mourning the loss of her body heat.

Far from looking affronted, she smiled and lifted one hand as if she were about to touch him, then thought better of it. "I want what you want, Will."

Fuck, she knew his name?

"So if we want the same..." she whispered.

She blinked slowly, the action mesmerising, reeling him in, encouraging him from the safety net he'd created around himself the past few months, leaving him floundering.

"Close your eyes, Will. Tell me everything."

Her eyes flashed a brighter green, and his reflection was in them, miniatures of his face, his expression showing how startled and confused he was. He attempted to adopt a better look, one she might find attractive, but failed. He closed his eyes, turning his body the other way so she couldn't see *him*—his inadequacy, his inability to even be with a woman these days without feeling useless and fumbling. Giving her his back was rude, but he had no other choice. She was too *there*. Too *within reach*.

"If I tell you, it makes me sound like I just want you for sex." There, he'd said what was bothering him.

No woman ought to be made to feel that way. He was a gentleman, or liked to think of himself as such, and telling her that he just wanted to lose himself in a fuck was... That God-awful embarrassment blazed hotter in his cheeks, and he gritted his teeth, internally struggling with the useless prick he had become yet wanting to be so much more. He *could* be more, had been once, but when *she'd* left him, his nerves threadbare, his heart broken, soul with a great big fissure in it, he hadn't found the impetus to pick up the shattered pieces and put himself back together.

"And why shouldn't you just want me for sex? If we both want the same thing, what's the harm?"

Oh, she was good. Very good. As though she'd placed the images there—somehow, some way, just like she'd arrived from nowhere—he imagined her body beneath his, her legs wrapped around him, her wet cunt settled over his cock. Warmth burst in his groin, and his cock sprang to life, his balls tightening with his need. He covered them with one hand to prevent his hard dick being evident. Shame splattered a cowl of heat on his face, paling the embarrassment into insignificance.

"Wouldn't you love to sink that hard cock inside me, Will?"

He almost nodded but bit his bottom lip instead. He couldn't tell her, could he? Admitting he was hard—even though she knew already, damn it—was admitting his need. He couldn't take her when he didn't know who she was and where she'd come from...

could he? He wasn't the kind of man to fuck for fucking's sake, never had been, but Christ, he knew he could be if he'd just learn to get rid of the shackles that bound him to propriety.

"Tonight you can do whatever you want," she said. "You just have to say…"

Her breath cooled his back.

Fuck it.

He took a deep breath and spoke before he could convince himself not to. "Yes, I want to shove my cock inside you." He closed his eyes. *As if doing that will make this any easier.* He cringed at his words—he'd swear they still echoed around the room, mocking him, a faint tinge of laughter at their edges.

"What else, Will?"

"I want to…" *Say it. Just say what she wants.* "To fuck you hard."

"And…? Tell me more. *Everything* you want."

"I can't. Fuck, this is so… it isn't me. Isn't who I am."

"It is, if you want it to be. If *I* want it to be."

She blew on his uncovered shoulder, a heady breeze infused with… something?

Whatever it was, it made him say, "I want to slap your arse and make you cry out, make you come." Now he'd started, the words waited in a queue on his tongue, crowded his brain like an insistent mob. "I want to suck your nipples, pull them, tug them, and have you begging me to do it harder. I want everything you have to offer, but I want to call the shots. I need… I *need* you to do what I say, to be an active partner yet—"

"Subservient?"

"Yes." Shit, his cock and balls ached.

"Then come and get me, Will."

He swivelled to face her, the sheet bunching between them and exposing his arse. Will reached back to cover himself, but she grasped his wrist—he *felt* her; she was there, real.

"Relax," she said, "and just be you. Act how you want, how you've always wanted to. Do it. Become who you really are. No woman should have reduced you to this. I've come to help you. To make you believe in yourself."

She leaned forward and brushed the briefest of kisses on his mouth, drawing back to observe him through heavy-lidded eyes. She licked her lips, pink tongue coming to rest in the seam. He wondered what it would feel like on his cock, licking, laving, curled around his hard-on as she sucked up and lashed it over his tip. Whether she'd flatten it against his balls and—

Courage filled him, grew from his damn toes right to the top of his head. His *self* as he knew it receded, fading out of him, replaced with another Will who knew what he wanted—a man who wasn't afraid to reach out and get it, either. How this had happened he didn't know, but if he questioned it he might talk himself out of what he knew was to come. His mind fuzzed; he blinked and shook his head, stared at her with new... new what? Clarity? Awareness? Enlightenment?

She wanted him, he sensed it coming off her in surging waves, and by fuck he wanted her.

And he was going to have her.

"Go and stand with your hands against the wall," Will directed. "With your arms up. Spread your legs."

She eyed him for a moment, that sexy smile of hers doing things to his cock it shouldn't be doing. How could a mere smile *do* that? Make him harder than he'd been before? Make the need in him so fierce he struggled to keep it contained? She wasn't of this world, he knew that all right, and if she *was* a figment of his imagination, he didn't give much of a shit. Not when he felt like this—so powerful, so wanted. And she *did* want him; the curly hairs of her cunt glistened as proof.

She got off the bed with graceful, gliding movements, nothing hurried about her. As she reached the foot she glanced at him over her shoulder, eyes ablaze, and damn her, she smiled that smile again. Will dug an elbow into the mattress and braced himself on it, taking in the curve of her waist, her generous figure, an arse that reminded him of an upside-down heart. Skin, smooth and shouting for him to run his hands all over it, to taste, to suck, to pet. But he wouldn't—not yet. He wanted to savour every minute with her.

But what if she disappears before I get the chance to—

"I won't," she said, doing as he'd instructed and pressing against the wall in a star shape. "Not now you've told me what you want."

The rounded swells of her breasts caught his attention then, only semi-circles of them visible due to her position. He wondered if the wall was cold and whether her nipples were painful buds as they grew from the contact. His mouth watered—he wanted those nipples between his lips, his teeth.

"Open your legs wider," he said, amazed at his commanding tone and her compliance. "That's it. Just like that."

He sat, yearning to get out of bed and grip her long hair in his fist, yanking on it so her head tipped back.

"So do it," she said.

Will threw the sheet off and it seemed he stood behind her within a second, her body heat once again warming him. He smelled her—ripe strawberries and the unmistakeable musk of her cunt—and his cock pulsed in time with his heartbeat.

"Fuck, I want you," he said, voice rough, jagged.

He slid his hand between her legs and held his breath for a second before touching her wet slit. Silky, so smooth he'd swear he'd never felt anything as glossy. His cock jerked, and he bunched his arsehole tight in an effort to stop pre-cum pooling on his tip.

He failed.

"Jesus Christ, woman..."

Gently, he explored her, brushing a fingertip over her clit, learning its shape, embedding it in his mind in case she never came back after tonight. Would it feel the same beneath his tongue? Would her taste match her aroma? He drew his touch down, circling her entrance, loving how wet she was, how creamy and ready for him. With deliberate slowness, he pushed his finger inside her, bringing it back down until it was almost out then inserting it again. She whimpered, a delicate, breathy sound that further hardened his cock, and fuck, if she was this tight now, what would she feel like clamping his cock?

He swept her hair away from her shoulder, gripping it in his fist and acting on his earlier impulse. She arched her neck, offering it for him to kiss. He leaned forward and pressed his mouth to her shoulder, the heat of her skin burning, an electric-like current skittering through his lips and spreading down his throat to his chest. His nipples hardened, tight points of rigidity, and he snatched in a breath at how contact with her threatened his equilibrium. His knees toyed with buckling of their own accord, and his lungs felt empty despite the breath he'd sucked in. With every finger-thrust she grew wetter, her juices thicker, and she jutted out her arse.

"You want more?" he asked.

"Do *you*, Will?"

God, yes, he wanted more—he wanted everything.

He stepped back, withdrawing his hand, and brought it up to his mouth. Her scent was something else—strong, enticing—and he wetted his lower lip with her cream. Sliding his tongue out to taste it, he reeled a little, tongue on fire, an explosion of *her* filling his mouth. Greedy for more, he sucked his finger and swirled his tongue around it, cleaning off every bit of cunt, swallowing the taste of her.

It wasn't enough—would never be enough.

She shoved her arse out again until the crease almost touched his dick. Going with his urges, he flattened his palm on her mound and coated it with her cream, drawing his hand up the shadowy crack of her arse over and over until it was slick. He settled his cock between her arse cheeks, pumping his hips so his length glided up and down. She reached back, cheek to the wall, and squeezed her buttocks together, creating white-hot tightness around his cock. With one hand on her shoulder and the other still clutching her hair, he used her for leverage as he watched his cock moving.

"Oh, yeah, that looks so fucking hot," he said, sweeping his gaze from there to her hair in his hand, to her awkward position, then back to his cock. All of it was too much, too damn sexy. "Put your hands back on the wall."

She did, and he nestled the head of his cock at her wet cunt hole. He waited a beat before sinking inside, and she clenched him, sucking him up until his balls met her dampness. His head lightened, and as he eased out a bit to set up his rhythm, he dipped his head to flash his tongue along the curve of her neck.

"You like that?" he asked beside her ear. "You like my cock inside you, and not being able to move because you're pinned?"

"Fuck, yes," she said on an exhale, jerking back onto his cock. "Fuck me. Do what you will. Fuck me until I can't breathe. Can't think."

He shoved into her—hard—shunting her body upwards. She cried out, clutching at the wall with useless fingertips, soft pants coming out of her—pants he wanted to make jittery, uneven. He gained a furious rhythm, rutting in and out with a force he hoped would give maximum pleasure—to her and to him.

She moaned, releasing a volley of "Ah-ah-ah!" that sung of an orgasm looming in her immediate future. Holding himself back, he pumped on and lightly bit down on her shoulder. She gave a long, drawn-out groan.

"That feel good?" he asked, then licked her neck, her earlobe. "That feel good with me fucking you like that?"

She nodded. "More. Give me all you've got. Fuck my cunt."

He ramped up the speed, increased the force of his thrusts, his balls slapping her. Almost at the point of no return, he pulled out and landed a different kind of slap—to her arse.

"Yes," she hissed. "Do it again."

He stepped to one side, held onto her hair and delivered smacks to her lower cheek, his fingers making contact with the wet flesh at the very top of her inner thigh. He struck on, slapping her arse red. She sagged against the wall, her cunt growing wetter, her cream drenching his fingertips. His cock expanded and lengthened, and he released her hair to clutch at his dick. She dragged herself down the wall so she bent over, her back a straight line.

"Fucking hit me," she said. "Harder!"

He obeyed, slapping her and jerking his cock, digging his toes into the carpet pile. Her body spasmed with every hit, and once again the excitement became too much. He let go of his cock, unable to stand it being touched, his over-sensitive tip thrumming with pressure. Her arse bore a large patch of claret, so startlingly vibrant next to the untouched skin that he momentarily wondered if she was in pain.

"Oh, God," she said. "This is it. I'm going to—"

Will rammed inside her, holding her in place with a rigid grip on her left shoulder. He pulled her up a touch then curved his free hand around her and delved between her legs. Rubbing her clit, his fingertips bumping his cock every time he withdrew, Will fucked her hard and fast. She grunted and hung her head, giving out those stuttered "Ahs" he loved hearing.

"You watching that?" he asked, not expecting an answer. "You watching my cock going in and out of you? See my fingers on your cunt? You see that?"

She moaned, long and loud, rearing back onto him as though he was never going to drive deep enough. He took that as a sign to work faster and jerked in and out, rubbing her slippery clit with more pressured strokes. She wailed, her cunt pulsing around him, sweat popping up in the slight dip between her shoulders.

Will couldn't hold back. His cock stretched both ways, seeming to grow so much bigger before his balls scrunched, his asshole puckered, and he yanked himself out, jerking off and spewing cum over her hot, abused arse. It kept on coming, creamy ropes that jetted onto her skin, and as he closed his eyes to better feel the myriad sensations speeding through him, she bucked and gyrated over his rubbing fingers. She came, her pussy a wet mass, surrounding hairs soaked. Will's release gave way to throbbing after shocks, painful tingles biting into his cock and savaging the end. He let his dick go, holding her by the waist with his cum-soaked hand while she rocked with jerky movements over his other.

He opened his eyes, slowing on her clit.

"Fuck," he said, breathless, his heart thumping. "Just…fuck."

* * * * *

She stood at the foot of the bed, hair sweat-slicked, face flushed. He realised, as he stared at her from his prone position on the mattress, knowing she would evaporate any second, that he hadn't touched her breasts, hadn't kissed her. He'd got caught up in the fuck, in doing what he'd wanted—like she'd told him to.

"Maybe next time," he said, testing whether she'd know what he meant.

Her edges faded. "You don't need me here again. You'll be all right now."

Her voice was thick. Laced with tears? She nodded, her body ghosting.

"When? When will I be all right?" he asked.

"Next time you think you can't give your heart, think of me. Think of what we just did—what you achieved."

He swallowed, wishing she'd stay, wishing she wasn't disappearing like that. Only a very pale version of her remained, and he crawled to the end of the bed, reaching out to touch her, to make her come back.

"No," she said, voice as weak as her image. "Don't do this. Don't…"

"Don't you want to come back?" he asked, lowering his hand.

Goddamn it, you have to come back. You're mine. You belong with me.

"I do, but—"

"So when?"

"I can't. I don't think it's possible. I'm not meant to—"

"If you could, when would you?"

"That would be now—I'd never leave. That would be always, me staying here with you."

"Then why don't you?"

"I can't stay. Not as I am, like this." She sighed then swallowed. "Someone else is out there for you. Someone who will stay. Can stay. You just have to find her. But you had to find yourself first."

"Won't you at least try?" Panic welled inside him—*she* was who he wanted. She was the someone out there for him. The thought of her going, of never seeing her again, opened a new gash in his soul, merging with the one already there. The void promised to swallow him whole. "Please, please come back."

"I'll try. I swear I'll try…"

She vanished then, leaving behind the soft scent of her cunt and the unmistakeable echo of a sob.

* * * * *

Will browsed the aisles, sick of microwave meals for one. He was tempted to get take-out again, something more substantial than what was on offer in those small boxes—a meal for half a person, more like. Life had gone on much as it had before—work, home, sleep, work, home, sleep—and he wondered where the fuck that *someone* was. He sighed and selected a roast beef dinner and a macaroni cheese, dropping them into his basket then stepping back from the freezer. Something solid met his back, and a bump or two beneath his heel told him he was standing on toes.

Fuck.

He took a step forward, ready to turn and apologise, but a distinct aroma assailed him. Hers. The spectre that had come into his life abruptly and left just as fast. He'd grieved for her, thought of her every day since that last night, waited in bed for her to appear, that beautiful hour glass who would warm his heart and life.

Spinning, he came face to face with a woman. His breath caught in his throat. Goose bumps coated his skin. A smile spread as he gazed at her blue-tinted black hair and the freckles scattered across the bridge of her nose. She was here—not faded, not ghosted, but here.

"You came back," he said.

She smiled and jammed one hand on her hip. "I did. So, tell me, Will. What do you want?"

* * * * *

More about Natalie Dae

Natalie Dae writes mainly BDSM erotica. She loves a Dom/sub relationship and is fascinated by how it all works. The trust issue is the best thing about it for her, so creating characters who have to adopt trust is one of her priorities. "Watching my characters bloom under tuition is such a treat," she says. "I find it such a privilege to be able to write about something that makes me learn something new with every book."

She lives with her husband and children in an English village and spends her spare time reading—always reading!—and her phone, complete with Kindle app, is never far away. "I can't imagine not reading or writing," she says. "It's a part of who I am. Without it I'd be more than a bit lost."

Natalie has many more BDSM tales swimming around in her head, so her workload for the future is very full. "What better way to spend a weekend than writing?" she says. "Saturdays are my main writing days, so I get up, open up a work in progress and rarely leave the desk. Unless I really have to!"

Her other pen names are Sarah Masters, Geraldine O'Hara, Emmy Ellis, Charley Oweson, and she's one half of Harlem Dae.

Links

Website: http://www.emmyellisblog.blogspot.co.uk/
Facebook: www.facebook.com/emmy.ellis.503

Praise for Natalie Dae

"My reaction to this book was WOW. I love dark erotica and this is definitely up there among my new favorites." **Amazon Review**

"WOW! Just WOW! This was one of those books where you stay up to all hours of the morning reading and then read as much as you can during your lunch break at work just so you can see what in the heck will happen." **Amazon Review**

The Wrong End of the Stick

By Lucy Felthouse

Bonnie stifled a sigh. He was doing it again. Staring at her, as he had been every day that week. She was on a fortnight's training course through work, the only one from her office who'd been sent. As a result, she knew no one and ended up sitting alone in the college's cafeteria at lunchtimes. She'd had a couple of invites from kindly people also on her course, but she'd turned them down. It wasn't that she was being rude or anti-social, she just hated people to see her eat. She was a big girl—that was putting it politely—and when people saw her have a meal, she could feel the judgement rolling off them in waves, the thoughts that she was fat because she ate so much.

It wasn't true. About what she ate, that was. She *was* fat, and there was no denying it. But it certainly wasn't her doing. She'd been born to large parents, and despite a healthy diet and plenty of exercise, she was still overweight. All she ever managed to shift was a pound or two here and there, and that was hardly noticeable, particularly on a woman her size. She kept at it, though, resigned to being a larger lady, but determined not to get any bigger.

Because she'd always been big, she was used to the snide comments, the dirty and derisive looks, the open stares. So it didn't upset her any more, but she still got irritated when people simply gawped at her. Surely one glance was enough for them to ascertain that yes, she was a shapely girl, and then move on. In most cases it was, particularly if she glared at the person in question. But not with this guy. Bonnie was sure he was trying to be subtle, because he often averted his gaze as she trained hers on him. But even if he'd looked away, she could tell by the position of his head and body that he'd been peeking at her. Again.

Now, on day seven, she was almost at boiling point. What the hell was his problem? Had no one ever told him it was rude to stare? She was on the verge of doing just that.

Eating her lunch was an unpleasant task, knowing she was being observed. If she hadn't been so damn hungry, she'd have left it. But she'd been running late that morning and had committed that mortal sin—missing breakfast. So her chicken salad—with no dressing—was absolutely necessary to avoid making herself feel ill, or passing out, so she devoured every last morsel. She ate faster than she normally would, not because she was being greedy, but because the sooner she finished eating, the sooner she'd stop feeling so damn self-conscious about the guy across the room watching her.

She decided to give him one last chance. When she'd finished her lunch, she'd drink her carton of apple juice, then sit for a few seconds, doing nothing. If he continued to look at her, she was going to stomp over there and give him what for. If he didn't, then she'd carry on with life and do her best to forget about him and his rudeness.

Deep down, she knew she was going to have to go over and say something to him. After seven days, he wasn't going to suddenly amend his habits. She was just being a bit of a wimp, really, hoping to find some way of getting out of confrontation, because she didn't like it, not one bit, and it was absolutely a last resort. Unfortunately, she couldn't think of a single other way of stopping him from doing it. Perhaps she could put up a sign in front of her saying "Please stop staring at me." But if he couldn't take the hint when she'd glared at him, he wouldn't take any notice of a piece of paper.

Several minutes later, her salad was gone and she moved onto her drink. With a sinking feeling in her gut, she saw he was just as interested in her now as he had been when she'd been eating. Damn, confrontation it was then.

Draining the carton, she gathered her plate, cutlery and other rubbish onto her tray, stood up and slid it onto the rack nearest her. Then she returned to her table, grabbed her bag, pulled in a deep breath through her nostrils and marched over to the Peeping Tom. She slid out the chair opposite him and sat down on it.

"Can I help you?" she asked. Now she was close to him, she couldn't help noticing that, annoying gawping habit aside, the guy was pretty cute. He had strawberry blond hair, pale skin, eyebrows and eyelashes to match, startling blue eyes and full red lips. Every time she'd seen him he'd been sitting at a table, so she had little clue about his height or physique, but his face was a damn good start. He looked about her age, too, mid-thirties. She chastised herself—she was meant to be telling him off, not lusting over him!

"W—what do you mean?" he replied, the blood draining from his face and making him even paler.

"I think you know, Mister. I've been attending this college on a training course for seven working days now, and on every single one of them, I've caught you staring at me at lunchtime. And you haven't even been subtle about it, either. You've gawped openly and it's doing my head in. Which is why I've come to find out exactly what your problem is, and to ask you to please pack it in."

"M—my problem?"

"Is it because I'm fat? Haven't you ever seen a fat person before? If you haven't, you've led a very sheltered life. And regardless of whether you have or not, hasn't anyone ever told you that it's rude to stare?" She was getting into her stride now—as much as she hated it, he'd driven her to this. She thought she'd kept the volume of her voice pretty low, but apparently not enough, because they were drawing stares from other tables nearby. But at least they had a valid reason to look—not many people could resist checking out an argument or a fight.

"F—fat?" The colour that had drained from his face came back, then heightened further and further until he began to resemble a tomato. He clutched the edge of the table so hard that his knuckles went white. "You're not fat. Y—you're beautiful." He dropped his gaze to the table then, and remained resolutely silent until Bonnie spoke again, which was a good few seconds later, as what he'd said sunk in.

"Hey," she said quietly, and, she hoped, kindly. "Look at me." Considering the whole point of their conversation, she was aware her words were ironic, but she only had another twenty minutes before she had to be back in her class, so there was no time to waste. He looked up.

"What's your name?" she asked.

"Owen."

"Well, Owen, I'm Bonnie. Would you like to go somewhere a little more private and talk? We seem to have amassed quite an audience here." She indicated the people at the surrounding tables, who quickly looked away.

He glanced around, and a smirk tugged at the corners of his lips, then immediately disappeared again, presumably as he realised the seriousness of the situation he was in. He nodded, then excused himself to put his own tray on the rack, before returning to where Bonnie still sat. "Okay," he said, "but I don't have long. I have to be in class in just over fifteen minutes."

"Don't worry, so do I. Let's just go and clear the air and sort this out, then we can get to where we're meant to be, all right?"

He nodded again, then followed her from the cafeteria and out into the corridor.

Bonnie turned right down the passageway, heading to the door that led out into the courtyard. She'd been able to see it from the classroom she'd been in for her course, and noticed that not many people used it. Probably because the lecturers could see it easily. The younger students would prefer to bunk off and mess about somewhere else.

She pushed open the door, shivering slightly as the cool air rushed at her. Holding the door for Owen, she waited until he'd closed it behind them, then spoke. "So, we're alone. Let's get this misunderstanding sorted out, shall we? Starting from the beginning, why on earth have you been staring at me?"

"I told you," he murmured, staring at his hands, which he was twisting together. "I just couldn't help it. I think you're beautiful, Bonnie. As soon as I first saw you, I thought so. It was kind of like those people in the cafeteria who were staring at us—I just couldn't help it. I tried really hard not to, and every time I looked away, it was like my eyes had a mind of their own. I'm really sorry if I made you feel uncomfortable, or upset."

Bonnie puffed out a breath. "It's okay, Owen. Well, sort of. You shouldn't have kept on doing it, whatever your reasons were, because you *did* make me feel uncomfortable. I ignored it for as long as possible, but you were annoying me. Now I know you weren't staring at me because I'm fat, I'm not quite so angry, though."

"You aren't?" His eyes grew wide, and he looked hopeful.

"Nope. Don't get me wrong, I'm still a little pissed off at you. Why the hell didn't you just come over and say something?"

"Because I'm shy. I'm shitting myself now, just standing here talking to you. I feel a bit better now I know you're not going to slap me, but I'm still nervous. I am absolutely crap at talking to women—well, women I like, you know, in *that* way—and although the whole time I was looking at you, I was trying to psych myself up to come and talk to you, I just had no idea whatsoever of what to say. I was terrified of making myself look like an idiot."

"Well you achieved that without even talking to me, didn't you? You made yourself look like some kind of creepy stalker. Now I know you a little better, I realise that's not the case. But just for future reference, although eye contact is great, follow it up with a smile, or a wink. So the woman knows you're interested in her, as opposed to just being a total weirdo. Then get off your arse and go and speak to her!"

"Um, that's not going to happen."

"Why not?"

"Because I don't want to let another woman know I'm interested in her. I like you, Bonnie. And you already know I'm interested, so I'm not going to wink at you. I'd probably end up looking like I'd got something in my eye. But what I am going to do, before I lose my nerve, is ask you out. So, would you like to go out with me? For a drink, or dinner?"

Bonnie raised her eyebrows. The rushed, breathless way Owen had spoken showed just how much effort he'd made to get past his nerves and say what he wanted to say. And now she'd ascertained that he wasn't crazy, he was just a nice guy who liked her but was too shy to say so, her opinion of him had completely changed. Her annoyance had evaporated and had been replaced with a feeling of fondness. Owen *was* incredibly cute, after all, and he was the first guy to show an interest in her since... she didn't even want to think about how long it had been since she'd last been on a date. Way too long.

"Yes, I'd love to. I find it difficult to eat in front of other people, though, so maybe just a drink? Unless you can promise you won't watch me eat."

"I can't promise, but I'll do my level best."

"That will have to do."

"Great. So when do you want to go out?"

"I don't mind. I don't have much of a social life, I'm afraid, so I'm free pretty much whenever. God, don't I sound like a total sad case? Are you sure you still want to go out with me?"

The smile that crept onto Owen's face threatened to make her melt into a puddle of lust. It lit him up, transformed him from shy and retiring to smokin' hot sex god. It was the dimples that did her in—she'd always been a sucker for a man with a nice smile, and dimples were the big, fat, juicy cherry on top of the cake. Delicious.

"Are you crazy? Yes of course I still want to go out with you. I'd say tonight, but is that too soon for you?"

Part of Bonnie wanted to say yes, it was too soon, and make her appear less eager. But then she remembered she'd already told Owen what a pitiful social life she had and he didn't seem to mind. So why not boost her social life by going out with him? Who knew, if it went well, she might end up going out with him the next night, and the night after that, too. She sternly reminded herself not to get too carried away. This thing had already gone from nought to sixty in less than fifteen minutes—she should try and take it easy. He could still turn out to be a nutter.

"Nope, that's fine. Where shall we go, and when?"

"Shall I pick you up at seven thirty? Is that too early—what time do you finish here today?"

"It's okay, I'll meet you somewhere. And half seven is fine. I finish here at three thirty and I don't have to go back to the office, so I have plenty of time."

"Excellent. How about the place on the corner of Cromwell Street? Do you know it?"

"Yep, that sounds great. And good choice, they have a great menu, something for everyone."

"That's why I chose it. Oh, I suppose we'd better go, huh?" He glanced at his watch.

"Yeah, I don't want to be late. Especially since I can see the classroom from here, and anyone in it can see me. That would be taking the piss to roll in late, wouldn't it?"

"Just a bit," he said with a smile. "Okay, I'll see you at about seven thirty then." He moved over to the door back into the building and gestured Bonnie to go in ahead of him.

"Thanks," she said, turning in the direction of the classroom she needed. "See you later."

"Looking forward to it. Oh, and Bonnie?" he said just before she started to walk away. "Good call on not letting me pick you up. You don't want me knowing where you live, do you? I could be anyone." He grinned, before turning around and walking away.

She was so stunned by his words that she just stood and stared after him as he left. It was like he'd read her mind, or something. Granted, she'd called him a creepy stalker not so long ago, but they seemed to have gotten past that phase pretty quickly. Despite that, she'd wanted to exercise just a little bit of caution—she'd heard enough horror stories to warrant that. But he'd smiled, so he obviously understood. With a decisive nod, she decided not to worry about it—she'd turn up at the allotted place at the time they'd agreed, and see what happened next. Right now, though, she had a class to get to.

* * * * *

In the end, she got there early. She had never been much of a girly girl, and she figured that if Owen had seen her in the smart-yet-comfortable outfits she'd been wearing to attend her course, then he wouldn't exactly run away screaming if she turned up in her best jeans and a nice top. The restaurant they'd decided on was the sort of place you could go to in tracksuit bottoms, if you wanted, so dress code was strictly up to the wearer.

She headed inside, immediately feeling self-conscious. It was tipping it down with rain, so standing outside to wait for him was not an option, unless she was going for the drowned-rat look. The trouble was, the place was huge and if she went and found a table, he might not be able to find her. Plus, if he was there already, she might not be able to find him. They hadn't exchanged mobile numbers, either, so it wasn't like she could ring or text him. She scolded herself.

Come on, Bonnie, you're a thirty-five year old woman, get a grip. Just wander around casually and see if you can see him anywhere. If not, find a table and he'll come to you when he gets here. Unless he stands you up, of course.

Now she was getting really frustrated. She knew that if he didn't turn up it was because of nerves, rather than having changed his mind. Wasn't it? Surely that was the case, as he'd been the one staring at her for seven bloody days, then had confessed to liking her. Why would he do that if he didn't mean it? It could all have been a terribly cruel joke, she supposed, but deep down, she knew it wasn't. Over the years she'd become a very good judge of character, and although she'd not had a high opinion of Owen to start with, now she knew the reason for his behaviour, she had a good feeling about him. Even if nothing happened between them, she knew he was a nice guy. He was just timid, particularly around women.

A hand on her shoulder made her jump and spin round to face her assailant. She was about to start scolding when she realised it was Owen.

"Hey," he said, holding his hands up in mock surrender, "I was just coming to let you know I was already here, to save you wandering around looking for me. You seemed lost. I've been here about ten minutes already and bagged us a table. It's there, look." He pointed to a table tucked into an alcove. "Now, go and sit down.

What would you like to drink?"

"Diet Pepsi or Coke, no ice."

"I can't tempt you with something a little more exciting?" He wiggled his eyebrows.

Bonnie giggled. "Are we still talking drinks here?"

Almost immediately, a blush swept across Owen's cheeks, and she felt bad. She'd have to tone down the teasing a little, otherwise the poor guy would spend most of the evening embarrassed. She got the impression he had about as much dating experience as her—in other words, not much.

"Sorry, Owen. I'm just teasing you. No, a soft drink is fine, as I'm driving. These days, it's not even worth the risk of having just one alcoholic beverage. My driving is bad enough, without being under the influence, too!"

He gave her a curt nod, then headed over in the direction of the bar. Sighing, Bonnie went to sit down at their table. They'd barely started their date, and already she'd done something wrong. It didn't bode well, not at all. She'd have to get Owen used to her somewhat wacky sense of humour, otherwise they'd never make it beyond their first date. And there was no point trying to hide it, or change herself, because well, if things progressed, then it wouldn't be a real relationship, would it? He'd effectively be dating a woman that didn't exist. No, there was no way she was going to fake anything. He either liked her as she was, or he didn't. He could take her or leave her.

That decided, she shoved the unpleasant thoughts from her head and worked on cheering herself up. By the time Owen returned from the bar and put her drink down on the table, her misgivings had all but disappeared.

"Thank you," she said, picking up the drink and taking a sip. "Ah, that's better. I didn't realise how thirsty I was. They're busy in here, aren't they? Mind you, they always are. I guess it's the good food and even better prices."

Owen grinned. "I think you're right. Shall we look at the menus? If they're busy, it might be a good idea to order quite quickly, because otherwise I might die of starvation."

"You're not exaggerating, are you Owen?" She beamed back at him, and their earlier awkwardness was forgotten. They were just two people, enjoying one another's company.

"Me? Never." He smirked, then pulled two menus from the

holder and passed one to her. "There you go, m'lady. Now, I love pretty much everything on this menu, so I may be some time deciding. I apologise in advance."

"I know what you mean," she replied, "same here."

They fell silent for several minutes as they perused the menu. Suddenly, a loud noise sounded and Bonnie jumped. Clutching her chest, she looked up to see Owen with a sheepish look on his face. He'd closed his menu a little too enthusiastically.

"Sorry," he said, "I was just drawing a mental line under my decision, telling myself I wouldn't change my mind."

"It's all right, you just made me jump, that's all. Okay, well I think I've decided, so how about I give you some cash and you go and order before we both change our minds?"

"You'll do no such thing. I asked you out, so I'm paying."

Bonnie twisted her face into a wry expression. "Fine. But I'm paying next time."

"There's going to be a next time?"

"Hurry up and order my food, and I'll let you know."

Owen quickly slid off his chair and, after checking their table number, scurried off to the bar.

Bonnie waited expectantly, and sure enough, a couple of seconds later, Owen was back.

"What was it you wanted, Bonnie?"

She bit back a laugh. "I'm going for the steak and ale pie and chips, please. Hopefully the ale won't put me over the legal limit." With a smile, she tucked her menu back into its holder.

"Okay. I'll try again, shall I?" He didn't wait for her answer, and headed back to the bar.

Bonnie couldn't help but think how damn cute Owen was. He'd loosened up a little, sure, but he was clearly still quite nervous about this whole thing. The place he'd chosen to stand and wait to be served actually gave her the perfect view of his arse, encased in dark blue denim. A filthy thought ran through her head—how she'd like to clutch those pert and delicious buttocks as he pounded into her. That was it... she was lost. A full on sex scene between the two of them took hold of her imagination, and she revelled in the erotic fantasy until the sound of someone clearing their throat yanked her out of it.

"You all right?" Owen said, sitting down again. "You had a look on your face that made you seem like you'd rather be somewhere else."

God, how on earth could she respond to that? She *was* kind of wishing she was somewhere else—in bed, to be precise—but she wanted to be there with *him*. "Oh no, definitely not," she replied, scrabbling around for something to say, "I was just daydreaming, that's all. I do it a lot."

"Care to tell me what you were daydreaming about?"

Bollocks. Just when she thought she'd gotten away with it, he had to ask her that! "Um... not really." The heat rushed to her cheeks in an almost overwhelming blast and she grabbed her glass and pressed it against her face, desperately trying to cool herself down.

Owen's amused expression didn't help her embarrassment. He leaned forward and lowered his voice, presumably so no one around them could hear what he was saying. "Oh my God, Bonnie. Are you having smutty daydreams in the middle of a crowded restaurant?"

That was it, she couldn't take any more. If any more blood shifted to the surface of her skin, she was afraid her head would explode. Slumping, she laid her forehead on the table and closed her eyes. Maybe if she ignored him, he would shut up. Or at the very least, say something to reassure her. Even better, he could change the subject altogether.

What she wasn't expecting was for Owen to speak directly into her ear. She jumped, knocking her glass over and spilling Diet Pepsi all over the table. Grabbing a bunch of napkins from the holder at the other end of the table, she hurriedly threw them down and started to mop up the liquid. The commotion had drawn attention from people on the surrounding tables, and she felt like she was back in the college cafeteria. Only now, rather than Owen being the one made to blush, it was her.

He chuckled. "Bloody hell, Bonnie, I only asked if you'd been daydreaming about me."

"I think I preferred you when you were shy and retiring," she grumbled. "What happened to that, anyway? Were you faking it?"

"No. I'm just shy about meeting women and talking to them in the first instance, I guess. I'm pretty much okay when I've established some kind of rapport with someone. Although I seem to be turning this date into a bit of a shambles." He paused. "Tell you what, I'll go and get you another drink, and then when I come back we'll start again, shall we? Maybe if we stop embarrassing each other, things would be better."

Bonnie nodded. "That sounds like a great plan. Thanks."

She refused to watch him as he walked away. Looking at his backside would only cause trouble all over again. Fanning herself with a dry napkin, she tried to waft the heat from her cheeks. When he came back, she would be as cool as a cucumber and try to steer the date in a less embarrassing direction. It was hardly surprising things weren't going perfectly, though. They were both horrendously out of practice at the dating game. She resolved to try harder. She could make this a success—she could.

* * * * *

"Well," she said as Owen walked her back to her car, which, it turned out, was only one row across from his, "thank you for a lovely evening. After a false start, I think we did pretty well, don't you?"

"Yes," he replied, "we got there in the end. I'm doing my best to end it on a perfect note. I can't walk you to your front door, so I'm having to make do with your car door."

"You can walk me to my front door, if you like. I'll even let you in for a coffee." Whoa, where the fuck had that come from? Talk about rushing into things! She'd never slept with someone on a first date. Nor a second, or a third. If a guy made it to a fourth date then she was sure he knew what he was letting himself in for—but that hadn't happened all that often, really. So why on earth was she propositioning a man she'd only just met?

As he stared at her, clearly trying to formulate the correct response, she realised why. Because she really liked him. Like, really. Despite the fuck-ups, the embarrassment, the unusual way they'd met, she felt a real connection to him. Something that was physical, sure, but beyond that, too. After the spilt drink episode, things had looked up considerably and they'd spent the rest of the evening getting to know one another and having a laugh. They'd barely noticed the restaurant emptying out, and only made a move when the staff very conspicuously started to clean the tables around them, got out the vacuum cleaner, turned off the music... they'd reluctantly headed outside where, mercifully, the rain had stopped.

"Oh, um, really?" he said, clearly as surprised by her words as she had been. "You don't have to, you know. Though I would suggest we exchange numbers so we can arrange another date—you're not going to be on your course with work forever, after all. More's the pity."

His kind words, the way he'd given her a chance to back out of her proposal, cemented the idea in her mind. "No," she replied, "I'd love you to come in for coffee. I'll give you my phone number then. If you want to, that is?"

He nodded. "Of course I do. I was just making sure you didn't think things were going too fast, that's all."

"They probably are," she said, matter-of-factly, "but you know what? One of us could get run over by a bus tomorrow, so we should live for the moment."

"That's a very good way of looking at it, if a little maudlin. But I'm not going to disagree. Lead the way, fair lady." He kissed her cheek then waited for her to get in her car and closed the door behind her.

She watched in her mirrors as he hurried across the tarmac to his own vehicle and got in. A few seconds later he flashed his lights, so she put the car in gear and drove straight forward—the car park was almost empty by now, so there was no car in front of hers. A shiver ran over her body as she made her way out of the car park—one, she suspected, that was a mixture of fear and anticipation. The anticipation was delicious, but the fear tried hard to throttle it. What if he changed his mind when he saw her naked? What if he just couldn't do it after seeing just how big she was, when she was totally on display?

Shaking her head firmly before pulling out of a junction and heading towards home, she told herself that was not going to happen. It was blatantly obvious, clothed or unclothed, that she was a big girl, and he can't have failed to notice that. And they'd got on so well—teething problems notwithstanding—there had been a definite spark between them, an undercurrent of attraction, of flirtation. No, there was no way he was going to baulk when she revealed her curves. And if he did, well then that was his loss, wasn't it? She could just as easily decide he was too skinny!

Ten minutes later, she was manoeuvring her car onto her drive, making sure she'd pulled far enough forward that Owen could get his car on there too, rather than having to leave it on the street. Really, it should have been the last thing on her mind, since there was a damn good chance she was going to get some sex very soon, but it seemed her brain was trying to distract her in order to keep her nerves at bay. She let it; nerves had almost fucked up her evening already, she wasn't going to let them ruin its potentially fantastic ending.

She got out of the car and locked it, then waved to Owen to park his car behind hers—he'd been about to park on the road. He saw her gestures, then backed up a little and turned onto her drive. A few seconds later he was beside her.

"Thanks," he said, "I was just gonna park on the road."

"Nah—there's plenty of room there, and no danger of anyone driving past and smashing your wing mirror."

"True."

A few seconds passed in silence, and Bonnie finally broke it. "So, let's get some coffee, shall we?" She knew her voice was too bright and chirpy, almost like she was talking to a small child, but it was too late to take it back now.

"Absolutely. Sounds great."

He followed her up the drive and to her front door, which she managed to unlock without too much fumbling. Once they were inside, she took his coat and hung it in the hallway closet along with hers.

"How do you take it?" she said, as she wandered into the kitchen and flicked on the kettle.

"Hot and full-bodied, thanks."

His voice had come from right behind her and she shrieked, dropping the container of coffee. Mercifully she hadn't opened it, so it didn't make a mess. The spoon she'd also been holding clanged to the floor. She was about to bend and pick it up, but Owen reached out and took her wrist gently, tugging her towards him.

"Leave that. I'm not thirsty anymore."

"Y—you're not?"

"Nope. But I fancy the pants off you, Bonnie. I know this is incredibly forward of me, particularly since we only met today, but would you like to go upstairs?"

She was pressed so tightly against him that she could feel his burgeoning erection trapped between their bodies. She couldn't trust herself to speak, so instead she nodded rapidly.

"Okay," he said, shifting his grip to her hand and leading her behind him, "so where's your room then, gorgeous?"

"Top of the stairs, second on the left."

He moved quickly to where she'd directed him, and she was suddenly very glad that she was a tidy person. She didn't have to worry that he'd walk into something resembling a bombsite, with dirty washing everywhere, or dust lining the windowsill. Hopefully, though, her bed sheets would be in need of a wash come the morning. She grinned, pleased he couldn't see her suddenly smug expression.

Immediately, he crossed the room and pulled the curtains closed. He turned and smiled at her, then his expression turned serious for a second. "Do you have protection?"

She nodded. God knows why, but she had a packet of unopened condoms in her bedside table. They'd been there a couple of years—hopefully they had a long expiry date.

"Good." He kicked off his shoes and socks, then sat on the edge of her bed. "Come here, you."

Wordlessly, she did as he said, shifting into the space between his parted legs. He was much taller than her—most people were, actually—so now he was sitting down, they were a similar height.

He slipped his arms around her, pulling her closer. She took the hint and went eagerly into his embrace, putting her own arms around his neck and leaning down just a little to kiss him. By the time their lips met, his were already parted, and, after a couple of seconds of relatively chaste kissing, they quickly moved into something altogether more needy, more passionate. They continued until they were breathless, pulling away to suck in some necessary air.

"Fuck, Bonnie," Owen said, "I want you. Bad."

"Mmm-hmm," she replied, pulling away and kicking off her own shoes, then bending to tug off her socks. Then she met Owen's eyes. He was studying her carefully, his eyelids hooded, his gaze laden with intent.

"Take off your clothes, sweetheart," he said.

"Oh, um... can we do it with the lights off?" She hated herself for saying it, but she was pretty sure that even if she was skinny, she'd find it difficult to strip off with confidence.

Owen sighed. "Yes, if you want. But I'm only agreeing to make you happy. I think you're beautiful and I want to see you naked. I'll just have to use my hands to explore your body instead of my eyes, won't I?"

Bonnie gulped. She desperately wanted his hands on her—the growing warmth between her legs was a testament to that. Moving to flick off the light, she started tugging off her clothes as soon as the room was plunged into darkness. She could hear rustling from the direction of her bed, so she knew Owen was doing the same.

As her eyes grew accustomed to the darkness, she scurried over to the bed and slipped underneath the covers—then came to the unfortunate realisation that because she'd turned out the lights, she would have to try and find the condoms in the dark. Damn. She set about that particular task immediately, wanting to get the protection ready for when she and Owen were, rather than interrupting their foreplay and potentially ruining the moment.

The mattress dipped as Owen clambered onto the bed beside her. Tentative hands reached out to find her in the darkness, then, realising she was under the covers, he joined her. "What are you doing?" he asked.

"I'm looking for the condoms. So we don't have to... you know... stop."

"An ingenious idea. Do carry on."

It was difficult to search when Owen was pressing kisses to her naked back and shoulders, but she forced herself to carry on. Eventually, she had the box in her hand, had torn off the cellophane, retrieved a foil packet and placed it within easy reach on her bedside table.

"Okay," she said, turning to face him. "It's ready when we need it."

"I'm glad to hear it," he replied, the heat of his breath on her face telling her just how close he was, "because I don't think it's going to be long before we do." He took her hand and guided it down to his shaft.

She gasped as she curled her fingers around his girth—and what a girth he had. Not so large as to be uncomfortable, but it would most definitely do the job. She stroked him gently, gratified when sounds of pleasure tumbled from his lips. They spurred her on to grip him a little tighter, tug him a little harder, and after a few seconds, he clasped his hand around hers.

"As amazing as that feels, babe, if you carry on it'll all be over."

She couldn't help it—she giggled. It had been a while since a man had made her feel so desirable. She wanted him too, of course, but his need for her ramped her own arousal up several notches. She felt as though she would climax with just a fingertip pressed lightly to her clit.

"Sorry," she said, "but I'm glad I make you feel good."

"Oh yes, you do. Now pass me that condom. I'm going to fuck you now. I just have to get it out of my system. Then we'll start all over again, and we'll take our time."

"I like the sound of that." Her voice was barely above a whisper. His response was a kiss so slow, so heated, that her toes curled and a fresh trickle of juice seeped from her pussy. She did as he asked, and she heard the telltale sounds as he made short work of the condom wrapper and sheathed himself.

"Now, come here, gorgeous." He clambered between her legs and knelt there for a second or two, exploring her curves with his hands. Her breasts, her tummy—it took all her willpower not to suck it in—as much of her bottom as he could grasp as she was on her back, and finally, her thighs. After what felt like an age—a supremely sensual age—he pushed her legs further apart, stroking his fingers between her swollen lips. "Good God, you're wet. That is so fucking hot."

He teased her a little longer, drawing her to the very edge of orgasm, then removed his fingers. She barely had time to whimper when he was on top of her, sinking his thick, rubber-clad cock inside her.

An animalistic sound left her lips and she wrapped her arms and legs around him, pulling him harder, deeper into her. She was so wet that he met no resistance as he penetrated her and before long, his balls were pressed against her body.

They lay, gasping, for a second or two as they grew used to the sensation. "I can barely see you, sweetheart," Owen said, pushing his weight back onto his arms, then leaning down to drop a kiss on her lips, "but what I can see, you have no reason to be paranoid about. Everyone has different tastes. And mine happen to run to women that have something to hold on to, curves I can explore, get lost in. You, specifically, are gorgeous both inside and out, and I know we've gone crazy fast with this thing, but I definitely don't regret it."

He shunted his hips back, then sunk into her again in one long, slow stroke. Their groans mingled in the air, as did their pleas to gods and bouts of bad language. Repeating the process, he fucked Bonnie long and slow, seeming to deliberately ignore the way she thrust her hips up at him, or clutched his bum cheeks to pull him harder into her, faster.

Soon, it seemed, he couldn't hold back any more, and Bonnie got her silent wish. Owen's movements grew faster, the friction of his cock in her cunt quickly growing her pleasure to delicious proportions and causing her labia and clit to swell further.

"Unnh... gonna come!" It was all she could manage before she tumbled into blissful oblivion, vaguely aware of Owen's increasingly short, jerky movements and then a growl as his own climax took over. Her walls clenched and released his shaft, milking him, their respective orgasms making them fill the room with blasphemy and carnal sounds.

The last thing Bonnie heard as she slipped into a satiated doze was: "God, you're perfect."

As much as she'd hated him staring at her to begin with, now she was really glad he had, and that she'd gotten the wrong end of the stick. Fat or not, Owen liked her, and she liked him right back.

*****

More about Lucy Felthouse

Lucy Felthouse is a very busy woman! She writes erotica and erotic romance in a variety of subgenres and pairings, and has over 100 publications to her name, with many more in the pipeline. These include several editions of Best Bondage Erotica, Best Women's Erotica 2013 and Best Erotic Romance 2014. Another string to her bow is editing, and she has edited and co-edited a number of anthologies, and also edits for a small publishing house. She owns **Erotica For All**, and is book editor for **Cliterati**.

Links

Website: http://lucyfelthouse.co.uk
Twitter: http://www.twitter.com/cw1985
Facebook: http://www.facebook.com/lucyfelthousewriter
Goodreads: http://www.goodreads.com/cw1985
Pinterest: http://www.pinterest.com/cw1985
Newsletter: http://eepurl.com/gMQb9

Praise for Lucy Felthouse

"I know that I can't go wrong with a book by Lucy Felthouse: trust me, if you want sexy, steamy shorts with a dash of humanity and humor this is an author to add to your list." **Gaele, The Jeep Diva**

"Ms Felthouse writes sex that makes your palms sweaty and heats you up..." **Scorching Book Reviews**

"If you enjoy erotica that is well-written, steamy and satisfying you will adore Lucy Felthouse." **Ashley Lister**

Stones

By K D Grace

*Stones would play inside her head
And where she slept, they made her bed.
Neil Diamond*

"A 7 a.m. start will help you avoid the worst of the heat, Mr. Danson."

It was difficult to focus when Magda Gardener's voice sounded like sex itself — low for a woman, slightly gravelly, like she'd not had enough sleep for reasons other than insomnia.

"It's badly overgrown, I'm ashamed to say, but I've been away a while attending to my affairs."

Thoughts of her affairs made my cock twitch. Stupid really. I'd seen the wreck of a house. She was more likely a Miss Havisham than a sex goddess. She needed the grounds cleared. She didn't want a crew. She wanted one person only. Time didn't matter. Cost was no object.

"I'm a bit of a recluse," she said, apologetically. "I value my privacy."

Until she called I thought the old Victorian heap was derelict. The grounds were a jungle, just the type of challenge I liked. It was high summer, so all of my crews were busy, but I was the boss, and I was due an intriguing side project.

"I want someone experienced in gardening and landscape, not a lawn boy. Some of the statuary has sentimental value."

"I'm your man," I said.

"I thought you might be, Mr. Danson." Her voice was barely more than a honeyed whisper.

She wasn't wrong about the grounds. Even I wondered if I'd bitten off more than I could chew when I saw the ocean of tangled bramble and ivy and the shaggy topiary run amuck. The reflecting pools were long since evaporated and filled with who knew how many years' accumulation of leaf mould and detritus. They were lined with marble benches smothered in moss and mould.

I'd worked half a day in heavy heat before I uncovered the first of Magda Gardener's statues. My gloved hand, groping through nettle and vine, came to rest on an erect stone penis. Before my brain registered what I'd grabbed, the vine I was tugging gave way, revealing the statue attached to the formidable hard-on, and I tumbled back on my ass.

It wasn't the Greek motif I'd expected. The man's cock was exposed above rumpled trousers gathered and bunched just below his ass. Next to him on the bench, stiff nippled, teacup breasts forced above the low cut front of her gown, sat a young woman. Her skirt was scrunched high, her legs akimbo. Her exposed pussy was splayed thick with arousal so real that the stone looked dewed with her juices. My heart battered inside my chest. My cock raged against my fly. It was so lifelike, so arousing, and yet so eerie, unlike any garden statuary I'd ever seen.

The hard-on threatening to unload itself in my jeans was tempered by the expressions of the lovers. Their gaze wasn't locked on each other, as the situation dictated, but instead on some invisible point over the man's left shoulder, over my left shoulder. The look of heat that accompanies a good fuck was caught between ecstasy and something else, something that squirmed its way up from my unconscious to coil in my belly tight and low. And when it struck, I shuttered my load in my pants, gloved hand over my mouth to hold back a cry that was too oppressive to be simple release.

Once I'd recovered from my unexpected jizzing, I noticed the sculptor had caught his subject at a similar vulnerable moment. Heavy droplets of semen glazed the length of his cock, dropping onto the bench only inches from the woman's begging pussy.

Horror and ecstasy blended together in whatever it was the couple saw over the man's shoulder. Over my shoulder.

A thick breath of air brushed my ear. The unkempt topiary behind me rustled. The sound I uttered was girlish, I suppose, but then I'd already shot my dignity thick and sticky into my boxers. The hair on my neck rose, and I was suddenly as unable to move as the statues sprawled across the bench. My breath abraded my throat, my pulse was a drum roll. Terror, the kind that only invades nightmares and makes no sense in the light of day, washed over me. I stood staring in wide-eyed horror at the couple on the bench, unable to turn and face my tormentor.

Then into the cocktail of fear and heat, my cell phone rang and I practically pissed myself.

"Mr. Danson... Goodness, you sound winded. Are you all

right?" The sexy voice of Magda Gardener filtered into my ear.

"I'm fine," I gasped.

"You seem to be making good progress. I've been watching from my study."

I could just make out a slender figure standing half-hidden by the drapery.

"Mr. Danson, it's starting to rain. I'm tired. I think we should call it a day don't you?"

I hadn't noticed the beginning of the drizzle that was suddenly a downpour. Thunder clapped. Lightning flashed, spotlighting Magda Gardener just before temporarily blinding me. But during that split second, I could have sworn she stood at the window naked. And Miss Havisham, she most definitely was not.

That night I dreamed of Magda Gardener's statues, caught mid spurt just at the tipping point. But on their faces there was never ecstasy without terror. As I pulled away ivy and bramble, they grabbed at me with stony fingers, women begging with open legs, men shooting their wads like geysers, unable to run, unable to stop their rut, unable to escape the terror that was always right behind *me*.

I clawed my way into the waking world drenched in cold sweat, gasping for breath. My cock was harder than the statues in Magda's garden, and fear dissolved into urgency. I stumbled to the bathroom holding myself, desperate for relief, but equally desperate to be free of the bed and the fetid breath of nightmare that still lingered.

I dry humped over the toilet, squirming and writhing in spastic grunts until I could feel the slap, slap of my balls, until I could no longer breathe for the heavy need rising between my legs, climbing up over my belly and chest. I clenched my buttocks, closed my eyes and jerked like my life depended on it. Then just before I shot the toilet full, the image of Magda Gardener flashed white hot behind my eyes, an image far more detailed than I recalled seeing. Now my view was close-up and personal, her breasts were full and high, nipples jutting like cherry gumdrops, her perfect pale skin glowing brighter than the lightning flash. In that split second my eyes followed the slope of her belly down to the dark golden curls nestled against her mons. Then, eyes lowered as though she were suddenly shy, she slid her hand between her open legs and with splayed fingers exposed the hard node of her clit and the moist gouge of the valley beneath. I came. I came until the very violence of it threatened to jerk me inside out, as though all my life I'd been holding myself for a tiny glimpse of Magda Gardener.

Not wanting to risk another dream, I settled on the sofa with my laptop. I found myself looking at the works of great sculptors, Michelangelo, Bernini, Rodin, trying to think what made Magda Gardener's sculptures different. There was sex, there was passion, there was violence, even rape. All were themes of the great sculptors. Bernini captured the very essence of Hades dragging Persephone off to hell — her terror, his lust — and no one could look at that sculpture and doubt what would happen next. Yet the horror was once removed, as though the stone itself has rendered safe and distant what was savage and terrifying, what was a breach of human decency.

But Magda's sculptures practically burst from the stone into life, into whatever mute terror secretly torments them, as though the sculptor fully understood that our most hideous nightmares are the ones born from the twisting and disfiguring of our most vulnerable passions. Could there be anything more horrendous than our deepest fear realised at the very point of ecstasy? Horror films capture it perfectly. The young couple, caught mid-fuck, always see it coming, and their last battle is the battle between ecstasy and horror.

The next day I uncovered three more sculptures. There was another couple, also caught mid rut. The woman's jeans were dropped to her knees, the detail of the riveting and the stitching around the back pockets clear, the texture of denim almost tactile. The man mounted her from behind, the droplet of pre-cum pearled for posterity on the head of his cock, just ready to plunge into her plumped wet gash. They both looked over their shoulder, the expressions on their faces, arousal infused with horror. The other two sculptures were solitary males, stiff and ready to fuck, their hands groping for the invisible objects of their lust, their cocks clearly at the point of no return. The same mix of horror and lust sculpted each of their faces. I wondered if their female counterparts had been destroyed or perhaps were still to be uncovered. My phone rang.

"It's hot, Mr. Danson. You've not had a break. Come, let me fix you a cool drink."

Magda Gardener gave me no opportunity to turn her down,

which I would have. I'd been working with my cock at half-mast since I'd uncovered the first statue of the day. And the last two, the two men, made me think of her, think of what it would feel like to reach for her, to do to her what the two stone men were so obviously planning to do the their missing women.

I walked slowly up the length of the garden trying to rein in my cock by thinking about how I would clean the reflecting pools. At the back of the house, beyond a patio flanked with an overgrown stone menagerie of dogs, cats, birds, rabbits even a rodent or two, the door stood open and I heard her call from inside. "Mr. Danson. I'm in the kitchen."

I wasn't prepared for the gloom and nearly tripped over a plant stand cradling what might have been a long dead dieffenbachia. Then suddenly, startlingly, she was at my side, brightness against the gloom, in a pale clingy dress that fell to her knees. "I'm sorry for the dark. I have a medical condition. My eyes can't tolerate bright sunlight." Even in the gloom, she wore mirrored sunglasses that sat close against her face.

"You're not a vampire, are you?" I felt stupid the minute I said it.

Her soft chuckle went straight to my cock. "I'd be a terrible vampire, Mr. Danson. I'm a vegetarian." She ran a hand over my damp brow and pushed my hair back. "I'm certain you're not a vampire, slaving away in the hot sun." She handed me a glass of weak lemonade and I drank it back in thirsty gulps.

"I'm fascinated by your strange statuary." I handed her back the glass. "If you're not a vampire, perhaps you're Medusa then."

For a brief second her hand froze over the glass, then she offered a tick of a smile. "They are my work, yes, from a very dark period in my life as you've no doubt figured out."

I released my breath slowly as she handed me another lemonade. "Then you're a sculptor?"

"Not any more, not with these eyes." In the silence of the room I could almost hear her pulse accentuating each word.

"I'm sorry."

"Don't be. You see how disturbing my efforts are. It's a relief really, not to create such horrors, and yet..." She laid a hand against the swell of her breasts, and now that my eyes were adjusted to the gloom, I could see the shape of her, not disguised by the thin dress. The crown of large nipples, the crinkle of tight areolae made my cock jerk against my fly.

"I should get back." I breathed.

"Sit down Mr. Danson. Take a break. Your work's not easy." She moved closer to me and rested a cool hand on my arm. My skin practically leaped at her touch, my nipples tightened to aching points at the feel of her breath against my neck. For a second I thought I'd come in my pants again, so intense was the feel of her flesh against mine. Oblivious to my distress, she guided me to sit at the kitchen table then sat down next to me, leaning close as though she would whisper in my ear. She seemed unaware of the way her top sagged giving me a view that as much as I'd have liked, I felt compelled not to take.

"Tell me, Mr. Danson," she half whispered, "what exactly do you know about Medusa?"

"I know she was once beautiful, that Athena turned her into a monster because she caught Poseidon raping her in her temple. And after that anyone who looked into her eyes was turned instantly to stone."

There was a slight lifting of the corners of her mouth, but I was pretty sure it wasn't a smile. "Don't you think it rather strange that the goddess of wisdom would curse a young girl for being raped?"

Before I could speak, she leaned even closer and curled her fingers around mine. "Don't you think perhaps it more likely that the goddess, in her compassion, offered the poor girl a way to avenge herself, a way to ensure no one would ever violate her again?"

"It's just a myth," I said, my throat strangely dry in spite of the lemonade.

She offered me a smile that was genuine this time and sat back in her chair. "Of course it is. Besides, what a terrible gift to offer a young girl whose anger and hurt and fear must have known no bounds, and who would have had little worldly wisdom and life experience to help her cope." Without warning, she leaned close, so close that I almost thought she would kiss me. Her hand slipped off the table, and for the briefest moment brushed my lap. "I'm not sure even the goddess of wisdom could have calculated the destruction wrought by one angry, wounded girl seeking vengeance on all men in lieu of the god she was helpless against."

The chair screeched on the tiled floor as I shoved back away from the table. "Thanks for the lemonade," I croaked. "I'll get back to it now."

I practically ran back to the cover of the topiary, nearly falling over a stone poodle in my flight. Behind an unruly hawthorn hedge, where I was sure I couldn't be seen from the house, I barely got my fly open before I unloaded. I've always had a strong libido, and I do my share of wanking, but I'm always in control, and I come when I choose. I felt like a teenager in the grip of a wet dream. This place, that woman. My god, I wanted her. As disturbing as I found her, I wanted her.

The next day I felt hungover and achy after a night of more dreams. The sky was heavy with clouds and the air was gravy-thick. There were more statues, lots more statues. Some were shoved together like chess pieces pushed off the side of the board. Some were tumbled and stacked against each other in careless disregard for erections and bare cunts. The whole thing sickened me even as it aroused me, which sickened me even more. I was so caught up in the train-wreck of it all that I hardly noticed the rain. It poured in torrents as I jerked and fought mechanically with a hefty vine entangling a tumble of statues.

A strangled cry broke my trance. I turned to find Magda Gardener, still hidden behind her mirrored glasses, wet dress clinging to her breasts and belly, hair dancing around her face in the wind like a wild thing. "This is not what I wanted, never what I wanted!" Her voice rose to a wail. Lightning split the sky with the reek of ozone. Magda pulled me back just as a large chunk of topiary exploded and burst into flame where I'd been standing. A branch flew through the air and struck her on the cheek sending her glasses flying into the hedge before I could shield her with my body. Embers showered us in a hot pelting of sparks that smoked and hissed in the heavy rain. We ran for the house, forcing our way through the driving storm.

Inside, she buried her face against my chest and sobbed. "I can't bear it. I can't bear it anymore. So many memories, such awful feelings. I never should have involved you in this. I'm so, so sorry."

"Shh. It's all right now." I kissed the wound on her cheek and tasted blood, warm and strangely soothing against my tongue. Heat snaked down my throat and spread in my chest warming places I didn't know were cold.

"It'll be all right now. Whatever it is it's the past." I stroked her wild hair.

When I brushed her still-closed eyelids with my fingertips, she flinched. But she kept her eyes tightly shut.

Then her lips sought mine. Her kiss was ravenous, like there could never be enough to satisfy her. "I want you, Paul Danson," she breathed into my mouth between sobs and tongue kisses. "I need you to make love to me. Please."

With the storm adding to the gloom, I could barely make out shadows and shapes. But her pale beauty shone like light. I lifted her onto the kitchen table, surprised at how slight she was. I worried the wet dress up over her head. She was naked beneath. A soft rise of goose bumps moved over her chilled flesh just beneath the skim of my hands. I took her breasts like an adolescent who'd never touched a woman before and yet she happily sighed my name. "Paul, oh Paul." She guided my hand between her legs into her soft moist folds. "Make love to me, Paul. Make me come. Help me forget, just for a little while."

I lifted her legs onto my shoulders, for the first time noticing that her feet were bare and soaked and the bottoms cut and bleeding, but she was already pulling my face to her pussy spread plump and heavy before me. I buried my face in her, and she made little kitten sounds, grasping at my hair with slender fingers. She tasted like the beginning of everything, dark and primordial, and I ate like she existed only to feed me, inhaling great gulps of her until my head buzzed from her heady feral scent all over me.

"I want you inside me," she gasped.

Breathing like the storm had migrated into my chest, I eased into her, carefully, gently. Suddenly, she seemed so fragile I feared I'd break her. She was tight, tighter than any woman I'd ever been with, whimpering and sucking little gulps of air at my thick invasion. When I was in she released a long slow sigh, grabbed the edge of the table for leverage and humped up to meet me, legs wrapped tightly around my waist. She rode me in serpentine undulations, with a relentless grip, a grip that took all my will power not to succumb to, not to empty myself into her grasp.

With each thrust visions of the statues in the garden pushed and shoved at my consciousness until the weight in my balls was balanced by a heavy knot of horror in the pit of my stomach.

"I've wanted you from the beginning," she whispered. "I've dreamed about you all my life, Paul. I pleasure myself thinking of you."

I cupped the swell of her breasts and kneaded and stroked. "Will I end up like them?" I felt like my balls were heavier than all the stone statues in Magda's garden.

Her eyelids fluttered, her breath bunched in her chest. "Why would you think that?"

"I want to be with you," I breathed. "If that's the cost, then I'll pay." It surprised me to realise I meant it.

She let go of the table and pulled her body upright against mine so tight that with each thrust our bodies battled each other for space to breathe. "You can't be with me if you're like them. And you're not like them, darling. You could never be like them." She wrapped herself around me and clamped down until I cried out in something not far from pain, then she spoke against my ear. "I don't want you like them. I want you warm and sweaty and full, so full just for me." One more squeeze from her gripping hole and I came. Sweet blessed relief, I came. The knot in my stomach dissipated and I emptied myself into her. She trembled and quaked like the willows outside in the storm. "Oh yes, dear goddess, yes," she spoke between shudders. "This is what I want. This is what I've always wanted."

And I swear, in spite of everything I'd seen, everything I'd experienced, in that moment I felt bliss.

When I arrived the next day the garden gate was padlocked shut. A man in a black suit waited for me. "Mr. Danson?"

Before I could answer, he handed me a thick envelope. "Your services here are no longer required. Remuneration has been deposited in your account for the whole project, since the breach of contract was not yours. Any tools or equipment left on the site will be returned to you as soon as possible."

"This is Magda Gardener's place," I said. "I want to speak to her."

The man shook his head. "This is not Magda Gardener's place, Mr. Danson. She's only allowed to use it, and this time she's overstepped her bounds."

I was desperate to find Magda, but I didn't know where to look. I talked to a paralegal at the firm which looked after the estate. For some reason the woman took pity on me. The property was held in perpetuity by some trust in Greece. It had been for as long as the firm had existed. Before that, she couldn't say. She could tell me no more.

There were no other leads. Magda was gone, and I had nowhere to look. Over time, the more disturbing dreams dissipated, and I was left with only one. In it Madga wandered her garden, talking to her statues, calling them by name. When she saw me, she pulled me down on the grass. We made love with wild abandon while all the statues looked on. But Magda kept her eyes closed. "Theirs is not your fate," she kept telling me. I always woke feeling better afterward.

Eventually the house was torn down and the property sold. I don't know what happened to the statues.

I was just beginning to feel myself again when the package arrived. It was larger than a case of wine and heavier. There was no return address. Inside was a bust carved in stone. The face made my heart stop, then clench, then beat faster. My cock tightened and my stomach knotted cold and low. The bust was Magda as she'd been in the storm, wild hair flying around her face, full lips parted, but this time her eyes were wide open, and the expression on her face was the same as that of the statues in her garden, terror and longing, lust and fear flowing endlessly into each other. Around her neck, like a silk scarf, was a single slender serpent, so detailed that the scales seemed to undulate in the midday light. It encircled her slender throat and paused, mouth open, tongue flicking at her ear lobe, frozen there for eternity, as though it were just about to impart a secret.

Topiary

By K D Grace

"Isn't it time yet? Surely it must be."

Aden ignores me, lost in concentration, delicately clip-clipping the unruly new growth from a perfectly spiralling boxwood.

I can always find him beyond the hedged labyrinth surrounded by fantastical shapes and patterns all sculpted in evergreen, each time a new shrub, each time a new shape. Aden is an artist when it comes to shrubs. He hired me to do the kitchen garden. I grow vegetables. I don't understand his fascination. But there's no denying Aden is the Topiary King.

"Surely it must be time." I squirm on the stone bench, feeling the discomfort of my condition.

"These things can't be rushed, Bess. All gardeners know that." He's working gloveless, like always. He says he needs to feel what he does. No one would ever believe what delicate work he can do with hands so hard. With his thumb and first two fingers he patiently teases and coaxes out the tiniest of wayward shoots until the hard swell of a budding leaf close to the top of the spiralling shrub is visible, something no one else would have noticed.

As I watch him, I bear down against the cool stone of the bench and shift from buttock to buttock. The nip of the secateurs is crisp, precise and I catch my breath with a little moan. "At least check. Please."

His shoulders rise and fall in a sigh of resignation. His gaze stills on the shrub, checking for other unruly bits to be tamed. Carefully, he lies down the secateurs and slowly, still studying his efforts, moves toward me.

I brace against the bench and shift my weight backward, ready for him.

"Timing is everything," he lectures. "There has to be enough growth to do what I envision, and what I envision must be there already waiting to be exposed."

I lean back a little, feeling the clench and the flutter in my pussy that comes from knowing it's almost time. I can barely stand another second of the heaviness, the chaos. I long for order, his order, which he never gives until conditions are just right. Please, dear God let conditions be just right. My impatience feels heavy and swollen like the buds Aden examines and caresses and nips.

"Open up."

I do as I'm told. He kneels in front of me and pushes chlorophyll-stained fingers under my skirt. He's hard. He's always hard when he shapes the shrubs. The first time he fucked me, he'd been shaping the same spiralling boxwood. He burst into the kitchen garden while I was bent over weeding the young carrots. It was all over in a few minutes, me gasping my orgasm with my shorts around my ankles, and him hammering into me, coming in hard shudders. Now, most of the time he lingers, like he does with his shrubs. The memory makes me clench and rock against the bench.

I feel heat rising off him. I smell his sweat all piquant and woodsy. I'm so tight and tetchy that even the first graze of his fingertips against my muff makes me gasp and wriggle.

I never had a muff — at least not a real one — until I met Aden. I was smooth and naked. I wore bikinis and thongs. But Aden doesn't like bare ground where something should be growing.

In the beginning it itched. Every night Aden tended me with soothing lotions and oils while he admired my new growth, tiny and prickly like young grass. He promised me it would be worth the wait. With time the new growth thickened and grew soft and escaped the edges of my panties like it was always migrating toward his touch. The more it grew, the more his hand was there to caress, to examine. Then I stopped trying to contain it. I stopped wearing panties and let Aden's garden grow unhindered. All that soft springy growth was new to me. I could barely keep my hands from straying under my skirt for a stroke. I never missed a chance to admire its rude, rambunctious fullness when I was naked, or when I was in the bathroom. My muff exerted more control over us than I would have ever imagined. One of us was always touching it or talking about it or thinking about it. That led to sex. Lots of sex.

And when we fucked, my god, there was rough, uneven texture that hadn't been there before. It was a primordial act when he fucked me in the topiary. It was fur against fur, catching and holding the animal scent of us, humping and growling and spreading our smell on the grass like the rest of the wildlife.

He shivers his fingers up through my lush growth and sucks his bottom lip in concentration. I practically catapult off the seat as his thumb rakes my clit. "Maybe," he says, shoving in closer until I can feel his breath against my inner thigh. "Could be."

"Please." I squirm against his open palm. "I can't wait much longer."

He shoves at my skirt with an impatient hand, raking and caressing, pushing my legs apart, examining. His nose is scant millimetres away. I know he smells the heat of my pussy. He's close enough to taste me. It takes all of my self control not to thrust myself full-on at his face.

The frown of concentration hardens to satisfied resolve, and he drops a breathy kiss against my mound. "Wait here, darling. I'll be right back, and don't touch." He slaps my hand away.

It feels like he's gone for ages. I grind my bottom against the stone and imagine penis and pussy shapes in the shrubs of Aden's topiary. When he returns, I practically sob with relief.

"Take off your clothes. All of them." His voice is firm, certain, like he knows exactly what he's about, like he has a plan. He watches as I strip off t-shirt, bra, skirt. My skin goes all goose fleshed with the warm breeze making my body hair stand at attention, making my muff feel bigger than the spiralling boxwood Aden has been tending.

But he doesn't notice the goose flesh. He doesn't notice the lead weight of my nipples, or my kittenish whimpers. He sees only my verdant dark patch, the patch that now pillows his weight every night when he mounts me, the patch that always makes him hard.

He orders me to straddle the bench and scoot down until I'm sitting at the end, legs splayed wide apart. Then when he's satisfied that I'm right where he wants me, he kneels in front of me and opens a leather case, which contains a comb and several small pairs of scissors. "They're newly sharpened," he says. "I knew you were close. I didn't want to be caught unprepared."

I thrust my hips forward. Everything between my thighs feels expanded and puffy.

At first Aden simply strokes my heavy curls, his face in deep concentration. His creative juices, like my own, are flowing. I begin to thrust lightly against his stroking, impatient for him to get on with it. But he won't be rushed. A stroke with the comb here, a shove of my leg there, a shivering with his fingers as he plumps and fluffs. "Yes, I see it now," he breathes. "I know exactly how it's supposed to be."

He begins.

He combs and snips and says half under his breath, "Mmm

hmm, uh huh, just a little more. That's right. Perfect." Then he switches to another pair of scissors. I can tell no difference, but he says he needs to create texture, depth, a sense of perspective.

"The landscape should always showcase its finest feature." His fingers press in around my clit, and he rubs and strokes it to prominence.

I try to sit still as he clips and combs, but I'm slippery and swollen and all of the fantastical shapes in Aden's exquisite topiary now appear orgiastic, spreading wide, thrusting upward, pouting and arching. The bench is damp beneath me and Aden's trousers look as though they're about to lose the battle for containment. He breathes like there's a wind storm in his lungs, and with each snip, he squirms and shifts.

With a weighty grunt he brushes away the hair he's trimmed and buries his face in my pussy. "Perfect," he says when he comes up for air. Then from inside the case, he pulls a gilt hand mirror just the right size for admiring personal gardens. He holds it up for me to see.

I'm splayed wide on the bench and the dark red of my pout swells like a wet cavern beneath the bonsai-delicate sculpting of my curls. As I admire his artistic skills, Aden frees his cock from his trousers and the naked weight of it presses insistently against my thigh.

"Very nice." His breath steams the mirror, obliterating the view of my private topiary. Then he pulls me off the bench onto his lap, wriggling and positioning until his cock is pressing between my labia. He holds me there just long enough to torture us both. Then he thrusts into me, all the way in, and I'm slick and gripping as he rolls me onto the grass.

He rakes across my pubic landscape with each thrust, and he does it slowly so we can both feel the texture and the depth of what he's created in my bush. "Perfect, exquisite," he grunts. "Can you feel it? Can you feel how it changes everything?" He arches upward and runs his hand down between us to fondle his work. "The angle is now better for penetration. It makes no sense, I know, but it is. Can you feel it? And your clit is now better exposed for stimulation." He tweaks my clit and I nearly buck him off for his efforts. He chuckles at my sensitivity, then he rubs against me. I lift my legs and wrap them around him, and we come together.

There's a view of the topiary from the patio. We eat there in the evening. We eat salmon and new potatoes, then feed each other strawberries fresh from the kitchen garden. Beneath the table, Aden wriggles his bare foot up under my skirt. I slump in my chair and go all vacant-eyed while I bear down against the press of him until I come in gasps and shudders as his toes circle my clit and dip into my pout. Then he beckons me to him and pulls me onto his lap like he's Santa Claus and I'm trying to convince him I've been a good little girl. But Santa Claus has a raging hard-on, and I'm definitely not a good little girl.

I wake from sex-crazed dreams. Sunlight streams through the bedroom window, there's water running in the bathroom. I yawn and stretch and shove myself into a sitting position against muscles that are tender from the celebration of my pubic sculpting. It began on the patio, then moved into the topiary under the full moon. At some point, we ended up sweating and grunting in the middle of Aden's big bed.

"Darling? Are you up?" Aden calls. "I've drawn your bath."

I don't bother with a robe. I shuffle into the bathroom displaying Aden's masterpiece proudly between my legs. He's waiting next to the tubful of lavender-scented water, lavender that I've, no doubt grown for him. I'm surprised to find him dressed in his gardening clothes. He barely notices his artwork as he takes my hand and helps me into the tub. I'm a bit confused, but it's early and my brain is still pretty sex-addled. I lie back and close my eyes. He sponges me all over, lingering to lick the water droplets off my breasts. Then while he slides the sponge between my legs washing the parts of me that are still tender and raw from last night's orgy, he fellates my toes one by one, and when he's finished, I'm spread wide and ready, grinding my bottom against the marble tub, not caring how bruised my pussy is. I want him.

But when I reach for his fly, he pushes my hands away. "Not yet, Bess. There's something I have to do first."

I offer him a pouty little whimper, which he ignores as he takes my hand and helps me to stand. Then he begins to wash my sculpted pubes, soaping them until they're white, pressed to jagged sudsy peaks like small glaciers. Running his fingers through my curls seems endlessly fascinating to him, so I stand in growing impatience with my legs open and my pussy gaping to be filled.

And still he lathers me.

"Aden, please," I beg. "I need you to fuck me."

"Not just yet." His voice sounds like it does when he's in the topiary, concentrating hard on his latest creation.

"Aden?"

It's then I notice the razor on the countertop and I nearly lose my balance in a tidal wave of water that drenches both of us. But Aden steadies me. "Stand still, darling." He reaches for the razor. "One day's growth can change everything. With one day's growth I can see how I might have done better, how I could do better next time."

"Next time? But—"

"Shh." He eats my mouth until I'm unable to protest, until he knows I'll do whatever he wants. Then his words come in a breathless rush. "Listen to me, darling, yesterday was just our first attempt. It was a magnificent attempt, granted, but think of what we can create once we've had a little practice." He's hard, nearly to bursting, as he lays two fingers against my labia. I hold my breath as he gently makes the first scrape with the razor. "It'll only be bare for a little while," he reassures me.

I watch through a mist of tears as in a matter of minutes he scrapes away his lovely creation, which has taken me months to grow. At last I'm smooth and naked once more. "A blank slate," he whispers, as he rinses away the last of the soap and bends to kiss the naked skin.

I stand crying quietly while he towels me dry. All the while he speaks softly to me, comforting me, promising me that next time it will be even better.

He carries me back to the bed and soothes my rawness with luxurious lotion, massaging in slow, even strokes that end with his thumb circling my clit. I quiver against him and lift my bottom to show him what I need.

"You'll see, love," he breathes. "It'll grow back so quickly and so beautifully." He stands to undress. "When it does, it'll be good. So good."

When he pushes into me, I feel the hungry rub of him against my new nakedness, and even through my loss, I find myself already anticipating the itch of new growth.

*****

More about K D Grace

K D Grace believes Freud was right. In the end, it really IS all about sex, well sex and love. And nobody's happier about that than she is, otherwise, what would she write about?

When she's not writing, K D is veg gardening. When she's not gardening, she's walking. She walks her stories, and she's serious about it. For her, inspiration is directly proportionate to how quickly she wears out a pair of walking boots. She also enjoys martial arts, reading, watching the birds and anything that gets her outdoors.

K D has erotica published with SourceBooks, Xcite Books, HarperCollins Mischief Books, Mammoth, Cleis Press, Black Lace, Erotic Review, Ravenous Romance, Sweetmeats Press and others.

Links

Website: http://kdgrace.co.uk
Twitter: http://www.twitter.com/kd_grace
Facebook: https://www.facebook.com/KDGraceAuthor
Goodreads: https://www.goodreads.com/author/show/2791969.K_D_Grace
Pinterest: http://www.pinterest.com/kdgraceauthor/

Praise for K D Grace

Body Temperature and Rising

"This well-written, full-length erotic novel comes from the pen of well-established writer K. D. Grace… easily one of the best books I've read!" **Jade Magazine**

"I am a huge fan of K.D. Grace's explicit, well-crafted writing (I've selected and published her work in multi-author "Best" collections), and this novel did not disappoint me. It's the first of a hardcore paranormal trilogy, and many readers think it is her best work to date." **Violet Blue**

Secret Servicing

By Lily Harlem

Chapter One

"Who the hell do you think you are?"

"Jen, please, don't… we need to speak."

"Fuck you." I pushed at the door and shut my eyes. I didn't need reminding how damn gorgeous Kingsley was. Not in a model way, but in a rugged, been-around-the-block macho way.

"No." He shoved his big black boot over the threshold, stopping the door connecting with the frame. "Let me explain. I've done nothing wrong."

"I don't want to hear it. Any of it." Still I kept my eyes tight shut. He'd ripped open my heart three weeks ago. I'd barely patched it up enough to get through each day. The last thing I needed was to see the way his lips flattened and his brow furrowed when he was professing his love, his passion—or in this case, his innocence. It would have me coming undone in a very unsightly tangle.

Bastard.

"Go," I said, shouting over the noise of the pelting rain that was hammering onto my paved driveway. "I need you to go. You're not part of my life anymore."

"But I am, please. If only you'll let me explain what happened that night."

I opened my eyes. "That night. That fucking night? What about the night after that, and the night after that? You've been gone twenty-one nights in total. It was as though you'd been abducted by aliens or something." I jabbed at his boot with my toes. I only wore fluffy pink socks so it hurt, and of course, he didn't budge.

"I was, kind of."

I laughed, without humour, a sound that was bitter and twisted. "Yeah, right. And I'm the goddamn Honey Monster. I've been with enough shitheads full of bull to know when I've got one on my doorstep."

"I'm not a shithead, Jen, you know I'm not. Fuck, let me come in."

I rammed the door again with flattened palms. It didn't move.

Kingsley had his shoulder against it, and he was a big bloke. My efforts were futile.

"Oh, what the hell." I turned, letting the door fly open to the night and felt the tiniest twinge of satisfaction when I heard his boots slap onto the wooden floor.

"Thanks," he said in his usual guttural tone.

He always spoke like he'd just knocked back a sharp whiskey and his throat was hot and rasped. It was one of the first things that had turned me on about him. That and his flashing dark eyes that promised as much sin as I could handle. He'd been so different to my usual blue-collared boyfriends with his quiet but solid demeanor and rugged arctic-truck-driver ways.

The door clicked shut, and he huffed out a breath—relief that I'd let him in, or just glad to be out of the storm?

Quickly I headed to the kitchen. I needed a damn drink. I'd been minding my own business watching *X Factor* in my fleecy pyjamas, enjoying wallowing in my misery on an evening off work, when suddenly he'd burst into my sanctuary. His presence was like a hurricane creating a whirlwind of emotions.

Vodka and Coke should settle them. Or at least be a start.

I banged through cupboards, gathering a tumbler and the bottles. I was aware of him looming in the doorway, his wide shoulders blocking out the hall light and his shadow stretching over the white linoleum.

I didn't bother to offer him a drink.

He wasn't staying.

"Go on then," I said, taking a slug and wincing at the sharpness. "Let's have it."

"Not like this." He paused.

I turned to him. I could make out the bulge of his biceps through his black leather jacket and the spread of his hard, muscular chest. Raindrops sat in his hair, there were shadows beneath his eyes, and he wore a couple of days' worth of stubble. His jeans were wet and ripped over his right knee, his boots grubby, and marking my floor as the rain slithered from them.

"What's the matter with you?" A sudden fizz of doubt wheedled its way into my mind.

He didn't look quite right—tired, a bit unkempt. "You living on the streets or something?"

He snorted and stepped into the room. "Might as well have

been." He pointed at the vodka. "May I?"

I shrugged then leaned back on the counter. My heart was skipping. Standing next to me was the man who I'd thought I had a future with, dreams in common with, and to whom I'd given my heart.

He sloshed vodka into a mug then knocked it back neat. "I won't stay long."

"Why, you on the run?"

He slammed the mug down and stepped up to me, fast, his chest rising and falling and a droplet of rain rolling from his temple.

"We need to hash this out, Jen. There's lots to say, lots to decide." He slid his fingers through his hair. It flopped messy and damp over his forehead and around his ears. His leather jacket creaked, filling the quiet kitchen. "Can we stop pissing about and start now?"

"Whatever," I said, feigning nonchalance.

"Remember that night, at the party?"

I clenched my jaw and swallowed down a rise of pain as my throat constricted. It had been the worst night of my life.

"It hurt me, too, to go like that. Without explaining."

I didn't trust myself to speak so instead I gulped on my drink.

"If there'd been any other way." He frowned and shook his head.

"I went to the bathroom, came back, and you'd just vanished." My hands were shaking. I placed my tumbler down. "I sat on the bench outside, waiting for you. No one had seen you even leave."

"It was the only way."

"I rang the police."

"I know."

Now it was my turn to frown. "You do?"

"Yes."

"But—?"

"Jen. I had to help someone." He reached out and touched my shoulder. "It was urgent."

What could have possibly been so urgent that he'd just walked away from me?

I shook him off. It was bad enough that he was here, ripping wounds open, but to touch me too? That was more than I could cope with.

Pushing away from the counter, I slipped past him and rushed into the living room. My mind was spinning and my eyes struggling to focus as I stared at a boy band on the TV screen. They were leaping around the stage in tight jeans and big bright trainers, yelling about the best song ever.

"Jen."

Out of the corner of my eye, I saw him toss his jacket onto the single armchair in the corner of the room, the way he always used to.

Damn, I missed him. Missed the way he moved his big body with grace around my small home. How he sometimes lost it when we made love and took me with him to wild, untamed places where pleasure rocked my world. The sound of him coming, grunting, panting for breath was a beautiful ghost of a noise that would haunt me until the end of my days. And the way he traced my skin after we'd fucked, as though it told him a beautiful story. It was enough to make my flesh goose bump just at the memory.

I loved his body, defined and powerful, because he worked out to prevent his sedentary driving job taking its toll. He had a smattering of chest hair, coarse and masculine, that wound down to his navel and thickened at his groin. On the underside of his upper right arm was a tiny tattoo. A dagger with wings; it was only small but it was super-sexy and tasted delicious when I ran my tongue over it.

"You just left," I said, muting the sound on the TV. "You just bloody left."

"I had to—"

"Without saying anything to me? Really? What kind of bastard does that?" I spun around. "No, don't tell me. Clearly the type of bastard that you are." I jabbed my finger at him.

"I'm not a bastard, though you have every right to think of me that way." He frowned and dropped his gaze from my face to my toes then back up again. He licked his lips.

"Don't!" I said, marching up to him and shoving his jaw to turn his head away. So that he couldn't look at me. "Don't act like you still find me attractive, that you still want me, because it's clear you don't."

"I do."

I kind of growled in frustration. A noise I hadn't heard myself make before. "Funny way of showing it."

He caught my wrist in his hand and turned back to me, holding my arm between us. "I'm here, aren't I?"

"Too little too late."

"I got here as soon as I could."

"What, like you couldn't call? Couldn't send me a text? An old-fashioned letter?"

"No."

I wriggled free from his grip and stared up into his eyes. "You better explain, Kingsley, because I've had the worst fucking few weeks of my life wondering if you were dead or alive. Wondering what the hell I'd done to deserve a man I thought I had a serious relationship with just vanishing like that." I paused, huffed. "Sometimes I even thought I'd dreamt our time together, or that you'd been a figment of my imagination."

He smirked, and I itched to slap the tilt of his lips.

"Funny, is it?" I snapped. "Funny that you made me fall for you and then trampled all over my heart?"

He grabbed me, both hands on my shoulders, and pulled me close. He stared down at me, his dark eyes flashing and his nostrils flaring. "I told you, I didn't want to go but I had to. And as for trampling all over your heart, do you think leaving didn't break mine?"

He was so big towering over me. His body heat was burning onto my skin, his gripping fingers pressing into my flesh. My traitorous hormones perked up. The feel of him against my chest, my legs, the breeze of his hot breaths on my face was creating a bundle of erotic memories of our time together.

I didn't want to still need the man who'd left me, but I did.

"So why did you?" I whispered. "Go, that is?"

He lowered his head so his mouth was a hairsbreadth from mine. He had a tiny dink in his bottom lip, right in the centre—it was a part of him I adored.

Suddenly he kissed me, soft and gentle, his tongue just peeking into my mouth.

I was so shocked I didn't respond, just stood there letting my arms hang limp and my mouth be caressed by his. But his flavour was too intoxicating, hot and peppery with a hint of vodka, and I soon found myself matching his kiss, winding my tongue with his.

It had been so long. I'd fantasised about this, being in his arms again. Kingsley fitted me so well, and I fitted him. We were two halves coming together.

What the hell am I doing?

I jolted away, freeing myself from his grip then spinning to face the TV again. "What the fuck…?" I muttered, wiping my mouth on the back of my hand, "do you think you're doing?"

"I—"

"No, don't speak." Heat was flaming on my cheeks. Indignation crawling on my skin like a swarm of ants. Did he think he could kiss me again and I'd fall at his feet? Oh, no, I wasn't that much of a pushover. Not by a long shot. "Just leave." I indicated to the door. "Now."

"But, Jen, let me explain. I'm not supposed to, not yet, we've still got lots to talk about, but I will."

"Don't do me any favours. We're over."

"Clearly we're not if that fucking kiss is anything to go by."

"Yes, we are. How could I ever trust you again? How could I even let you go into another room and be one hundred percent certain that you'd come back?"

"Trust," he said, "is delicate, I agree. And the fact that I shattered your trust in me was not within my control, but I promise, it'll never happen again. Not once I've explained."

I kept my back to him, staring at the screen as a new singer silently performed a ballad.

I wanted Kingsley to go. He was talking in riddles and he'd just pulled off the Band-Aid I'd wrapped around my delicate heart. The pain was too much to bear.

There was a rustle of material behind me.

"Jen."

"What?"

"Please, look at me."

"No." I knotted my fingers together. I was shaking.

He appeared around my right side and stood between me and the TV. He'd removed his t-shirt and I found myself staring at his bare chest. Oh, fuck. That little scribble of hair on his sternum and his tight, dark nipples could be my downfall in resisting him.

The bastard didn't play fair.

"You think you're going to win me back with your body?" I asked with a huff, peeling my gaze away. I had to hand it to him, it was a decent plan.

"No, but I need to show you this." He raised his right arm,

exposing a tuft of black hair and the small tattoo etched onto a paler patch of delicate flesh.

I rolled my eyes and shook my head. "Really?"

"This," he said, poking the tattoo, "doesn't exactly have the meaning I first told you."

I scowled. "What?"

"I told you it was a symbol of my great grandfather's regiment, in the army, didn't I?"

"Er, yes. I think so." What was he on about?

"It isn't. It's the symbol for the regiment *I'm* in." He paused and tugged at his bottom lip with his teeth. "Now."

Chapter Two

"The regiment you're in now? But..." I was struggling to make sense of his words. "You're not in a regiment. You're... you drive a truck."

He lowered his arm, cupped my jawline in both hands and frowned. "I lied to you, and for that I'll always be sorry, but it's how it had to be. The only way it *could* be." His voice was so husky it was like his throat was made of sandpaper.

"You lied? About being in the army? Why would you do that? Why would anyone do that?"

"I had my reasons." He pressed his lips together and lowered his face to mine.

I could smell him, his skin. Warm, salty flesh laced with dark earthy cologne. "I... I don't understand."

"Jen. That night. I had to go, immediately. I got a call from my superior. Something had come up. Something of vital importance both from a professional and a personal point of view. There was no time to explain to you, not from the beginning anyway. And without starting at the beginning it would have scared you, confused you more."

"So try now." I moved away, not wanting him touching me while I forced my muddled brain to follow what he was telling me.

His touch was too distracting. His nearness made my knees weak and my heart beat fast.

He folded his arms, his knuckles pressing into his biceps, and studied me. "I did try and find you that night. You'd told me you'd gone to the bathroom, but you weren't there. I checked out a couple of bedrooms but I had a twenty-minute window until rendezvous and that had to be my priority."

"Rendezvous?"

"To get to headquarters. Across town. I was in the air within an hour of us last being together and I only landed and debriefed earlier today. I came straight here."

"Oh." I pulled the sleeves of my soft pyjama top over my hands and bunched the material in my fists, thought back to that night. I had gone to the bathroom, yes, but then I'd headed off with Cassie to borrow a pair of stockings as I'd laddered mine. Her room was in the attic, and we'd ended up giggling about the guy she fancied who'd just given her the eye. I'd only been a few minutes, and then when Cassie and I had rejoined the party Kingsley was gone.

Vanished.

"I went with Cassie, up to the top of the house."

"I figured as much, and I wished I could have pulled you to one side, taken the time to have the conversation I want to have with you now. But I had barely one minute to leave the house if I was to make my deadline."

"You make it sound like it was life or death." I tsked.

"It was."

Something about the set of his jaw and the furrow in his brow made me realise he'd meant what he'd said. Did I even know the man I'd fallen in love with? The notion that maybe I didn't sent me jittery, unsure of everything I thought I believed in and knew about other people. We'd spent so much time together, intimate time, fun time, when he wasn't on a long distance drives we'd been inseparable for a blissful summer of love and lust. His confident but understated manner had won me over, and the raw maleness of his desires had set my world alight.

"You better get on with this conversation," I said as I folded my arms. I didn't know what else to do with them. I didn't know what to do with myself. "I'm running out of patience."

"Jen." He stepped closer and held his hands out. "Don't. I've gone over this conversation in my head a million times. Please…"

I moved backwards, until my legs hit the sofa.

He sighed and shrugged. "I'm a soldier; I'm on active duty with a special forces division."

"But… but you said you worked for a long-distance haulage company?" I stared at his face, the shape of his nose, the bump in the middle. So familiar yet somehow not.

"That's just a cover. My true profession is classified information. But I need friends and acquaintances to think I do something for a living. I don't want to be thought of as a bum or generate suspicion if I'm away for weeks at a time. Truck driver fits the bill."

I had so many questions but I started with the one that prodded me the hardest. "Classified information. What are you talking about?"

"I'm legally not allowed to tell people what I do, Jen. Only close relatives are permitted to be told, and… and, well, spouses obviously."

"But you've told me now. I think."

He tipped his head and smiled. His whole face softened, and the shards of steely determination in his eyes mellowed. "Not all of it, but yes, you now know more than most." He scrubbed his hand down his cheek, creating an abrasive sound as his palm scoured against his stubble. "Which must surely prove something to you."

I panted out a breath. A sudden, vibrant image hit me of his bristles grazing the inside of my thigh as he pleasured me with his tongue. Damn, the man was good at that. In fact, he was bloody good at a lot of dirty deeds. *And* he was a hot soldier? Really? Fuck!

"Jen, are you keeping up?"

"No."

"I'm telling you this because you're special, important to me." He paused, pulled in a deep breath. "I need to be with you. I need to know that you'll be waiting when I get back from a mission. That when I'm in some goddamn shit-hole being fired at by hostiles that you're here, that you're mine. That I'll hold you in my arms again, make love to you, be with you."

"Hostiles? Being fired at?" Alarm socked me in the guts like a real punch. He got shot at? People wanted to kill him? This man of mine?

"Don't look so alarmed, Jen."

"But what if you got hit?"

I couldn't help but scan his body for signs of gunshot wounds. He had a few dinks and imperfections yes, but nothing too lethal looking.

"I won't get shot. I'm really fucking good at my job." He gave a lopsided grin. "And that's all it is, just a job. I get downtime, but occasionally I have to go, for a few weeks or months, on a moment's notice."

"Like you did in August."

"Yes." He reached for my left hand and unfurled the cuff of the pink patterned top that was covering my knuckles. "And if you'd known, if we'd been a proper couple, without secrets, I could have told you in an instant what was going on and you'd have understood." He lifted my hand, turned it over and pressed a kiss to my open palm as he smoothed his fingers over mine. "I wouldn't have wanted to leave you. Wouldn't have wanted to go without a proper goodbye." He smirked, a sexy little twitch of his cheeks.

"You know what I mean by proper goodbye, eh? A long, lazy fuck and a whole night of me adoring every inch of your beautiful body."

"Er, yes, I know." I pressed my knees together as a glut of heat shot to my pussy. It wasn't hard to remember just how good he was at making every erogenous zone I possessed sing to his tune.

He tugged me close, slowly, like I was a deer that might bolt, and carefully rested my hand on his warm, bare shoulder. He wound his arms around my waist and settled me against the length of his body.

"So what do you say, babes?"

My breath hitched at his use of his pet name for me. "About what?"

"About forgiving me, taking me back?"

I stared into his dark eyes and studied the black line around his irises. Could I forgive him after all the pain he'd caused me? The panic, the torment, the sleepless nights, and the soul-aching grief he'd put me through?

I honestly didn't know.

"Please," he whispered, a line furrowing between his dense eyebrows. "I'm in love with you, Jen. It doesn't seem worth it without you. It did before but now, now it's you I want to do it all for."

A sob brewed in my chest and burst from my mouth, spluttering out as it shook my whole body. "But it hurt... so much."

His face twisted, as though he was in pain. "And I'll spend the rest of my life making it up to you. I promise. Because we can work this out, I know we can, we're strong."

He tightened his grip on me, and I couldn't deny that being in his arms lifted the aching anvil of sorrow that had been following me around for so long. "But how can you promise me that if... if like you say, you might have to go again, any second?"

"It's true, there are times when I have to go in an instant, but usually I have notice. It was just..." He glanced away, seemingly staring at something in his mind's eye.

"What?"

"It was just a colleague. No..." He shook his head. "More than a colleague—a mate, best mate, who was in trouble. I had to go. I had to be the one leading the rescue mission. If I hadn't gone and he'd been killed I would never have forgiven myself."

"And did you save him?"

I smoothed my hands over his shoulders, wondering what hell I'd go through if it were Kingsley in trouble and in need of saving. But, no, Kingsley was too tough, too sure of his every move to get into a deathly situation. He'd always made me feel safe and protected when we were out together. Now I knew why.

He was a trained killer.

Shit.

I shoved at his shoulders and twisted away. My stomach clenched. All the things he must have done and seen and been involved in. I wasn't stupid; he was in the SAS. I'd seen films, read books. Suddenly my imagination couldn't keep up, and I wasn't sure if I wanted it to go there or not.

"Hey, hey, yes, we got him out. He's fine, at home with wife and kids and making a good recovery. He looks a mess, but he's an ugly fucker anyway." He laughed. "Matt is a great soldier but came unstuck when he was outnumbered. He'd have come to get me if I'd been captured, no doubt about it, it's the way we roll."

"That's good, great but… you killed people to get him out, right? That's what you do?"

"People, no, I kill shit-for-brains lunatics who are trying to harm this country, the people *of* this country and who want to undermine all the things I believe in." He pressed his hand into my lower back, squeezing our pelvises together. "Have you any idea what I'd do to someone who tried to hurt you? Even just a hair on your head?"

"No, I… oh…"

His erection jammed up against my belly, and even through clothes I could feel how hot and hard he was. "Kingsley?"

He pressed a quick, strong kiss to my lips and then pulled back. "I'm sorry there's a part of my life you didn't know about, but that's all it is, one detail. I'm still the same man who craves a hot curry, hates soppy movies, and loves having you hug me tight shouting 'faster, faster' as we burn rubber around town on my Harley." He brushed his hand over my hair. "It's still me, babe, it's just now you know everything."

"I guess I do." I licked my lips, taking in his delicious flavour that lingered there.

Suddenly a glint, a sparkle on my left hand caught my eye. There was a ring on my finger. A new ring, one I hadn't seen before. It was a ruby surrounded by diamonds and set in gold. Big and beautiful, it fractured the light from the TV and sent it glittering over my fingers and onto the back of my hand.

I snapped my palm from his shoulder. "What the…?"

"I'll promise to do my best to make you the happiest woman on Earth, Jen, but I won't promise to play clean." He reached for my hand, closed his fingers around mine and the ring. "Dirty is my middle name, especially when it comes to getting the result I want."

My throat was tight, my mouth dry. "Which is?"

"You."

"But I—"

My words were cut off by his ravenous kiss. His passion unleashed he ravished my mouth in a way that had my pussy clenching and my clit buzzing. Kingsley was a man who put everything he had into whatever it was he was doing, which made him one hell of a kisser, one hell of a lover.

In that moment, as his breaths quickened and he cradled the back of my skull, I knew I'd forgiven him. Knew I'd need this for all of time. Okay, so he wasn't who I thought he was, he was so much more. He was layered, mysterious and, so it seemed, mine.

"Wait," I panted, pushing at his chest. "But, the ring."

"You're still wearing it, which is a very good sign." He shifted his eyebrows upwards as though daring me to say otherwise.

"But what does it mean? Are you asking me to—?"

"Marry me, yes."

I paused for a moment and then, "Well, in that case, soldier…" I tilted my chin and stepped back from his embrace. "You'd better get down on one knee and ask me properly instead of presuming."

For the first time since he'd walked out, for the first time in weeks, a smile, a real, genuine smile pulled at my mouth. It felt good—more than good, it felt fantastic.

Kingsley dropped to the ground in front of me, a wicked smirk on his face and a damn dangerous glint in his eyes. "Yes, ma'am."

Chapter Three

I held out my hand, the ring a bright beacon on my finger.

Kingsley took my fingers in his and dropped a kiss over my knuckles. He closed his eyes, and I studied the way his eyelashes were like little fans, spreading shadows on his cheeks. He could be so gentle, so sweet and delicate, and although I'd always known he had power and energy lurking beneath the surface, now I knew the extent of that muscle and skill.

It turned me the hell on.

"Babe," he said, looking up at me. "Marry me, be my someone to come home to." He didn't blink, just stared into my eyes. "I love you so much and I'll work forever to making this last few weeks up to you."

I blinked back a well of tears that were building on my lower lids.

"You're a complete bastard, you know that?" I said, swallowing even though my throat had thickened with emotion. "And, yes, you will have to work very hard to make it up to me."

"Does that mean you will? Marry me, that is?"

I gulped for air, tears threatening to overtake me completely. How fast my life had spun around from sitting alone and sad to being deliriously happy and excited. A life with Kingsley, my whole life?

I loved him so much and always would. He'd stolen my heart the way he'd no doubt sneaked in and saved his soldier mate, with stealth, precision and absolute determination.

"Yes, yes I will." The last word came out as a squeak.

"Thank fuck for that." He stood, grinning and showing his chipped top right tooth. "Babe." He slid his fingers beneath the base of my top. "We got some lost time to make up."

"I guess we have, fiancé."

"Mmm, I like being your fiancé, and I'm going to like being your husband even more."

"Why?"

"Because then I'm going to be the luckiest man alive." He tugged my top off and tossed it onto the sofa. "Fuck, I'd remembered how beautiful you were, but seriously, reality is so much more fun than tossing off to memories."

"You, tossing off? Really?"

"Babe, it gets pretty boring holed up in hell sometimes. And this last trip, I had a whole load of sexy encounters with you to relive when it was dark and cold. Can't blame a bloke for getting turned on and needing some relief."

"I like that, that you thought of me."

"There is only you."

My bra released, slackening around my chest. He slipped it down my arms and it landed on top of my sweater.

Kingsley dipped his head and suckled my right nipple. I arched my back, set my hands on his damp hair and closed my eyes. Damn, I'd missed his clever mouth. He always applied just the right amount of pressure, the perfect squeeze with his teeth, and the way he gently kneaded my flesh with his calloused hands was enough to have me toppling towards orgasm.

"Ah, I forgot how good you taste, babe."

He straightened, towering over me again. There was a feral look in his eyes, a wildness that told me this wasn't going to be a slow reunion. He was on the edge, desperate for it.

Just as well, because I was too. I'd waited too long for this, given up hope of it. So now that I had my beautiful rough-around-the-edges man back, I was going to take everything that I could, and more.

With my fingers all in a fumble, I released the belt on his jeans. It was the same brown as his eyes with a diamond shape pressed into the leather. The buckle was silver, and it took me a moment to open it.

When I did, he groaned and cupped himself over the denim. "Jesus, this is getting painful."

"Let me help you out with that."

"Fucking excellent plan."

The buttons on his fly were easier to manage than the belt. He assisted my access by shoving the denims to his thighs.

He wore tight black boxer trunks. No designer label, no pattern, that wasn't his style, and they tented impressively as the material struggled to contain his bloated cock.

Over warm cotton I curved my palm around his shaft. "So how long until this grenade goes off?" I asked with a smirk.

"I'm guessing about sixty seconds, but I promise, I'll make it good for you too."

I didn't doubt it for a moment, but before I could say

anything I was flat on my back on the sofa with him over me. He grabbed for my pyjama bottoms and pulled them off, efficiently removing my knickers in the process. He left my fluffy socks on, though, they didn't appear to bother him. Seemed the exciting bits were accessible and that was what was important.

"Open up, babe, let me get you as close to coming as I am. We gotta explode together on this one."

He parted my thighs, settling between them. His shoulders pressed against my flesh, and the sweetest ache formed in my hips as he opened me wider.

"Damn, I've missed this," he said, planting a kiss on my soft pubic hair. "And this." He swirled his tongue over my clit.

"Oh, fuck, me too." I fisted a cushion that was lodged at my side.

He nuzzled into my pussy, his tongue licking, exploring, probing into my entrance.

I thrashed my head left and right, found myself staring at the TV again. Some young female singers were getting raunchy in military outfits as they sang a fast-beat song. Or so I guessed because the volume was still down, but their dancing was rapid, their hips rolling.

I set my attention on Kingsley, no pretend military outfit necessary. My trucker boyfriend, it seemed, was a master of disguise and also a master at cunnilingus.

My thoughts began to scatter. A pressure was building in my pelvis. A delicious, deep pressure that started in the very centre of my womb. "Oh, yes, fuck, just there."

Kingsley reached up, cupped my breast and massaged. I placed my hand over his, letting him know how much I liked his touch, silently telling him that it went straight to my core and added to the already blissful sensations he was creating.

He wasn't building me up slowly, he was going for it, slurping, fretting, taking me on a fast ride to Heaven. He added his fingers, too, toying with my clit then heading lower.

He paused at my entrance, slid his fingertips through my wetness, then pushed, what I imagined, two fingers deep inside me.

I bowed off the sofa, wanting more, loving him burying higher, harder, hitting the spot I needed him to most.

I groaned, long and loud, grabbed his hair and pushed my pussy into his face.

He lifted up.

I whimpered in complaint. The tension had been growing, my belly quivering, my pussy sopping.

"Please," I begged. "In me, now."

"I am." He grinned wickedly and waggled his fingers.

"Ah, yeah," I managed, staring at his damp face and the tiny beads of my moisture sitting in his stubble. "More, now."

"Still greedy, eh?"

"Only for you."

"Good, because you can have as much of me as you want."

"I want your dick." I paused to suck in air as he stroked over my G-spot again, pressing in a way that made me want to pee at first but then set me up on a deeply satisfying climb to orgasm. "Now. Now, Kingsley."

"Are we still flesh on flesh?" he asked, his lips against my cheek and his breaths coming hot and fast.

"Yes, yes, it's all fine, please." I should have been impressed that he had the good sense to ask the question, but all I could think of was getting him inside me in the fastest way possible. Yes, I was still on contraception; yes, I was still clean. There'd been no one but him all year.

He grunted, reared back and pushed away his boxers. They bunched around his jeans, which still sat at his thighs. His cock sprang out, as thick and dark and domed as I remembered. A small bead of glossy pre-cum sat in the slit.

My pussy fluttered at the sight of his erection, and I clenched my stomach.

"You ready?" he asked, taking his cock in his fist and stroking to the end. He smoothed the pre-cum away with his index finger and sucked in a breath through gritted teeth.

"Yes."

"Thank fuck, 'cause I've been ready for this for weeks."

He lowered and fed the first inch of himself into me.

I tried to relax but he was big—big and hard and hot and determined.

"Bloody hell, I've missed how damn tight you are, how well we fit," he said, his hair flopping forward as he watched his entry. "Damn, I love you so much, Jen."

"And I love you... oh..."

I gasped then held my breath when he pounded balls deep,

my juice creating a wonderful, fast glide to full depth. He stretched me width-ways and lengthways, and I felt like he'd consumed me, taken over my body.

I clenched around him and he groaned, lowered his head and caught my mouth in a frantic kiss.

"Fuck me," I managed against his lips. "Fuck me, Kingsley, I need it now."

"Roger that," he said, kissing over my cheek to my eye, my forehead, my temple. "Hold on."

He withdrew, not all the way, and I gripped his tense biceps.

With one powerful thrust he forged back in.

He knocked the breath from me and I huffed. He was so deep, so perfectly thick and had rubbed all my hot-spots deliciously. His domed head rammed over my internal nub, and his pelvis battered up against my needy clit.

"Yes, yes," he hissed, "this is where I needed to be."

I couldn't answer, my body was shaking and tense and focused on his cock as he pulled out then pushed back in again. Once more I was shunted up the sofa. He didn't let up, though. His pace quickened, and he dropped his weight, inflicting my clit to even more wonderful stimulation.

I swept my hands down his smooth, hard shoulders, gripped his taut buttocks, and wrapped my legs over his thighs. Hanging on, I met him thrust for thrust. We were wild, animalistic. I gave into it all, let heartache melt away and be replaced by joy and pleasure.

Kingsley was back.

We were getting married.

He was one heck of a hot soldier who wanted me forever.

I squeezed my eyes shut and was aware of tears flowing down my cheeks. I was close to coming. It was within reach. My dark world flashed as his stormy breaths blasted into my ear, swirling with the sound of my rapid pulse.

"Oh... oh... it's here," I managed.

"Thank fuck!"

He lifted up, and I looked at him. Through blurry vision I could see his face, hot and red, his jaw tense and his lips pulled back.

I spiralled into ecstasy.

He drove deep and deeper still. Our bodies worked so well together, perfect harmony and in tune.

My pussy contracted wildly, and my clit bobbed against his

relentless grinding. On and on I spasmed through my orgasm. Not breathing, not thinking, just owned by an almighty climax.

And then Kingsley gave in to it too.

With a roar of release he spurted into me. His muscles turned to granite, and his buttocks clenched.

"Ah, fucking hell, that's it, Jesus, fuck, fuck, bloody Nora…" he shouted, throwing his head back and pushing into me as though he wouldn't be happy until he nudged my diaphragm. "Yes."

His shaft was thumping inside me, and I hugged him with my pussy, dragged in a deep breath and reached for his face.

Sharp stubble grazed my palms, and I wondered at the beauty of him in the final throes.

Through gritted teeth he sucked in a breath, stilled, and lowered his face.

"That was," I panted, "amazing." I relaxed my hips and within my socks uncurled my toes.

"Fuck yeah."

His eyes were glazed and his mouth slack. I stroked my thumb over his bottom lip, caressing that little dink I loved.

"So that's what you'd been thinking of, when you were away?"

"That was just number nine hundred and ninety-nine of the fantasies I had when I was hiding out. We got a way to go yet, babe." He frowned. "Are you crying?"

"No, I—"

"Shh. It's okay." He kissed the dewy dampness on my cheeks.

"I'm not sad."

"Sure?"

"Yes, I'm happy—happy that you're back, happy that you want me."

"I will want you forever; you're my reason for living, reason for coming home."

I pushed a lock of his hair away from his eyes. It had curled like a comma and was tickling against his lashes. "But you will always come back?"

"Nothing in life is a guarantee, not in my world, but I'll do my best."

"I couldn't be without you again."

"And I couldn't be without you." He kissed me, long and

slow, his tongue dancing with mine and his breaths calming.

I looped my hands around his neck and hugged him tighter. I never wanted to let him go, but I knew I'd have to. I knew that when he was gone I was going to pace the floor, hardly sleep and pray for his safety. But that was the price I was going to have to pay for being a military wife, a *secret* military wife.

The thought was scary, daunting, but it was also exhilarating to think that soon I'd be walking down the aisle to marry my hunky 'truck driving' hero.

*****

More about Lily Harlem

Lily Harlem lives in the UK and is an award-winning author of contemporary erotic romance. She writes for publishers on both sides of the Atlantic including Ellora's Cave, HarperCollins, Totally Bound, Xcite and Sweetmeats Press. She also self-publishes novels that range from emotionally charged erotic romance, to steamy ménage a trois and, with Natalie Dae, (Harlem Dae) dark BDSM that pushes all the boundaries.

Her HOT ICE series regularly receives high praise and industry nominations and Lily is sure that she'll never run out of inspiration for penning more sexy stories about her bad boys of the ice and the women who tame them.

One thing you can be sure of, whatever book you pick up by Ms Harlem, is it will be wildly romantic and down-and-dirty sexy so make sure you hang on tight for the ride!

Links

Website: http://www.lilyharlem.com/
Blog: http://www.lilyharlem.blogspot.com/
Twitter: https://twitter.com/lily_harlem
Facebook: https://www.facebook.com/lily.harlem
Facebook author page:
https://www.facebook.com/LilyHarlemAuthor
Goodreads:
http://www.goodreads.com/author/show/4070110.Lily_Harlem
Pinterest: http://pinterest.com/lilyharlem/
Google+:
https://plus.google.com/u/0/106837751333678531161/posts
Newsletter: http://www.lilyharlem.com/newsletter-subscription.html

Praise for Lily Harlem

Breathe You In

"The level of emotion Ms. Harlem evokes not only from the characters but the reader as well shows a rare gift."

Scored

"As always in a Lily Harlem novel, the sex is HOT! Ms. Harlem writes mind-blowing scenes."

The Glass Knot

"I'm not even done & I'm in love with this book. I can tell it's going to be a favorite re-read. Lily has a way of writing that is so engaging, raw & real."

Hired

"The way Lily Harlem draws you on is so refreshing; her voice is refreshing and real. Lily is rapidly becoming one of my favorite authors. I loved everything about this book!"

Breathe You In

"This is one of those emotional reads that just makes you say "wow" when you read it."

Hired

"Great characterization, believable dialogue, hot hot hot love scenes. Even the hockey game is exciting. Lily Harlem has joined my auto-buy list."

End Result: A Raw Talent short story

By Lily Harlem and Lucy Felthouse

Chapter One

I stood in the home team's private box, tapping my long fingernails together and trying to slow my racing heart. My fiancé, Luke Hale, had been chosen to take the penalty in the eighty-ninth minute. I was some distance away, but I could sense the determination oozing from him. His wide shoulders, beneath his red footballer's top were stiff and set back, his chin tilted toward the London sky and he walked like a man who meant business.

Good, because we needed him to do what he was paid to do. He had to hit the back of the net. If he did, the match would be a draw, if he didn't, we'd be one down. The thought of losing didn't bear thinking about, not against Rovers, our archenemy. The team would be in a sour mood, Luke included, and it was me that had to go home with him at the end of the day.

The end of the day. Mmm… that held a lot of meaning for us as we'd come up with an ingenious way of coping with the highs and lows of professional football.

Victory celebrations were always wild fun, the best, we'd knock back champagne and then drive each other crazy, neither of us top or bottom, just going for what felt good. Losing, well that definitely had its benefits, despite his sullen face, and I enjoyed wearing my Domme heels and wielding a flogger. Seeing big, bad Luke get to his knees and beg for release was always a treat and it certainly took his mind off his woes. And a draw, well I *really* liked that because then I had Luke, at his best; determined, focused, dominant and ready to let all that tension go in one big burst of energy. He had considerable skills on the pitch, and when it came to getting results in the bedroom, he had a whole other set of talents for that. My body, my satisfaction and my unique set of needs were in capable hands and well looked after.

He set the ball down, swivelled it in the mud until he was happy it was in the optimum position, then straightened, stared at the goal and walked backwards ten paces, not taking his gaze from his target.

His team mates watched the way the fans did—nervously biting nails, hands pressed to foreheads and arms folded tight.

"Get it in," I muttered, "just hit the back of the damn net."

Luke clenched and unclenched his fists. He hopped from foot to foot; his wide thighs flexing and his shorts stretching tight over his groin.

I licked my lips. They tasted of cherry gloss. His favourite.

The goalkeeper hunched over and swayed left to right, his big, gloved hands spread wide and his expression deadly serious.

The whistle went.

Luke blew out a breath then raced at the ball. The *thwack* of him kicking it reached me a split second after impact. The ball whizzed through the air, he'd put a spin on it and the curve it took towards the goal meant it was on a perfect arc to meet its destination.

The goalie dived to the right, the exact opposite way the ball was heading, and as the back of the net punched out, he hit the turf and skidded along the slick ground.

The stadium erupted. Home fans leapt out of their seats, punching the air and stamping their feet. The noise was deafening and I added to it with my own shouts of delight. "Yes, that's it. Yes! Whoop, well done. Yeah!"

Luke was the best shot in the league, just one of the many reasons why he was captain of the team and why the fans loved him so much.

I loved him too.

He turned to his team mates as they flung themselves on him. Vaulting high and landing on his back, his shoulders and then on top of each other until they were a red tangle of footballers.

Anyone would have thought they'd won rather than just drawn level. But not conceding a loss to Rovers was a win in itself. It had been a tough game, though with just sixty seconds left on the clock the final score was unlikely to change.

The ref blew the whistle to resume play. Left-winger Diego gained possession of the ball and knocked it around an opposition centre-mid. Luke got his foot to it and teased another Rover player with a couple of side-taps before booting it up the midline to a defender.

Another few passes, one minute injury time, and the final whistle screeched through the air.

I heaved out a sigh of relief. One-all we could live with.

Well, certainly I could, because I was looking forward to my evening with Luke in his masterful role. Far from being exhausted after a Champions League match he was always ready for action. It was as though the adrenaline of the game lingered in him and his body still needed to work, sweat it out.

Not that I was complaining, the sort of work I had in mind for him would keep *me* very happy indeed, equally sweaty and riding high on my particular brand of bliss. Or so I hoped.

Two hours later, Luke pulled the Range Rover into our garage and flicked the button on the remote to shut the door behind us. I liked it when he did that. It felt like we were shutting out the world, putting all the media and the fans and the pressures of him being a world-class footballer away for the night.

I flicked off Twitter and dropped my mobile into my Prada handbag, then reached out and rested my hand on his thigh, over his sweats.

He turned to me with his black eyebrows low and his mouth set tight. He hadn't spoken on the way home, which was often the way. I didn't mind, he'd explained to me how he liked to go over and over the shots in his memory while they were still fresh. Figure out what he and the team could have done better to win the ball and keep the ball, so that next time they'd be even better.

"Do you want to eat?" I asked, a little quiver attacking my pussy as I looked at him all big, dark and brooding with shadows slicing over his handsome face.

He turned off the engine and rested his big, warm hand over mine. "We'll eat later."

A bubble of excitement popped in my stomach. He wanted to get straight to the good stuff then. I was a lucky girl.

He leaned close and his shower-fresh scent and recently applied woodsy cologne filled my nostrils.

"I just need you, Emma. I just want to be with you."

"Well that can be arranged." I brushed my lips over his as a tingle ran up my spine and over my scalp. Luke might be a pin-up for many women, his on-pitch skills admired by a million men, but here and now he was mine, all mine.

Ever since he'd proposed three months ago I'd kept pinching myself to make sure it was real. We'd been childhood sweethearts, yet he'd been launched into the stratosphere of fame with his sporting achievements after he'd left the small town we'd grown up in. It wasn't until we met up again eighteen months ago through a friend of a friend that the spark was reignited. One glance across a crowded wedding reception and all the emotions tumbled back into me, and him too, so he'd said. It was like we'd never been apart.

He hadn't changed much. He still acted goofy and made me laugh so hard I had tears pouring down my cheeks. Continued to insist on a weekly trip to the cinema to see whatever latest action movie was out, and he always put me first. Whatever we were doing he'd make sure I was okay, that I was happy. Luke was attentive, considerate and caring both in and out of the bedroom. Loving him was easy. Famous footballer or not, it was Luke Hale who'd stolen my heart for all of time. Just him.

I smiled and looked into his dark eyes. His pupils were large, though his lids were heavy, the way they always were when he was thinking about sex; especially *equalizer sex.*

I knew damn well if I cupped his groin over his jeans he'd be hard. Desire was written all over his face and, it seemed, thoughts of what had gone down during the game had receded into the far corners of his mind.

He kissed me, harder than I'd kissed him, and peeked his tongue into my mouth. His delicious flavour, mixed with the orange sweetness of an energy drink, had me greedy for more.

I ran my fingers into his long strands of hair and clenched my fists. I held his head tight as I fed him kiss for kiss. My body came alive, heat spreading between my legs and my nipples pressing against my bra.

His breaths quickened, so did mine.

He cupped my right breast, squeezed and released, massaging just the way he knew I liked.

The urge for flesh on flesh became a desperate need. I wanted us naked, joined, writhing in ecstasy. I needed him to turn my skin pink and hot and make my body sing with edgy pleasure.

It seemed he wanted all of that too. He tugged at my sweater and slipped it over my head, our kiss only breaking for the briefest moment. A loosening around my chest told me my bra had gone.

"Baby, you taste so good," he murmured, ducking his head and suckling my nipple.

"Mmm," I moaned, still clutching his hair. My pussy was dampening, my stomach clenching and I arched my back, pushing into him for more.

He sucked and nipped, sending darts of desire shooting to my groin. I pulled at his t-shirt, dragging it from him and discarding it the way he had mine.

"I need to make you mine," he said, breathlessly.

"What here?"

"Yes." He paused, frowned and shook his head. "No, not here. That won't work for what I have planned. Inside. Now."

He pulled back and yanked the keys from the ignition so he could let us into the house. I paused for a moment to admire his wide shoulders and the acres of golden skin that rippled as the muscles beneath moved.

After slipping from the car, he hesitated before shutting the door. "Emma?"

"Yes Sir?"

"What are you waiting for? Come on." His attention dropped from my face to my breasts.

I was breathing fast, my chest rising and falling. My nipples were erect and moist, a little dusky too from his attentions.

"Yes Sir," I said, opening my door. "I'm coming."

He grinned sinfully. "We both will be soon."

Chapter Two

I almost burst into the back hallway in my eagerness to get Emma to our bedroom. Stumbling a little in my haste, I heard a brazen giggle from behind me.

"I saw that," she said, her blue eyes glinting with mischief and her luscious lips curving at the corners. "The famous Hale feet got tangled."

"Laughing at your Master are you?" I said, turning to face her and folding my arms.

"Yeah, I did. What are you gonna do about it?" The expression on her face indicated she knew exactly what I had in mind and she was quite happy about it—pushy little brat.

"I think, young lady, that you'll have to wait and see." I paused momentarily, hoping to lull her into a false sense of security, then reached out and grabbed her before slinging her over my shoulder.

She let out a shriek, which was quickly followed by a peal of laughter.

"What are you doing, you crazy person? Put me down! I'll break your back."

I landed a hearty slap on her jeans-clad arse and the satisfying sound rang around the room. "Shut up, woman. I'm a world-class athlete, didn't you know? I'm at peak fitness. I think I can handle carrying my fiancée to bed."

"Well, hurry up then. All my blood's rushing to my head."

"Seriously, you're pushing it big time, telling me what to do."

Kicking the door to the garage closed, I held on tight to Emma and strode across the ground floor of our house, before turning to head up the stairs, careful not to bash her against any of the door frames or the banisters.

She was silent now. I guessed she'd figured that was as far as she wanted to stretch her Master's patience for now.

My eagerness to fuck her carried me quickly up the stairs. Seconds later I flung open the door to our bedroom and deposited her in the middle of our queen-sized mattress. I didn't bother to close the blinds—we were far enough from the road in our expensive countryside property that even the most powerful telephotographic lenses couldn't capture snaps of us in our bedroom.

Joining Emma on the bouncy mattress, I crawled over her and captured her lips with mine. God, but she was perfect, she always had been, right from when we gave each other our virginity. My cock was straining hard against the inside of my jeans and she wasn't even naked. Yet.

We kissed long and hard, lips and tongues clashing and our hands wandering, grabbing, squeezing and stroking. Our oral attentions continued until we were both breathless, and I pulled away, shaking my head in the hopes of getting rid of some of my dizzying lust so that I could function. So that I could think, form words and orchestrate what was going to happen next and be what she wanted me to be.

After a few seconds, I managed to get a hold of myself and I flashed a wicked smile at my wife-to-be.

She writhed a little, saying nothing.

Good girl. Don't give me another reason to punish you.

"Okay," I said, "get off the bed and take off the rest of your clothes. Then you may remove the rest of mine."

Still remaining silent, she scrambled to do as I'd asked, her breasts and bottom wiggling enticingly as she moved.

My view was perfect as I followed her off the bed. Soon, she was naked, and I drank in the delicious sight of her, all blonde hair, perky tits and long legs. Legs I looked forward to having wrapped around me as I pounded into her tight pussy. Not just yet, though. We were going to have some fun and games, first.

Stepping towards me, Emma paused and looked up at me questioningly. She was asking my permission like a good little sub.

"Yes, you can take my clothes off now." As I spoke, yet more blood rushed to my dick and my heart rate picked up.

"Thank you, Sir," she said quietly, kneeling down on the thick carpet to unlace my trainers and remove them and my socks from my feet.

I helped her by lifting each of my feet when necessary.

Placing my shoes and socks carefully to one side, she remained stooped before me as she reached up and undid my belt, sliding it from the loops then popping it onto the bed.

I stifled a grin. She knew the drill, did my Emma. Always keep my belt handy, just in case I felt like using it to turn those perfect buttocks of hers red. Which I would, soon enough.

After undoing my button and my fly, she eased my jeans

down.

Once more I lifted each leg in turn as she pulled the denim away from me. Folding the designer jeans and putting them on top of my trainers and socks, she reached up for the last item of my clothing—my boxers.

The black cotton was tented, my cock sticking out rudely towards Emma as she carefully tucked her fingers into my waistband—she'd be in trouble if she scratched me with those nails without being instructed to. Slowly she pulled down my underwear. They pooled around my ankles and I stepped out of them, leaving her to add them to the neat pile of clothing next to her. It was the way I always insisted my clothes were stacked.

I wrapped my fingers around my aching shaft, pumping it up and down a couple of times, before fixing my fiancée with a stare. "Well, what are you waiting for? It's not going to suck itself."

Immediately, she shuffled into position in front of me. Swiftly pulled her hair into a messy ponytail which she then tied up with the elastic she sometimes kept around her wrist should she need it. That done, she placed her hands on my hips and began worshipping my cock. Emma didn't just give blow jobs. She took such time and care over sucking me off that calling it a blow job wasn't doing it justice.

I reached back with my right hand and rested it on the pillar at the foot of our four-poster bed. I knew once Emma got going that I'd need the support—my legs would get wobbly, they'd already worked damn hard today.

She wrapped one hand around the base of my shaft and used the other to cup my ball-sac. After a brief pause, she began to pleasure me—gently tugging and rolling my balls while her other hand squeezed and stroked my cock.

A guttural groan escaped my throat. I wanted her, bad, but when it came to Emma and giving me this kind of pleasure, the journey was just as good as the destination. I had to keep a lid on it, for now, harness some of that stamina that I was so good at summoning on the pitch.

Letting my head loll back, I closed my eyes and waited for the bliss to begin. I didn't have to wait long. Her warm, wet tongue began to lick delicately at the head of my dick, like she was savouring an ice-cream.

I may be the one in charge, ordering her to her knees in front of me she holds all the power. She's the one with my cock and balls in the palms of her hands and I love it. Love how we switch and change our dynamics around.

As she upped her game, covering my entire shaft with saliva and pressing a finger to my perineum, I knew I was in for a damn good time.

Before long, her lips closed over my tip and slowly slid further down my dick, enveloping me in her hot, wet mouth and applying just the right amount of suction. Once satisfied she'd gotten it right—the tension in my muscles, my breathing and the sounds I make are indicators, apparently —she began to bob up and down, her tongue flicking wildly around as she did so and her fingers pressing and rubbing at that sensitive patch of skin between my ball-sac and my arse.

It truly was perfection. Every millimetre of my cock and balls got her special brand of loving attention, and I adored her for it. Her wicked lips, teeth, tongue and fingers teased me closer and closer to climax, an incredibly gradual build up which felt amazing but ensured it wouldn't all be over too soon, despite my initial desperation. Not that it would have mattered to me—the woman always got me so damn hot my cock would be ready to go again in a minute or so—but Emma's always insisted that when she's in worshipping mode, she's there for the long haul.

Chapter Three

Pre-cum spread over my tongue each time Luke withdrew his cock to the outer edge of my mouth. When he pushed back in the saltiness spread up to my palate and mixed with the excess of saliva that was now wetting my chin.

"Ah, fuck, yeah..." he groaned. "Take me, all of me."

He laced one hand into my hair to keep me held still and ground his hips, setting the rhythm to just what he liked, fast and firm in short, sharp strokes.

I gobbled him down with each forward thrust. My heart was pounding and catching my breath was hard, but I felt so alive like this. On my knees before the captain of the team, my mouth his fuck-hole and my body his to do whatever he wanted with.

"Ah, damn it, what the hell are you doing to me back there...?" His voice broke off.

I continued with my questing fingers, rubbing the silky skin between his balls and his arse and with each slide round just teasing his anus. His firm cheeks clenched but then he spread his legs and I had even better access to his most private place.

"Emma..." he gasped, tightening his hold on my hair. "What...?"

My scalp complained at the sting but I didn't; I sent the sensation down my body, to my nipples, hard and tight, and then on to my clit, which was aching for stimulation. Feeling high and also daring, I settled my index finger over his arsehole and exerted a steady pressure in the very centre. My slow, gentle action was a stark contrast to the busy movements of my other hand on his balls and my mouth slurping on his cock.

"Fuck, did I tell you to do that...?" He suddenly stilled, completely. His cock bloated in my mouth and a tremble from his thighs shivered into me.

Yes. I had him on the edge. I might be kneeling before him but I owned him. What was more, despite his protest, he wanted me to do what I was doing. He wanted it bad.

For the first time ever I eased the tip of my finger into his arse. Poking through the tight band of muscle into a dark, soft space.

A strangled cry left his lips. It might have been shock at my daring or maybe the new sensation. I wasn't sure, nor was I sure what had come over me. I was flying on the desire to feed his hunger. His satisfaction was ruling my actions as was the need to take him higher than he'd gone before. I could do it, I could hold him there and then bring him back down, I just knew it.

I delved deeper into his edgy heat. Up to my second knuckle. Then bent my finger forward, onto the front wall of his insides and sought the tiny swelling I knew would be waiting for me.

His knees gave way and he sat on the bed, hard. Tipping backwards with a solid thump he dragged me with him by my hair until we were both horizontal.

The change of position was momentarily awkward for my hand and mouth but then he hoisted his hips up and spread his legs.

Slotted between his firm thighs, my arse in the air, I continued to bob up and down on his cock. The wet, firm pressure of my mouth was keeping his shaft granite-hard and pre-cum leaking from him. I waggled my finger, stroking his insides and pushing so that my entire finger was surrounded by his delicately soft insides and the base, by my knuckle, was hugged by his tight band of muscle.

"I…I…bloody hell, Emma," he groaned.

Out of the corner of my eye I saw his free hand fist the sheet, crumpling it into a ball. Damn, I'd be punished for this, in a good way of course. Taking him to such a point of desperation wouldn't bode well for the flesh on my buttocks once this was over.

Still exploring, I found the hard nugget I was looking for. It was hidden deep inside his body and I carefully stroked over it.

His whole pelvis jerked, his thighs clamped against my ribs and his cock nearly slipped from my mouth.

"Fuck," he shouted, his voice dark and hoarse and laced with desperation. "I'm gonna have to…really fucking teach you a lesson for…this…" he said, gasping for breath.

I didn't care what he doled out. It would be worth it. Having Luke writhing, panting, giving himself over to me was off-the-scale erotic. My pussy was moist and swollen with excitement. I'd never dreamed that I'd do this to a lover. He was so close to orgasm. Hovering, teetering, one more stroke. My God, if his fans could see him now.

I sucked him to the back of my throat, hugging his shaft with my tongue and creating a strong hold. At the same time I massaged his prostate, treating it to gentle circular movements and caressing it like it was the most precious thing I'd ever touched.

I heard him drag in a deep breath and hold it.

A pulse in his shaft thrummed around my mouth. The base tendon, at the root of his erection, elongated and rose against my lips.

I had him. We were at the point of no return.

"Fuck!" He jolted upwards as a ripple rose through his cock, culminating in a shot of cum into my throat. "Fucking…hell…"

I swallowed and kept up my assault in his back passage.

He bucked, groaned and clenched his sphincter around my finger. His legs relaxed, flexed then hugged me close against his body.

Another flood of cum as he pressed my face into his groin and his cock to the very back of my throat. His small internal nub of pleasure was firm yet pulpy against my fingertip and I worked it through his orgasm. My actions seemed to extend his pleasure taking him on and on, cresting over waves of bliss.

He was experiencing a whole body climax that sent shards of satisfaction through me, and his guttural groans were going straight to my clit. I'd never heard him so wild with release. Usually he had some modicum of control but this felt like his cries were being ripped from him and his muscles were spasming with near violence, over and over.

Semen seeped from my lips, catching in the thick hair that covered his groin. I struggled for breath and he released my head.

I pulled up, gasping, and grabbed his shaft as another string of pearly cum shot from him, landing stickily on his abdomen.

"Emma, Emma," he said, curling forward and staring at me with wide eyes. "Fuck, your finger…in there…doing that…"

"Feel good?" I asked, giving his prostate another swipe and sliding my hand up his cock.

His eyeballs rolled back and I saw white beneath his dark irises.

"You have to ask?" He suddenly shifted away and my finger slipped from him. "But that's all I can take, fuck, I feel like I'm still coming." He gripped my hand which was still grasping his cock and moved it up and down. He stared into my face as a shudder swept its way over his tense stomach muscles.

"Shh…" I soothed, kissing his thigh and up to the sexy groove on the inside of his hip. "Shh, I've got you."

He was silent for a moment, gasping for breath, and then

when he spoke his voice was hoarse. "That's my line."

Suddenly I was up and over him. He'd dragged me along his body and wrapped his arms and legs around me. Heat encircled my sweat-damp skin and his solid pecs pressed into my breasts.

"I'm the one calling the shots, not you," he said sharply. He rolled over so I was beneath him.

His weight on me always thrilled me, but he was careful not to crush me despite his chest still heaving as he caught his breath.

"I didn't hear you complaining ten seconds ago," I said, twitching my eyebrows in a way that I knew would make him strain to discipline me.

Damn I'm pushing my luck today, what the hell is wrong with me?

He caught my chin in his hand. "Complain? I couldn't even form coherent thoughts, let alone speak." He pulled back, set his lips in a straight line and a flash of excitement crossed over face. "And for getting me into that state you'll pay the price."

"Which is?" I slid my palms over his smooth shoulders and down the gutter of his spine before slipping over his hard buttocks and squeezing.

"For me to know and you to find out."

He pressed his palms onto the bed, either side of my head and straightened his arms. He looked down at my small, pale body beneath his.

"Now where did I put that belt?" he asked, licking his lips.

Chapter Four

I scooted off of Emma, looking for the belt, which I found on the floor next to the bed. It must have gotten knocked off during our sexy tussle. I clearly hadn't noticed—but then, there could have been an earthquake and I wouldn't have realised.

Christ, my mind and body were still reeling from what had happened and my arsehole buzzing at the new sensations it had been treated to. Jesus that had been intense, dirty little minx.

All I wanted was to continue the erotic game while my cock recovered ready for round two. And what better way than to reprimand my future wife for her disobedience? It didn't matter that the disobedience had resulted in the most powerful orgasm I'd ever experienced, she still needed to be punished. Feeling the kiss of leather on her buttocks would do the trick and I knew damn well she wouldn't have any complaints in that department. She was always greedy for pain, of the erotic variety.

Folding the belt and gripping the ends, I shifted my hands towards each other, then jerked them back out, making the sides of the belt collide with a loud *snap*. Emma jumped, her eyes wide with excitement and her hand clutched to her heart.

"Time for some discipline. Now be a good subbie and come here. I want you bent over the bed."

Wordlessly, she clambered off the mattress and assumed the position I'd requested; arse up, head down and elbows bent. Only when her back was turned did I allow myself the smirk I'd been holding in. I was going to enjoy this. But then, so was she. It had been a while since I'd used the belt like this and I knew it was her favourite implement of sensual torture.

Holding the belt in my left hand, I used my right to reach out and touch Emma's delectable buttocks. I stroked them with feather-light touches, caresses that I knew made the hair on her skin stand on end, a ripple of sensation that would be the complete opposite of what was coming next.

Sure enough, goose flesh soon covered her bum cheeks and she shuddered. Deliberately, I counted to five before switching the belt to my right hand, unfurling it and swinging it through the air at my side. The whooping sound dragged a gasp from her lips, but I hadn't yet aimed it at her, so it cut through nothingness, then gravity brought it back down to my side.

I chuckled. "Such a tease, aren't I?"

She didn't reply, but then I hadn't expected, or commanded, her to.

The next time I swung the belt I *was* aiming for her. As I gripped the buckle end and the leather strip landed squarely in the middle of her right buttock.

Emma grunted, but I didn't give her chance to fully process the pain, instead sending another line of fire racing across her left cheek. Pausing momentarily for effect, I then laid into her with practised skill, confident that I could bring her to the very edge of climax without hitting her too hard or leaving any lasting damage. Her arse would be beautifully pink, then red, but the marks would fade by the morning.

A glance toward the rest of her body showed both her hands gripping hard onto the duvet, and a tension that told me she was ready for anything. I continued to lay stripe after stripe on her pale skin, covering every inch of her bottom and the tops of her thighs until she glowed pink.

Then I began again, eager to make the pink turn a bright red, and for her to be so desperate for release that she'd probably come as soon as I buried my cock inside her cunt. I could hardly wait and my erection was growing, tapping against my abdomen as I moved.

Picking up my pace, I whacked my girl's bottom relentlessly until it was a vivid red and I could smell her arousal. Foxy and pungent, her need assaulted my nostrils and ramped up my own by several notches.

Writhing with pleasure, Emma moaned her approval of my precision and willingness to strike her just the way she needed it most. Her gorgeous body, and her rapidly reddening arse were a sensual feast for my eyes.

Abandoning the belt, I reached out and grasped her heated bottom, digging my fingernails in for no other reason than causing her additional pain—the kind she liked. Stepping forward, I nestled my cock in her cleft and pushed her no doubt smarting cheeks together, pumping my hips a handful of times to tease her, having my cock so close to where she needed it most.

She groaned and twitched, her head tossing from side to side and her hair landing messily over her face.

But I couldn't tease for long. I wanted her just as much as she wanted me. So I softened my grip on her arse, simply holding onto her, and manoeuvred until the tip of my shaft rested against her entrance. Already I could feel her heat, her slickness, and I held back for a second before giving in and plunging inside in one gliding movement.

She was so wet, so ready, her cunt gripped me snugly as each inch disappeared. The feel of her was already threatening to send me over the edge.

"Christ, you're tight, baby. Feels so damn good."

"Yeah! Fuck me, Luke, please."

I was already succumbing to lust so I almost let her comment slide, but pulled it back at the very last second. "Sorry? What did you call me?" I smacked her right buttock hard, wrenching a strangled moan from her throat.

"S—sorry! I'm sorry. I meant fuck me, Sir, please."

"That's better," I said, my tone laden with anger I didn't really feel. How could I be truly angry when I had it all; perfect job, perfect house, perfect woman? An exceptionally beautiful woman that was beneath me, begging to be pounded until we both came.

Shifting around until I was in the optimum position, I began to rock my hips, sliding my cock in and out of Emma's silky heat. My steady movements betrayed the desperation I really felt, but I couldn't hold out for long. I'd already come once, but it didn't matter. She'd done something to me with that finger up my arse, I was sure of it, made me even more sex-mad than I was before.

Pulling in a deep breath, I upped my pace, alternating between shallow and deep thrusts so as to hold off my climax that bit longer. Emma's pussy just felt so damn good that I wanted to fuck her forever and a day. But I also wanted to come. By the sounds Emma was making and the way her cunt gripped my cock, it seemed she was growing closer, too.

I slipped my right hand beneath our bodies, quickly finding her swollen clit. Gathering some of the copious juices from where our bodies were joined, I slicked them over her bud, repeating the action a couple more times until she was good and lubricated. Continuing to fuck her hard and deep, I scissored my index and middle fingers around the distended flesh, pinching it between them, then beginning to rub. She'd told me in the past that when I did that, it seemed to touch every last nerve ending in her clit. And I wanted those nerve endings sparking, ready to set alight as she climaxed on my cock.

I didn't think it was possible, but as I stroked her pussy, it gripped ever harder around my shaft. So hard it almost hurt. I didn't stop, though, didn't slow down. Instead I simply fucked her faster, deeper, the friction on my dick incredible, and the room filling with the sounds of our frantic lovemaking. Moans, groans, yelps, expletives, skin slapping against skin, and the delicious wet, clicking, squelching sound that Emma's cunt made as I pounded it.

The signals that I was about to come had hit me, and still I'd refused to let go. But, inevitably, my body overpowered my mind, wrenching my orgasm out of me with a ferocity that easily matched the one I'd had with my fiancée's finger up my backside.

Yelling and bucking into Emma with short, sharp thrusts, I tumbled into blissful oblivion, filling her delicious cunt with my spunk. My energy started to seep away and I collapsed onto her back, using my left hand to hold my weight as my right continued to strum her clit until she followed me into climax.

"Oh... Sir," she said, her voice hoarse. "I'm so close. Please, Sir, make me come. Hard. Bite me."

It took a second for my brain to register the last comment she'd thrown in there, but once I did, I happily obliged. Shoving her ponytail out of the way, I sank my teeth into the strip of flesh between shoulder and neck, hard enough to hurt, and to mark, but not so much it would detract too much from the other sensations she was experiencing.

It seemed the extra stimulation did the trick, and not a moment too soon. My right hand, still riding up and down the apex of her slick vulva, had begun to cramp, but I didn't stop until she was well and truly over the edge. She screamed her release, her internal walls gripping so hard they almost forced my cock out of her, then spasming wildly around me.

I waited several long seconds until the waves of Emma's climax had ebbed, then disentangled from her body, lifted her carefully further onto the bed, rolled her onto her side and tucked myself behind her.

She muttered something in her dazed state, something I didn't quite catch. I took a chance.

"I love you too, sweetheart."

Murmuring happily, she squirmed further into my embrace and gave a contended sigh.

Pressing a kiss to the side of her neck, I held her tighter. I really was the luckiest man alive. But then I couldn't lose, not really. Win, lose or draw, the end result was always orgasmic.

*****

More about Lily Harlem and Lucy Felthouse

Lily Harlem and Lucy Felthouse are both prolific writers who share a love of hot, toned-to-perfection athletes who wield their talents both in and out of the bedroom. With nerves of steel, precision timing and enough testosterone to fuel a jet engine, Lily and Lucy's heroes (and heroines) come in the shape of tennis players, footballers, hockey stars and more. And it's not just male/female loving going on outside of the court, rink or pitch either, these authors like to dabble with gay romance, ménage a trois and BDSM so there really is something for everyone. If you, too, appreciate guys and gals who insist on winning, strive for being the-best-of-the-best, then check out the **Raw Talent series**, **Hot Ice** and if footballers press your buttons try **Scored**.

Links

Raw Talent series: http://www.rawtalentseries.co.uk

Praise for Lily Harlem and Lucy Felthouse

"The characters are two incredibly strong individuals who learn that being together can make them stronger. I love the easy introduction into a light dominate, submissive relationship. Grand Slam is an amazing love story for the romantic at heart, with just enough BDSM to interest those who appreciate extra spice in their life. Ms. Harlem and Ms. Felthouse have an amazing talent of balancing the BDSM lifestyle with the romance of love." **Coffee Time Romance**

"The chemistry between Travis and Marie is hot. The sex scenes were sizzling. I can't wait to read the next book in the series." **Night Owl Reviews**

"This hot and steamy sports themed book has it all …very well written with a lot of attention paid to details – particularly the details of their sexual romps which are scorching hot! Overall, it's an erotic romance that teases and definitely pleases your literary senses." **The Jeep Diva**

The Wife

By Kay Jaybee

Jade walked slowly along the right hand corridor, wiping her clammy palms self-consciously down the front of her jeans. Barely noticing the hospital's sterile cream walls, hung with the occasional bizarrely abstract painting designed to cheer an otherwise depressing atmosphere, she turned left, left again, and then right, until she saw the small reception desk she'd been hunting for.

There were two women behind the desk, each with a computer terminal flashing before them, their fingers dancing over the attached keyboards. The identity tags they wore around their necks hung on long straps that reached below the line of the desk, so Jade was unable to see which of the women was the one she was hunting for.

"Can I help you?"

Jade had been expecting the question, but it still made her flinch as she was regarded by the pale blue eyes of a pretty blonde woman, with a young kind smile, "I um... I'm searching for Karen Marks."

The other receptionist looked up, a questioning expression crossing her oval face, "That's me."

She had a darker complexion than Jade had imagined. Long black hair hung loose down her back, her eyes shone green, and her skin glowed with the remnants of a tan. Jade suddenly realised she shouldn't have been surprised by that; after all, she already knew this woman had been to Spain within the last month.

Feeling her mouth go dry, Jade was unable to speak in the face of the striking thirty- something woman before her. Karen Marks was far more attractive than she had allowed herself to imagine. There was something disconcerting about the mistress discovering that the wife was an eye-catching self-assured woman, and not the cold harridan that had been portrayed to her. No, that wasn't true. Neil had never told her what Karen looked like; or even what she was like. Jade had never asked him. She had simply presumed. She had presumed wrong.

"I..." Jade licked her lips nervously, "I wonder if we could have a quick word in private."

Karen's eyes narrowed and the curt nod of her head told Jade that somehow she'd been expecting her visit, if not today, then one day. Referring to her colleague, she said, "I might as well take my lunch now," and rose from her chair before leaving the reception area. "This way," Jade had to jog to keep up as Karen's long slender legs marched down a neighbouring corridor, her heels clicking purposely against the tiled floor, before she disappeared into a side room.

The small space had once been a treatment room, but now it was a store for unused medical equipment. Boxes were haphazardly piled up and scattered around an old ripped examination couch.

When she finally turned to face Jade, Karen's expression was strangely calm, "So, how long?"

"Six months."

"And why come to me now?"

Jade could barely hear her own answers such was the hammering of the blood in her ears as she faced her lover's wife. Mustering all her concentration on keeping her voice level, she replied, "One of Neil's colleagues found out. He threatened to tell you. I didn't want you to find out like that."

Karen propped herself against the examination bed, holding her arms protectively across her chest. "You thought this less cruel?"

Jade nodded shyly, "It seemed like the responsible thing to do."

"Responsible?" Karen spoke the word with incredulity. She cocked her head to one side, an expression of disbelief on her face, rather than the angry or distraught one Jade had been mentally preparing herself for. "What does Neil think about this? He does know you're here?"

"Well, actually he thought it was a mad idea, but yes, he knows I'm here."

"Let me guess, he told you he didn't want you to come?" Karen sat further back on the torn couch and crossed her long legs, showing Jade how shapely they were beneath her black work trousers, making her wonder why on earth Neil had sought out her much shorter, more rounded frame. His wife certainly didn't appear to be the type of woman who'd be lacking in the sex department.

Jade bent her head from the increasingly uncomfortable stare of her opponent. Karen's sharp eyes didn't even seem to blink. This wasn't how Jade had imagined this confrontation at all. She'd prepared herself for anger, tears, accusations and perhaps even physical violence, but not mild disdain, and certainly not derisory amusement. As the quiet piercing gaze continued, Jade felt a steeling unease creep up her spine, "I should go; I thought you should know from one of us, not from some third party. That's all."

Karen snorted. "Third party! Isn't that what you are honey?" Her words cut like ice, her lips barely moving as she spat them out. "Wouldn't you say that this colleague was, in fact, the fourth party?"

"I suppose," mumbling her words, Jade hoisted her handbag up onto her shoulder. She'd been gripping it so tightly that the leather strap had begun to dig into her palm.

"Tell me," Karen re-crossed her arms, crushing her tits under her creamy satin blouse, so that her cleavage was pushed up even higher, "what makes you so sure that this *colleague* actually exists?"

"What?" Jade frowned.

"Couldn't Neil be bored with you, like he got bored with all the others before you?"

A cold wave of panic swept through Jade as Karen jumped from the bed, standing so near that Jade could feel her warm breath against her face. Trying to avoid the wife's glare, but also determined not to look at her undeniably gorgeous chest, Neil's mistress kept her eyes fixed on her feet, and attempted to step away from the receptionist. However, Jade was hemmed in and had no choice but to hold her ground. Confusion swamped her.

"You did know he'd done this before?" Karen tilted her head to one side, appraising her visitor. "No, I can see he has told you nothing of the other gullible children who have come to find me like this."

"What... I..." The words gullible and children stuck in Jade's ears, echoing over and over again.

Jade stepped sideways in an attempt to put some distance between herself and her lover's wife, but Karen's arm shot out, her hand catching Jade expertly around the wrist. Its cool tight grip pinched. "We are not done here yet honey." She gestured to the couch with her head, her sleek hair swaying with the abrupt movement. "Sit."

Her feet stayed where they were, the small hairs at the back of Jade's neck prickled as her mind raced.

"I told you to sit." Karen propelled the smaller woman by the elbow to the bed. "I advise you to do as you are told, after all, I think you'd agree that you and Neil owe me one — or probably more than one if I know Neil, which my dear girl, I do. Very well indeed." Karen closed the door of the room, pushing a few boxes in front of it, ensuring they would not be disturbed.

Jade's heart rate went off the scale as an unfamiliar combination of fear, panic, and intense curiosity filled her. She knew she should run, scream, call for help, but something about this woman made her stay precisely where she was. A vision of Neil flashed through her head. *Had he set her up to come here with tales of a fictitious colleague? Was he just trying to get rid of her, or, perhaps his wife had orchestrated this, perhaps it was her...*

The hand around her bare arm relaxed its grip a little, but Karen didn't let go, instead she began to trail her neatly trimmed black painted fingernails up and down a square inch of Jade's skin, sending electric waves of unexpected desire through Jade's body. "So, let me look at you properly, let me see exactly what my husband sees in a little girl like you."

Jade trembled beneath the woman's oppressive gaze. She felt as though she was being appraised before being sent to market. The slim fit jeans and respectable short-sleeved lilac shirt she had believed suitably dowdy for the occasion felt, not only slutty, but see-through. She longed to flick a stray red hair from her eyes, but any movement she made Jade felt would be wrong, forbidden even. Or worse, misinterpreted as encouragement.

The green eyes after which she had been named, felt dim next to the cat-like sheen of Karen's stare, which, starting at Jade's small booted feet, travelled up the length of her 5ft 2" pale frame, making Jade embarrassingly conscious of the hardening of her nipples. This was ridiculous. Although the thought wasn't unappealing, she certainly didn't really want to have her first experience of sleeping with a woman with an intimidating wronged wife, especially when she was the one who'd wronged her. *Why the hell is my body responding in this way? What is the matter with me?* "Let me go!"

"I don't think so, honey," Karen's tongue dripped scorn, "you owe me one fuck at least." Karen ran a sensual digit across Jade's chest, "and by the way your tits are reacting to me my dear, I'd say you quite like the idea."

Jade froze as Karen's palms pressed against her breasts, forcing her to shuffle backwards, so she was flat against the wall. Her feet felt glued to the floor as her treacherous teats pushed hungrily back at the uninvited pressure.

Karen came closer, dropping her hands to Jade's waist, her own rounded chest brushing her opponent's. She whispered into Jade's ear, "Neil tells me everything you know. Everything..."

Flinching, as the other woman's mouth came to her neck, Jade let out a muffled cry as her skin was nipped and lapped with long languid strokes. Unable to move, and with no choice but to endure the attention, Jade screwed up her eyes and tried to focus on Neil. *He hadn't really told his wife about her... had he? Had there really been others? Surely Karen was just trying to freak her out, trying to extract her revenge in the strangest way possible.*

When the red lipstick-covered lips met hers, Jade was totally unprepared for the current of electricity that shot from her mouth to between her legs, and was unable to hide the quiet groan that revealed her body wanted this, even if her brain screamed that she didn't.

Laughing, Karen said, "I knew it, you're like a bitch on heat." She pulled the shirt from Jade's trousers and thrust her hands beneath, scratching sharp nails across Jade's flat stomach. "I bet if I touched your pussy it would drip between my fingers."

Squirming, Jade tried to pull away, but was again prevented by Karen, the wall behind her, and the boxes that littered the floor. "I don't want this, you're crazy!"

Karen's hand moved so fast, that Jade didn't have time to prepare for the arrival of the slap that stung her cheek. "Crazy? I don't think so. Just curious girlie, curious about who is currently getting my husband's boxers around his ankles on a Tuesday afternoon."

Jade's throat instantly dried shut, as she croaked out a bewildered. "Tuesdays? How did you know that we met on Tuesdays?"

Karen laughed again, this time with less cruelty and more pity, which seemed somehow worse to Jade, as the woman stroked her lithe body. "I told you little girl, Neil tells me *everything*." She worked her hands up under her rival's bra, pinching her nipples until tears sprung up in Jade's eyes. "Haven't you worked it out yet?"

"I..." Jade couldn't think what else to say. Her arms hung limply at her sides as a hot tight pain coursed through her chest, and her brain tangled with conflicting messages, telling her to both run and hide, and stay and enjoy these strange new sensations as the warm body caressed her own.

"Let me tell you a few facts." Karen's eyes blazed as she spoke, her fingers continuing to work Jade's nipples. "One; Neil and I have an arrangement regarding third parties to our marriage. Two; Neil only goes for women he thinks I will find attractive — until now that is. You really are something completely different from his usual type, hence my curiosity. Three; he has been on a search, a quest if you like. A search I sent him on. I can't believe he found *you* though." She sneered in derision. "Still, I suppose he *might* be right. I find you something of a puzzle, little girl. You're fighting what I'm doing, yet you aren't trying to push me away. You are deliciously aroused, in spite of your natural personal feelings of wariness towards me." Karen squeezed Jade's tips even harder, making her sob gasps of air and pain, unable to believe what she was hearing, unable to comprehend that her body was responding so much to the other woman, as her sticky liquid glued her satin knickers to her crotch. Karen continued. "Usually Neil's conquests either break away from me and run away, never to be seen by either Neil or I again, or they willingly enjoy a quick tumble and leave. You my dear are different."

Ripping the zip-fly of Jade's jeans open, Karen thrust an arm into the gap and grabbed Jade's pussy through her panties, making her squeal in a heady mix of protest and dark pleasure. "I knew it!" The wife's voice was triumphant. "They're wet! You are one hot handful."

Jade said nothing, biting back tears of humiliation. Two conflicting voices shouted at the back of her head. One asking her why she hadn't run away, the other telling her to relax and savour the new experience.

"Now come with me." Dragging Jade by the crotch to the battered medical couch, Karen pulled down her jeans, saying, "Sit."

Jade found herself sitting, her body working as if on auto-pilot. She re-closed her eyes, feeling heavy, weak, confused, and helpless to do anything but obey, as her companion began to massage her cunt through the fabric of her damp knickers. Karen, commanding but calm, used her free hand to open the buttons of Jade's shirt, revealing the small neat globes with her bra hanging uselessly above them. "That's a good girl. Now, you stay precisely where you are."

The stale air of the medical junk room blew cool, feeling

unbelievably arousing against Jade's skin as Karen slid her pants down. Working skilled fingers over the sticky nub, Karen released a deep breath, a smirk of triumphant command across her face, as she dug a hand into her pocket and pulled out a mobile phone.

"I have her here." Clutching her husband's lover's snatch even harder, the expression on Karen's face dared her victim to speak as she chatted in relaxed tones to the anonymous recipient. "She is much younger and smaller than your usual type, darling."

Her face blanched. Jade realised that everything Karen had said was true. Neil had been in this from the start. He *had* known *exactly* what would happen when she came here today. She was about to speak when Karen eased a long index finger into Jade's soaked opening, changing her forthcoming words of protest into an unbidden sigh of lust.

"But you were right babe, she is one horny bitch." Karen chuckled at Neil's unheard reply. "She's done nothing but complain since she got here, but boy is she hot. You should see her right now, her clothes are in disarray, and she's skewered on my finger, moaning like a common whore."

Karen beamed into the receiver, and Jade could only guess what her lover was saying to his wife; flushing in shame as she accepted the truth of the situation.

Yet, the idea of Neil being high on the knowledge of her current situation was strangely erotic, as was the power of the woman whose finger was now sliding in and out of her with painfully slow regularity. Beneath the dark of her eyelids Jade could picture Neil, his trousers around his ankles, his boxers down, a firm hand around his hard shaft, yanking himself off as his wife described exactly what she was doing to his lover.

It was a thought too far. The images in Jade's head, the tightness of her breasts, and the finger that was probing up inside her, were all pushing her body further towards the edge. Shutting her eyes tighter, so as not to witness even a glimpse of the inevitable expression of victory on her companion's face, Jade allowed her body to receive the climax it so desperately needed.

"Oh sweetheart!" Karen's gloat down the phone only went to make Jade feel smaller than ever. "I hardly touched her, and she's fucked off against my hand."

There was a pause as Neil obviously spoke to his wife at length. Jade, her eyes still fused, hardly dared breathe, her ears straining to hear what he was saying. After a few moments of fruitless listening, she heard Karen say, "Okay darling, will do," before she ended the call.

"Well then," Karen drew her hand free, making Jade whimper at its loss, and her companion laugh, "you have just managed to make your master come. I hope you're proud." Jade said nothing. She had never thought of Neil in terms of being her master before. It was another disconcerting thought to add to all the others that were swimming around her head. "You are obviously a powerful force in my husband's imagination."

Suddenly Jade realised that she wasn't being touched or restrained any more, and gradually she opened her eyes. Karen was stood before the couch gazing directly at her. Her blouse was open, and one hand was twisting her right nipple, while the other was down her trousers. From the look on her face, she was fast bringing herself off. Jade couldn't help but wordlessly watch. She had never witnessed a woman wanking before, and felt her enflamed and confused body begin to respond as she observed the scene in fascination.

A sharp cry, and Karen, her gaze locked onto Jade's, indicated the start of a juddering climax which left her shaking for only the briefest of moments. Then, in a brisk business-like way, she did up her clothes, brushed herself off, and, with cold indifference, as if nothing had happened, said, "For God's sake woman, have some pride will you, get dressed, I've got work to do."

Shakily, Jade got to her feet, readjusted her clothing and picked up her bag. She wanted to run as far away from this strange woman as possible, but at the same time desperately needed to know what Neil had said to his wife on the phone. She had only taken two steps towards the door before she decided that as her pride and dignity had already been torn to shreds, she might as well ask. *What have I got to lose now anyway?* "What did he say on the phone?"

Karen smiled insincerely. "Ask him yourself little girl, he's coming to see you tonight." Then Mrs Marks pushed roughly past her husband's mistress before, without so much as a backward glance, adding: "and I'm coming too..."

Underwear

By Kay Jaybee

Straightening the black thigh-length skirt and matching jacket over her pristine white blouse, Leah checked her reflection one last time.

Finally satisfied with her look, Leah gathered her long chestnut hair into a neat ponytail, slipped her court shoes onto her stocking-clad feet, grabbed the holdall that held a stack of catalogues advertising the cosmetics and underwear she sold, and the items of lingerie her clients had ordered the week before, and headed out to work.

Smiling privately to herself, Leah knew the new underwear she wore beneath her suit was flattering her curvaceous figure, and she felt sexy and confident as she drove towards her target area, her mind lingering on one client more than the others.

Two hours, three sales and several positive enquiries later, Leah felt her pulse rate rise as she knocked on the door of his small terraced house. The door was opened almost the second she rang the bell.

"Good morning Mr Richards, I have the underwear you ordered."

"You'd better come in." Leah walked into the narrow hallway and on into the living room, where she had spent a pleasantly flirtatious half an hour the week before.

He followed her, his alert blue eyes appraising her round figure; his tall frame towering over her as she sat on the edge of the sofa, the holdall on her knee already unclipped as she searched through its contents for his order.

"Here you go Mr Richards," Leah placed the see-through plastic bag on the coffee table. "One set of 36C/14 bra and knickers, crimson lace, with matching suspender belt and black stockings as per your request."

"Sam." His eyes twinkled as he spoke.

"Sam?"

"My name is Sam." He perched next to her. "Mr Richards sounds a bit formal, don't you think?"

Inclining her head a fraction, but keeping her eyes lowered over her products, she replied, "I'm Leah." She could feel his eyes boring into her, and the tension in the room was pleasantly palpable as she fished her account book from her bag. "How would you like to pay?"

"Cash." He produced a battered wallet from his back pocket. "But first I'd like to make sure they fit."

All week Leah had indulged in the ridiculously unrealistic fantasy that this man was single, and that the underwear was for his sister or a friend. Feeling let down by her own flights of fancy, she said as lightly as she could, "Oh, is your girlfriend here then?"

"No she isn't, but you're about her size."

Lean laughed. "That's a bit cliché isn't it!"

"Maybe, but I'd still like to see you in them." He sounded serious, and as Leah risked a look at him, she could see he meant it.

"You have a girlfriend." Leah spoke with a finality she knew she didn't feel.

"Yes I do." He reached a hand out and picked up the lingerie set. "But I still want to see you in this first."

"If I was your girlfriend, I wouldn't want you to give me pre-worn underwear."

"Lucky you're not my girlfriend then, isn't it?"

Leah's hand hesitated over her bag. She had no doubt he was serious, and she had even fewer doubts that her body was already reacting to the closeness of his presence, but that didn't make the fact of his girlfriend's existence disappear.

As if reading her mind, he said, "If I'd lied and said I hadn't got a girlfriend, would you be trying the undies on by now?"

Raising her gaze to meet his, Leah spoke with a defiant edge. "That's not the point. The fact is, you do have one. Why else would you buy this stuff? It isn't exactly the sort of thing you'd buy your mother is it?"

"True." Sam stood back up. "It is also true that, spoken for or not, I haven't stopped thinking about you since last time you were here, and that I've told my partner all about you."

Leah's stomach began to turn cartwheels as she forced herself to hold his stare, trying to ignore the feeling that she'd stumbled out of her depth. "You told her what exactly?"

He took a step nearer. "That I'd met a beautiful door-to-door lingerie seller, who I'd like to fuck."

Her calm exterior broke instantly at his confession. "You told your girlfriend that!"

"It surprises you that she'd rather I told her about

encountering women I fancy, rather than keeping it quiet?"

The corners of Leah's mouth begin to curve as she struggled not to smile in incredulous disbelief. "Your honesty is indeed surprising." Closing her bag, Leah stood. "I should go."

Trying not to inhale the delicious aroma of aftershave and sheer maleness that emanated from his creased shirt, Leah was forced to physically shove past Sam to reach the hallway, making her more aware of his height and bulk than ever before. She'd just reached the door when he said, "I haven't paid you yet."

Leah knew that if she was going to hold onto her principles, she had to leave now. "There's an address on the bill, you can post me a cheque."

"Sarah will be so disappointed."

Something about his tone made Leah turn to face him. "Disappointed, why? You have her gift."

"No, I don't."

Her hand seemed to have frozen to the doorknob. Leah could feel her nipples hardening beneath her underwear, underwear which she knew was an exact match for the packet of lingerie Sam still held in his hand.

With a dry mouth, she stood there, statue-like. In two strides Sam was right next to her, close enough for her to feel his breath on her flesh.

Pushing her free hand into her jacket pocket and gripping the handle of her bag tightly with the other so that she couldn't reach out and pull his shirt from his jeans as she longed to, Leah said, "Explain."

"She wanted me to have you, and then tell her all about it."

"What?"

Sam put a hand on her shoulder, and immediately Leah felt a treacherous rush of heat flow through her.

"She gets off on it, and naturally, so do I."

Attempting to deflect her concentration away from the pressure of his palm, Leah spoke with far more defiance than she felt. "And how do I know that you're not just saying that so you can get your leg over?"

"You don't." He stroked a finger across her cheek, sending tiny shock waves through her nervous system. "But I know you want to find out."

"You're an arrogant git aren't you?"

Sam smiled. "Yeah I am, and I still want to see you in that underwear."

Leah levelled her gaze firmly to his. If she was going to do this, she was going to do it on her terms. "If I do this, I'm not coming back here again. Not ever."

His eyes blazed with a swift flash of victory, but wisely he said nothing, merely nodding his head.

Throwing her shoulders back, Leah walked back to the living room, ignoring the voice at the back of her head telling her to get the hell out of there, and listening only to her body, that wanted her client's cock inside her as soon as possible. Girlfriend or no girlfriend.

Determined to rob Sam of his assumed control, Leah thumped her bag onto the coffee table. With her heart beating fast and her hands on her hips, she said, "Right, stay exactly where you are. Do not move."

Sam looked more amused than put out and obediently stayed in the doorway between the hall and the living room.

"If you want to see me in that underwear, then you can."

Dropping her jacket to the ground, Leah maintained eye contact with Sam. If she looked away she was afraid that her courage would fail her, or worse, she'd start to think about what she was actually doing. Placing a hand either side of her skirt, she eased it to the floor, giving her solo audience the first indication that she was already attired as per his wishes.

Sam's arms dropped to his sides as he watched her, and he leant more heavily against the doorframe. Encouraged by the hunger in his eyes, Leah moved her attention to the small pearl buttons of her shirt. As she undid the top fastening, Sam gave an audible gasp, which made Leah speed up, and soon her top joined the skirt on the floor.

The voice at the back of her head was shouting now, telling her how important it was to keep control, to make him wait. Tilting up her chin, Leah said, "So, what do you think of the underwear?"

"Gorgeous." Sam lurched forward, so that they were stood either side of the coffee table. "I knew it would look better on you than in a lifeless packet."

Leah moved her hands so that her fingers could trace the lacy outline of her bra. "It certainly feels good to wear."

He almost whispered, "Are you the same size as Sarah then?

I hoped you were."

"It would appear I am." She took one hand from her chest and placed a single digit inside the top of her panties and ran it over the belly beneath. "The question is, what do you look like in your underwear?"

Sam's jeans were off so quickly that Leah struggled not to giggle at his eagerness and shatter the whole 'in control' illusion she'd been building up. Observing him closely as crisp black boxers appeared from beneath his trousers, and his shirt hit the table, she felt her crotch twitch with erotic anticipation.

His underwear was smart, designer with three little buttons at the fly, and more importantly, a telling bulge beneath. "Nice."

"Thanks."

Neither of them moved, the table acting as a barrier between them.

Leah licked her lips as the tension in the room continued to rise. "Your girlfriend must be a very unusual woman."

"Sarah is one of a kind. I'm very lucky."

"And you really are going to tell her how you fucked me?"

"Exactly how." Sam knocked the holdall and new underwear from the table, sending them flying towards the hall, and knelt on the unyielding wood, reaching his hands out to Leah's chest. "Action for action, groan for groan, climax for climax."

With a massive effort of will, Leah took hold of his wrists and lifted his palms from her breasts, stifling the whine of loss she felt when the removal of his exploring fingers left her feeling dangerously neglected.

"And how will she feel when you report that rather than you taking me," picking up his shirt, Leah twisted it into a long sausage shape, and moved to the other side of the table, "I took you?"

Deftly positioning her client's unresisting arms behind his back, and tying his shirt around his wrists, Leah instructed him to stand.

Sam, a sly grin on his face, said nothing, but simply waited, presumably curious to see what the saleswoman planned to do next.

"Sit on the edge of the table." Leah stood between his outstretched legs, glancing at the cock that was evidently stiffening further beneath his shorts.

She'd fantasised about having sex with this man all week, and although Leah hadn't really believed her dream would come true, she had a good idea of what she wanted to do.

Placing her hands on his shoulders, she trailed her painted fingernails down each side of his smooth chest, lingering over his stiff nipples, flicking their tips once or twice, watching with fascination as they hardened into peaks.

All the time Leah sensed Sam looking at her, his eyes boring into the top of her head. It wouldn't have taken much effort for him to break free from his restraints, but he made no attempt to escape as Leah slid her hands further south, exploring the outline of his toned torso down to his navel, which she circled with light scratches of his skin.

Dropping to her knees, she bought her mouth to his stomach. With long lingering laps that made him tighten his muscles further, she tongued his flesh an inch above the elastic of his underwear. Encouraged by the growl Sam wasn't able to contain, Leah's kisses grew firmer as she gripped his knees to steady herself, her chest rubbing against the lace that encased it.

Drawing back, Leah shifted her gaze back to his. The ache in her chest was becoming unbearable; she felt as if her breasts were actually inflating. Placing her hands behind her back, she unfastened her bra, freeing her tits from captivity. Sam's eyes widened at the sight of her creamy freckled chest and large nipples, which were pointing directly at him, as though they were accusing him of something.

Leah began to weigh her tits in her palms, easing a single finger up and over each teat, making herself gasp as she caressed her body in front of her semi-bound audience.

* * * * *

Following her every move of Leah's masturbation, Sam gulped as one hand entered her knickers. He stared as she closed her eyes, the hand obviously manipulating her mound, hidden by the red lace. Sam's cock dug painfully into his thigh. He wasn't going to be able to take much more before he would have to have his own underwear removed, plus, although Leah was blissfully unaware of the fact, time was running out.

His breath caught in his throat, as with her eyes still closed, Leah hooked either side of her knickers beneath her thumbs, and edged them to the floor. Ideally he would have liked to see this through, to see what this amazing woman planned for his domination, but he had instructions of his own to carry out.

It took only a matter of seconds to release his hands, and, while Leah was lost in her personal world of pleasure, Sam picked up his shirt and Leah's blouse, and tearing his eyes away from Leah, stood up.

Sensing movement, Leah's eyes flashed open, but Sam was too quick for her. In seconds she'd been picked up and pushed, back down, against the large coffee table, a knee pinning her stomach in place, while her right hand was yanked up and attached to a table leg with his shirt.

* * * * *

Shocked by the dramatic turn of events, Leah's left wrist was already being restrained before her voice came to her. "What the fuck are you doing?"

"Taking control." He stunted any further protests with his mouth, kissing her ferociously. "Trust me. This, you will love."

Leah's head spun. She'd been moments from orgasm, and she longed to come. She pulled at her arms, but the bindings held. As he spread her legs wide and attached her ankles to the table, she realised that he'd had as many plans for her as she'd had for him.

Robbed of the ability to move, Leah felt incredibly vulnerable. No one had ever secured her so completely. A natural control freak, she was always the one who did the tying up. This was new territory, and she wasn't sure if she was thrilled or terrified.

Sam swung a leg over the table, and stood astride the tethered woman, his dick still a prisoner in his underwear. "You look amazing." He leant forward and freed Leah's hair from its ponytail, so that she could rest her neck more comfortably against the wood.

Leah was about to speak when he placed his warm lips over her right tit, and her words of protest immediately morphed into a drawn-out mewl. The sensation was increased when a hand came to her other breast, teasing the slightly rough skin around the areole.

A gentle click bought Leah back to reality, and she pointlessly struggled to sit up. "What was that?"

"Nothing." Sam murmured through his mouthful of breast, and Leah sank back against the table. Her hair was already a mass of knots beneath her as her head moved from side to side in frustration at not being able to touch him, and confusion at her body's total enjoyment of being entirely at the whim of someone else.

As Sam worked, Leah could feel the climax she'd been denied rise again, increasing in urgency with every lap of his tongue and each flick of his fingers. "Don't stop, please don't... I'm so close."

* * * * *

Sam kept going, listening for the quickening of her breath that would tell him Leah could take no more. He was also listening for another sound, the sound of a packet being opened.

Leah's back began to arch against the table. "Oh hell Sam, I'm coming, I'm gonna..."

"Not yet you're not."

Sitting up abruptly, Sam looked towards the hall, the shift in his weight forcing Leah further against the unyielding surface of the coffee table. "You took your time."

* * * * *

Leah felt cold, as if someone had pressed the paused button on her orgasm, while her brain struggled to make sense of what her eyes told her was happening.

"You look fantastic sweetheart." Sam beamed at Sarah, who stood in the doorway dressed in her brand new lingerie.

Blinking, trying to extinguish the vision in front of her, Leah forced herself to digest the knowledge that she should have seen this coming. Horribly self-conscious of her nakedness, she wriggled against her restraints.

"Don't bother honey." Sarah swept her stunning red hair from her shoulders as she peered down at the saleswoman. "If Sam has tied you up, he'll have done it securely enough to make sure you can't escape."

Her throat had never felt drier, and yet Leah could feel the liquid continue to leak from her pussy as two sets of eyes focused all their attention on her prone body.

Sarah put out a hand and yanked Sam off Leah's stomach, so that they were next to each other. As if she was a lioness marking her mate, Sarah kissed him deeply, leaving Leah in no doubt as to whom this man belonged to. Then, glancing at Leah again, Sarah said, "You're right Sam, she is beautiful."

Leah's face turned from pink to scarlet as the other woman casually placed a hand, flat and unmoving, between her legs. "Tell me Sam, what's happened so far? What have I missed?"

Feeling like a thing, a mere object, a sex toy for two lovers, Leah listened as Sam gave Sarah a blow-by-blow account of everything they'd done together. As he told his lover about Leah's masturbation, she laughed, and Leah felt the blush on her face creep through her and swamp the rest of her shamed flesh.

Attempting to block out the conversation going on above her, Leah shut her eyes, but there was no escape from either the audible replay, or the pressure of the gloriously soft palm that remained fixed in place between her legs.

When Sam eventually stopped talking, Leah cautiously dared to open her eyes. The silence between the three of them was tense, the expressions of her companions unreadable. Leah felt the need to speak, to break the heavy expectant atmosphere that floated around the room. "You look nice."

Even as she spoke, Leah knew her comment had been rather lame, but Sarah smiled, "Thank you, so do you." She started to glide her hand gently up and down. "And you feel even better."

Leah moaned softly as her body leapt a little off the table. Immediately, Sarah removed her hand, making Leah whimper in distress.

Losing another chance to orgasm deprived Leah of the last vestiges of her pride, as Sarah adopted the position Sam had previously held over her hips, placing her hands on her own chest. "Gorgeous, this underwear you sell, but don't you find that the lace edging is a little scratchy?" Without bothering to let Leah reply, Sarah pulled the bra cups beneath her tits, and began to fondle her nipples. "How badly do you want to suck these I wonder? As badly as you want your own chest sucked I should think, but perhaps not as badly as you want Sam's dick in your pussy?"

Leah gazed up at the other woman, her brain racing. She'd been with women before, but not like this, not without some level of power, and not for a very long time.

"No answer?" Sarah continued to play with her breasts. "Perhaps you aren't that bothered about coming after all?"

"What? No! I have to, please..."

Sarah laughed again, but more kindly this time, as she turned to Sam. "Time to remove those boxers honey, before they cripple you for life."

Swiftly Sam obliged, and Leah sighed at the sight of him. His cock was as hard as any she'd ever seen.

Sarah pointed, and Sam went to the foot of the table, crouching by Leah's tethered feet. Then, moving so she stood over Leah's head, leaning forward so that her breasts hovered just centimetres from Leah's lips, Sarah spoke bluntly. "Suck me."

Engulfing the offered right nipple, a zip of electricity instantly shot through Leah at the sensation of having a woman's breast in her mouth. Then, as she got into a comfortable rhythm of licks and nips, Leah jolted. A tongue was working between her legs.

It only took a few seconds before the orgasm Leah had been denied twice before raced up her throat and along her spine. As her pussy quivered against Sam's greedy mouth, Leah's cries of pleasure were muffled as Sarah pushed her teat further into her mouth.

Exhausted, Leah felt the final flutters of her climax escape, and her kisses against Sarah's peach skin became lighter as the strain in her neck and the ache in her trapped body filled her with sudden fatigue.

Stroking a hand across Leah's forehead, Sarah wiped away stray strands of hair, before she signalled to Sam to untie their guest. Then they helped Leah to sit up, and allowed her to catch her breath for a moment, before Sam abruptly picked her off the table and laid her on the sofa.

Seconds later, Sarah was astride Leah's face, and Sam was sat over her hips, his cock pumping in and out of her as Sarah ordered, "Lick me girl. Make me come."

Flashing colours danced behind Leah's eyes as she worked her tongue frantically over Sarah's clit, while the gloriously thick dick of the client she'd fantasised about all week rammed in and out of her. A new climax knocked the first from Leah's mind with sharp intensity, as Sam spunked into her and Sarah spasmed wonderfully sticky juice across her lips and chin.

* * * * *

They left Leah to dress on her own. As she picked up her discarded holdall she noticed that a pile of cash had been left next to her bag, precisely the correct amount for Sarah's new underwear.

Feeling wobbly on her kitten heels, she took a final look

around the room, her eyes lingering for a moment on the coffee table, picturing what she must have looked like to her client and his girlfriend. Smiling to herself, Leah headed quietly to the front door.

Her hand was on the latch when Sam came up behind her. "Sarah really loves that underwear."

"Good." Leah didn't know what else to say.

"She wondered if you had another set of the same style in black."

"I'll have to order it, but yes."

"Will you bring it next week?"

"I said I'd never come back."

"I know you what you said, but will you bring it next week anyway?"

Leah fixed her gaze directly onto Sam's. "Maybe." She headed to her car, knowing as well as he did, that she'd be back.

*****

More about Kay Jaybee

Kay Jaybee has been writing erotica for almost a decade. Her work includes *The Perfect Submissive Trilogy - The Perfect Submissive, The Retreat, Knowing Her Place* - (Xcite, 2012-14), *Making Him Wait,* (Sweetmeats Press, 2012), and *The Voyeur* (Xcite, 2012). The novellas *Digging Deep* (Xcite, 2013), *A Sticky Situation* (Xcite, 2012), *Not Her Type: Erotic Adventures With A Delivery Man* (1001Nights Press, 2nd ed 2012), and *The Circus* (Sweetmeats Press, 2011). The anthologies *Take Control,* (1001NightsPress, 2014) *Christmas Kink* (KDP, 2013), *The Best of Kay Jaybee,* (Xcite, 2012), *Tied to the Kitchen Sink, Equipment (*All Romance, 2012), *Yes Ma'am (*Xcite e-books, 2011), *Quick Kink One, Quick Kink Two* (Xcite, 2010), *The Collector (*Austin & Macauley, 1st Ed 2008, 2nd Ed 2012, and the short story *Punished (*Sweetmeats Press, 2013).

Links

Website: http://www.kayjaybee.me.uk
Twitter: http://www.twitter.com/kay_jaybee
Facebook: http://www.facebook.com/KayJaybeeAuthor
Goodreads: http://www.goodreads.com/user/show/3541958-kay-jaybee
Pinterest: http://pinterest.com/kjberotica/

Kay also writes romance as Jenny Kane:
http://www.jennykane.co.uk

Praise for Kay Jaybee

"Most readers of the genre will be familiar with Kay Jaybee's high quality writing. Kay's short fiction has appeared in countless anthologies and **THE PERFECT SUBMISSIVE** is a testament to her skills as a phenomenal writer." **Ashley Lister**

"Just the table of contents had me intrigued about Not Her Type. But I didn't linger on what was to come, because, wow, wham, bang, that first scene threw me right into the action... the author expertly plays with the old idea of 'can a relationship just about the sex work' ... go grab a copy of this seriously hot book, though be warned, because I for one will never be able to look another courier man in the eye again!..." **Miz Crew Reviews**

"Making Him Wait held me captive, made me blush, had me yearning for more before I was even ready to let the previous chapter go... erotica's "Queen of Kink" sucks her readers into the fascinating domain of domination and submission. A realm where one's words must be listened to very carefully and choices are empowering..."
Rose Caraway

Corporate Punishment

By Ruby Madsen

Sitting in the management meeting I hold his gaze as I argue with him about the latest figures. I know that he'll punish me for it later, even though I'm right and that thought is making my knickers wet. I try to concentrate on what he's saying to me but I can't because I'm hoping that no one's noticed the flush across my neck and chest that my filthy thoughts have caused. His eyes drift downwards and it's obvious that he knows what I'm thinking about. I make my final point and he raises an eyebrow as I bite my bottom lip, my signal to say that I submit to him completely. I see him swallow hard just before I drop my eyes and go back to writing in my notebook. If the other managers notice anything, no one mentions it. He has no comeback and I smile as he agrees to let me look into it, even though I know how much trouble I'm in.

For the rest of the meeting I watch him, my head filled with thoughts of what he will do to me later. I can almost feel the rope around my wrists, taste the silk of the scarves that he might push into my mouth. I've never wanted anyone the way I want him.

Six months ago, I'd never so much as used a paddle in the bedroom. I owned a pair of handcuffs but they were more for decoration. I was too shy to ask anyone to tie me up, afraid that they'd think I was kinky. Now I have difficulty remembering how I lived before him.

When I hear his voice telling me to strip, when he tells me to kneel or when he makes me beg him to let me suck his cock nothing else matters; nothing. I never realised how much pleasure could come from submitting completely to someone. If you'd told me six months ago that I would be here now, I would have laughed in your face. No one told me what to do in a relationship. I called the shots and I knew what I wanted from the guys I dated. At least I thought I did until I started seeing him.

The meeting finishes and I go back to my desk but I'm not working. Instead I'm following him around the office with my gaze, watching as he talks to the sales team. I try to tear myself away but I can't. All I can think about is what he'll do to me later. How those big strong hands, currently being used to emphasise a point to the Sales Manager, will be all over my body, touching and teasing me and pushing me to my limit. He looks in my direction and I drop my gaze immediately. He doesn't let me look him in the eye when we play at home and I know that my action will make him think about fucking me. I want him to know that I'm thinking about him fucking me. Maybe he'll punish me later for thinking inappropriate thoughts at work. I hope so.

I look up again and he's deep in conversation with another director. I watch the curve of his lips as they curl up into a sneer; he must be pissed off. When he looks at me with that mean sneer, I know my chastisement will be harsh. I imagine his hand on my arse and it makes me shiver, catching my breath.

I try to do some work, I really do but I'm just rushing through the essentials desperate to get finished so that I can leave on time, and I can't stop looking at him. He's dressed casually, no shirt or suit today and no tie, which is a shame. A tie holds so many possibilities; the slippery smoothness around my wrists or tight across my eyes. Sometimes he'll wrap it around my neck and pull, gently at first but then when I whimper, harder; just hard enough to make the edges blur. It makes my pussy twitch thinking about it.

Today he's wearing jeans and a polo shirt. I watched him put them on this morning, stretched out in bed, warm in the post orgasmic glow of our early morning fuck. He's only popped in for the management meeting we had earlier so he'll be home again by the time I'm finished here. The polo shirt means I can see his tattoo, the sleeves short enough to expose most of it. It's a tribal thing, wrapped all around his arm, and ridiculously I'm jealous because I want to be wrapped around him. I watch as he picks up a pen to sign some cheques and his top pulls tight across his arms and chest, making me melt. My wetness soaks the tiny scrap of material he made me wear this morning and I can feel my suspender belt biting into the flesh of my thighs as I move around in my chair. The tweak of pain sends a frisson of lust through me, flooding my knickers again. I want to go to the bathroom but he'll see me go. He'll know what I'm doing. He catches me staring and winks, his mouth curling up at the edges and I know that when I get home it will be so good.

*****

My key turns noisily in the lock on the front door. My heart's pounding in my chest and my pussy aches with the need to come.

It's been two hours since he left the office and I wonder what he's been doing while I've been working my arse off to get his monthly reports ready. All I want is to submit to him and I'm not disappointed.

He's leaning against the doorframe between the hallway and the living room, a bottle of beer in his hand. His t-shirt has gone and my gaze is drawn from his chest down the sexy trail of hair to the button on his jeans as I bend over to put down my laptop and handbag. It's half undone, teasing me.

"Good day, baby?" he asks, smiling at me as he takes a gulp of his beer. I nod, my eyes drawn to his as I straighten, watching as they darken when I tuck a strand of hair behind my ear.

"Not too bad," I say, smiling back, "I had a little disagreement with my boss, but I think he came round to my way of thinking in the end."

He raises an eyebrow and I drop my gaze to the floor, my breath quickening, waiting for his comeback.

"You had a smart mouth this morning," he states, and I can only imagine his face as I study the carpet. It sounds like he's smirking, enjoying my discomfort as I squirm in front of him. He knows exactly how turned on I am and I know he's going to milk it.

"Yes," I whisper, my pussy warming at his words. I stifle a squeal as I feel his hand on my neck, his fingers strong but gentle, pulling me in for a brief kiss before he urges me to my knees, my face in his hands, yanking me towards his crotch.

I can feel the heat rising through my body at the feel of his fingers against my throat as my face grazes across the soft denim of his well-worn jeans. My nostrils are filled with the scent of him and I close my eyes imagining the soft warmth of his cock just millimetres away from my lips. My fingers scramble at his button but he stops me, trapping my wrists and pulling me back to my feet. A moan escapes from my lips, frustrated by his teasing and he grins at me.

"Not just yet baby," he whispers against my ear, his warm breath tickling me, making my pussy gush again. "I have plans for you first."

He pulls me into the living room and I can see he's been busy while I've been at the office. He leads me over to the coffee table and pushes me gently down until I'm kneeling next to it. He kneels next to me.

"Take off your jacket," he murmurs, his lips tracing the edge of my mouth and I hurry to do as I'm told, my fingers stumbling over the buttons in my desperate need to please him. As soon as my jacket is off, he pulls at my shirt. "This too, and be quick," he says and I can hear the hitch in his breath, probably as he thinks about me doing it. "I want to see you in that bra I told you to wear this morning."

He chose a tiny half cup push-up bra this morning when he dressed me. It's holding my tits so tightly I'm sure it's left red marks across my breasts. My nipples are hard, poking out over the lacy material and as I unbutton my shirt his appreciative moan makes my insides tingle.

A moment later he grabs my hair, pulling my head back against his chest. "Do you like the toys I got for you baby?"

On the table is a spreader bar, a heart-shaped paddle, a ball gag and a purple leather flogger. There's also an assortment of vibrators and dildos and my favourite silk rope.

"I think I need to remind you who's in charge in this relationship," he says, his voice soft and low, full of promise and his fingernails trace a sharp trail over my nipples as I writhe against him. "I'm the boss and you need to remember that. You do as I tell you and I won't have you argue with me."

A moment of madness makes me back-chat him, not caring if the punishment is harsher. "I was right though," I say, "in the meeting. I was right."

He grins at that, his eyes crinkling. "Oh dear." He shakes his head. "You are really pushing my buttons tonight." He shoves me forward so that my cheek is pressed against the cold glass of the table then roughly tugs my skirt up and over my hips, exposing the soaking wet scrap of material that's almost covering my sopping pussy. I spread my legs so that he can see more of me, the heat of his gaze making me wetter still. I can imagine what he sees, the bright blue material cutting between the swollen red lips of my cunt. Then with one pull he's removed my thong, exposing me completely.

"I've made you wet," he murmurs. "Were you like this in the office?"

"Yes," I whisper, my voice shaky. "All the way through the meeting."

His cock is pushing against my thigh and I feel it twitch as I speak. "Fuck," he hisses under his breath. It sends shivers through me, warming my insides. "That's so hot, thinking about you sitting at your desk all wet and desperate for me. You are a very bad girl." His words make me wetter and as he talks, he slides a finger into my aching hole and I moan again. I get a slap for my trouble. "If you can't keep quiet, I'll make you quiet," he growls.

I know what he means but I can't help myself and I whimper with lust, bucking back against his hand. He pushes me roughly against the table again and stands up. I don't move, waiting to see what he will do next. "Get up on your knees," he snaps and I obey immediately, biting my lip. His eyes are all over me but I can only imagine what he sees. My tits lined with red marks from the bra, squeezed into submission; my shirt hanging open, pussy exposed underneath my rucked up skirt. I can make out his erection straining against his jeans and I wonder if he's naked beneath them.

He's picked up the purple ball gag, winding the leather straps around his hands. "Open your mouth."

I do as he orders, my body quivering with anticipation. He slips the gag between my lips, pulling the restraints tight behind my head until my eyes water. "That should keep you quiet," he whispers against my ear, his hands sliding over my body, removing my shirt and tossing it across the room.

Pushing me forward again he pulls my hips up exposing my pussy even further. The back door is open onto the garden and I can feel a cool breeze caressing my hot, swollen lips. I ache to feel him inside me but I know he'll make me suffer first. I try to squeeze my legs together to bring some kind of release to the throb in my clit, but he sees and without warning slaps my arse with the leather paddle.

I squeal, the noise muffled by the gag, as the stinging heat warms my exposed bum. "I say when you can come," he says. The paddle comes down on my flesh again and again and I can feel the heat covering my skin. I know it will be red and I know how much he likes to see it like that. I try to turn my head to see if he still has his jeans on and he spanks me again. "Don't move unless I tell you to."

I close my eyes. The smoothness of the glass under my cheek makes me think of the soft skin of his cock and I really want to suck it. I want to feel the velvety warmth of his thick shaft pushing into my mouth, right down to his balls. I need him to use my mouth for his pleasure, his hot cum filling me, dripping down my chin as he wipes himself on my cheek.

My eyes open as he grabs my ankles and pulls my legs as wide as they'll go. My breath hitches as my clit throbs again, the hard nub desperate for his touch.

As if he can read my mind I feel his hot breath against me, his tongue darting between my soaking lips and I stifle my whimper, trying not to make a sound, desperate for him to carry on. I hear a heavy clank as the spreader bar hits the floor between my legs and I sigh as he shackles it to my ankles. I can hear him take a step back, admiring his handiwork.

"I should take a picture," he says, "a picture of you kneeling at my feet like the wicked little slut that you are." I nod, wanting to be able to see myself as he sees me. Nothing matters when we're together like this. All I care about is pleasing him, making him happy. I hear his phone click then the cool touch of his fingers on me. He pulls my wrists behind my back and shackles them together, my nipples grazing the smooth surface of the table top as I topple forward. I'm helpless, completely at his mercy, awaiting my punishment.

I hear him get up and from where my face is pushed into the glass I can only see his legs as he walks around me. He picks something up and then I hear the low buzz of a vibrator. My pussy twitches, the muscles clenching and I feel my wetness flowing, leaving a sticky trail down the inside of my thighs. Spread like this before him I can't hide my arousal and yet I have no idea how he's affected by the sight of me. I want to see his cock.

He's behind me again. "You're so wet," he murmurs and I feel the tingling buzz of the vibrator as he glides it slowly down my gaping slit, sliding it briefly inside me, my muscles grasping for it before he removes it again. I moan against the gag, saliva drooling from the corners of my mouth. He pushes the toy into me, this time thrusting it in and out, watching my pussy swallow it up and release it, a slurping wet noise cutting through the silence, punctuated by my muffled gasps.

He guides it all the way in and turns it to slow, holding it deep inside me. It's exquisite torture, a feeling of fullness but with the sensations too low to push me over the edge and make me come. His fingers slide between my legs and finally, at last, he pays attention to my clit. I feel the tears at the corners of my eyes as he strokes it, rubbing against the soft flesh with his rough fingers.

Then, shattering the silence, his mobile rings and he gets up to answer it, removing the vibrator and leaving me spread across the table, my clit aching for his touch again. It sounds like it is work and I hear him move into the other room.

Bastard, how can he leave me hanging like this? My body hums with longing, unable to do anything about the ache between my legs. I try to turn my head, the muscles in my arms burning, a frisson of fear licking its way through my insides. I can't hear him anymore. I don't know how long he's going to be.

The seconds tick by and it feels like he's been gone forever. I feel empty; my only existence is waiting for him to come back. I focus on the clock on the mantelpiece, my pussy throbbing with each tick. I know that he is teasing me, making me wait for him but closing my eyes for a second, every creak of the house is suddenly magnified as I strain to hear him return. The fear that he won't heightens the sensation even more.

Then I squeal through the gag as he brings his hand down on my bum, his fingers lashing my aching pussy. Fuck, he scared me to death creeping up on me like that.

"Did I make you jump?" he asks.

I nod, pushing myself up towards him. "Yeth, Thir," I say, the gag making me sound funny.

He winds his fingers into my hair, pulling gently, his nails digging into my scalp.

"Where were we?" Unclipping the gag he turns me around. I whimper at the sight of him, naked at last, his jeans shed along with his restraint; I can feel his desire like a naked flame against my skin.

"You are a fucking little tease," he moans against the soft skin of my neck. "The way you were looking at me this afternoon, all I could think about was screwing you over my desk. I don't know how I lasted this long before having you. If I hadn't needed to show you who's in control here I would have fucked you the minute you set foot in this house."

I close my eyes and let his words wash over me, smiling at the effect I have on him. Then at last I allow myself to look at him properly, to devour every inch of his body. His eyes are warm now; a deep, dark brown, his skin pale, his cheeks flushed with arousal. He's so beautiful; his body tight and toned, his obvious desire for me drawing my gaze between his strong thighs. I feel myself blush as he steps back to take in every part of me. I can't move, the spreader bar stopping me from standing, my hands still tied behind me and I feel exposed as he looks at me.

"I need to be inside you," he growls, unfastening the restraints on my wrists and ankles and removing the gag. As I stand, my legs are wobbly from kneeling for so long and he catches me, strong arms around my waist, pushing me backwards onto the sofa; soft fabric rubbing against my naked arse. His cock is hard, the end glistening with pre-cum, swollen and heavy, a deep, dark pink. I lean forward to take him in my mouth but he pushes me away, forcing me onto my back, his knees spreading my legs so that my pussy is exposed again. I'm so wet that my inner thighs are coated with the slick mess of my juices. I'm almost embarrassed but he slides his fingers against my skin, and without warning dips his head so I almost scream as his tongue slips inside my heated cunt. I give myself up to him as he laps at my core, drawing a low moan from my lips. I tangle my fingers in his hair and try and pull him deeper into me but he grabs my wrists and holds me back. He teases me as punishment until I'm begging him.

"Please," I whisper, my breath ragged, eyes half closed.

"Please what?" he asks, trailing his fingertips between my breasts, following them with his tongue which darts over the bullet tips of my nipples.

"Please baby," I whisper, "I need you inside me."

He kisses me then. I gasp, the shock of the sudden tenderness taking me by surprise. He never normally kisses me when we're playing, but as he sucks and nips at my lips, his tongue fucking my mouth, I realise that he's making me submit to him again, making me wait for his beautiful cock. His kisses are rough and demanding and they leave my lips raw; swollen with lust until they mirror the heaviness of my aching cunt. He tastes salty from the sweat on his top lip and it makes me shake as our teeth connect and I taste blood, my lip cut in the frenzy of our coupling. The metallic taste hotwires my pussy and I forget everything except how much I want him.

"Please," I murmur again, my voice disappearing into the depths of his mouth and this time with one swift move he's over me and I can feel the hot solidness of his cock sliding between my thighs. It rests against me for a moment; I look up at him and then he's inside me, buried to the hilt.

"Not so talkative now, are you?" he murmurs. "I told you I'd show you who was boss." He shoves my arms above my head, my nipples grazing his chest as I arch underneath him.

"No," I whimper. I can't help myself pushing against him, desperately grinding my clit against the hard curve of his abs. I need to come, to finish what he started this morning. My whole body is tense, I need the release of orgasm and I know he won't deny me for much longer as his fingers grip my arse, pulling me harder onto him.

I run my hands over his strong back, the feel of his soft skin under my touch making me shiver and I try to kiss him again. He pulls back, a half smile flitting across his face as he teases me some more. He pushes into me over and over, watching my face as he does and I can feel the beginnings of my orgasm deep in my stomach.

Just as I'm about to come, to finally get the release I've been craving all day, he pulls out of me and flips me onto my stomach. The emptiness inside me is almost too much to bear and I whimper into the cushions, cool and crisp beneath my face. I can't believe he's going to make me wait again.

For a moment he's gone and then with a rush of air I feel the burning sting of the paddle across my bum. He is relentless in his punishment, even when I know he is as desperate to come as I am and I moan and writhe beneath him. The heat fills my pussy until I cry out, begging him to fuck me and then he does; finally giving in to his lust and we fuck until we're both spent and I'm sobbing with every thrust against my burning skin.

As the last waves of my orgasm are subsiding, he pulls slowly out of me and wraps his arms around my body. I can feel the warmth of his chest as his breathing slows and the sweat trickles between us. He tucks a strand of my hair behind my ear, nuzzling against my neck and I feel safe.

I'm exhausted from the onslaught of his passion, enveloped in the animal scent of our lust. As my eyes close I feel his breath hot against my ear and he whispers the words that he'll never say out loud. I smile in the darkness. He might be the boss in the boardroom and he might be the Dom, but I hold all the cards in the bedroom.

*****

More about Ruby Madsen

Ruby Madsen is the living embodiment of Lexie Bay's dark side. She loves to explore the dangerous things in life, prefers the wilder side of romance and firmly believes that being naughty is more fun.

Ruby has a dirty laugh and she's been told, an even dirtier mind. She's a stocking wearing, chain smoking tease with a fondness for red lipstick and bad boys and she wishes she'd been born in the 1950s when men were men and women were pin ups.

This is her first published story, but she's working on some more and hopes to have her debut novel ready in the next few months. You can expect lots of kinky games, raw emotions and not so much of the happily ever after, because sometimes life's just mean and your heart gets broken. Although Ruby believes that there's always something better around the corner.

Links

Website: http://www.rubymadsen.co.uk
Twitter: http://www.twitter.com/rubymadsen
Facebook: https://www.facebook.com/rubymadsenwriter

Caught Naked

By Sarah Masters

The bright swathe of a flashlight cut through the darkness, the beam arcing across the concrete floor of the warehouse. Naked, Mark stood behind a pallet of boxes that stretched to twice his height. He held his breath.

Jesus fucking Christ. Go away. Don't find me.

He peered between his pallet and the next, the aisle too narrow for someone to walk through without their shoulders brushing the polythene covering the boxes. He'd hear whoever was coming, despite their barely perceptible footsteps—the polythene would rustle.

Unless they walk sideways. Shit!

Why the hell Jake thought it would be fun to meet and fuck here, Mark didn't know. He was all for having sex in unusual places, but the warehouse where they worked? Okay, they knew the layout, knew where all the cameras were outside so they'd avoid detection coming in, but bloody hell…

Seems someone's found me anyway.

Jake had texted five minutes ago to say he would be late. Stuck in traffic—what a damn cliché. Reckoned he'd be here in about half an hour, but that was no good to Mark. He'd left his clothes in his locker and made his way here to their meeting spot, not expecting security to be working this area.

He thought about his options. If he was caught he *could* say he'd forgotten his phone, had returned, using his keys to get in. Had heard a noise in the warehouse and was just checking it out when he saw the flashlight.

Sounds plausible…if I wasn't naked.

Someone coughed. Mark jumped and released his breath. It breezed out too sharply, despite his efforts to stop it, and jostled a loose strip of polythene hanging at head height. The plastic made a crinkling sound as it blew up then settled back down.

Fucking great. May as well have shouted, "I'm here!"

The flashlight beam stilled at the end of the aisle, a circular pool highlighting a divot in the cement where something heavy had perhaps fallen from a forklift during work hours. The flashlight doused, and the darkness was just about absolute. Mark held his breath again, waiting for whoever was out there to step forward and show himself. And it had to be a man, didn't it? No way a woman would break in to a bloody warehouse in the middle of the damn night.

Sexist fuck.

Mark's nerves were so taut he almost laughed. His sister would have something to say if she'd read his thoughts then, and sexist fuck was one of her milder admonishments. But he couldn't laugh. There was nothing funny about this situation. If it wasn't security prowling, it had to be someone else who shouldn't be here, and that someone might be armed.

A shuffle scuffed the floor, loud and abrasive in the cocooning darkness, its echo sending a chill up Mark's spine. His stomach rolled, and he clenched his fists, digging his fingernails into his palms to divert his mind to the pain there rather than the fear. He was so fucked—and not in the way he and Jake had in mind, either—if he got caught like this. He could face losing his job, something they didn't need, what with the high mortgage payments on their London apartment. And if it was Ben, the burly security guard with the attitude that stunk like donkey's bollocks, Mark might get to keep his job, but his discovery and how he wasn't dressed would be embellished and spread around the workforce in no time.

He imagined Ben's words now. "I caught the skinny little bastard in the nude. And yeah, he *is* a natural redhead."

He'd never live it down.

Like I need to worry about their opinions. Why the hell didn't I wait until Jake took my clothes off?

Footsteps clicked on the floor, the sound of them tinny. Mark secreted himself further behind the pallet, pressing his chest against the boxes; the shock of the cold polythene had him gasping. He silently cursed himself and stared down the aisle with only one eye, cautious in case the owner of those shoes came strolling along the narrow passage.

A figure ghosted past the opening then disappeared. The footsteps reverberated, fast strides that quickened Mark's pulse and ratcheted up his heartbeat. Could he make it back to the locker room so he could get dressed and get the hell out of here? He glanced behind him into the gloom, estimating the time it would take to run behind all those pallets without being seen, getting to the end before the figure reached there first.

Fuck it. Do it. Run!

He looked down for a moment, his mind a jumble as to what he should do. Making a snap decision, he turned and rushed forward, his mouth suddenly dry, his legs weakening. It seemed as though his breaths had amplified, would alert the other person to where he was. A more insistent thought of getting busted further ignited his need to get away, and he picked up his pace. Only two more pallets until he reached the end and the corner that would take him to relative safety.

For now.

His chest hurt, lungs constricting, and a sharp pain jabbed his side. That was all he needed, a damn stitch, but he pressed on, skidding around the corner, straight into…Jake.

"Fuck!" Mark grated out, almost shitting his damn self. "Some other fucker's in here. Quickly, I need to get dressed." He grabbed Jake's arm and pulled him towards the locker room, slowing as his mind registered Jake dragging his heels. "Come *on.* I saw someone down there. Security or a burglar, for God's sake." He tugged Jake harder.

The sod was smiling.

"What's so bloody funny?" Mark whispered, coming to a stop beside the door leading to the car park, and turning to face his lover. He peered over Jake's shoulder, waiting for whoever had been in the darkness to appear.

I just want to get dressed and forget this whole idea.

"Someone's in here, you say?" Jake cocked his head, his face half illuminated by the glowing fire exit sign on the wall beside them.

His brown eyes looked black, and one cheek had a spectral glow. A flop of blond hair hid his brow, and waves of it curled around his ear. He smiled again, that sometimes infuriating quirk of the lips that sent Mark nuts.

"We'd better go and see," Jake said. "We'll be in shit if we leave them in here." Glancing down at Mark's nakedness, he grinned wider. "Best you don't frighten them with the size of your cock."

Jake turned and walked back the way Mark had come.

What's he doing?

"Jake!"

Jake ignored him.

"At least let me get dressed first."

As Jake disappeared around the corner, Mark let out a ragged sigh and lifted his hands, dropping them uselessly by his sides. When Jake had a mind to do something, there was no stopping him.

"Fuck!" Following Jake, Mark rounded the corner and spotted him at their meeting place. He ran behind the pallets, coming to stop, out of breath from his quick sprint and the adrenaline rush. "I waited here like you said," he gasped out, glancing back then looking at Jake. "And someone with a flashlight—"

Jake pushed Mark up against the pallet, holding him in place with the press of his body. "So you waited like I asked, eh?"

"Yes. What are you *doing?* We're so going to get caught here, man. Pack it the fuck in."

"And you saw someone... So where are they now?" Jake's breath kissed Mark's neck a moment before his lips did the same.

"I don't know, do I? Jake, stop it. We have to go. We're going to get *caught*, for fuck's sake."

Jake trailed his soft lips up the column of Mark's neck. "Isn't that what you wanted?" he asked between kisses. "A little danger? Wasn't that what you said I could get you if I ever wanted to buy you a birthday present?"

Mark raised his hands then snaked them between him and Jake. He gently shoved at Jake's chest, trying to make him see sense. "Yes, but not like this. Not when someone else could catch us at it."

Jake took hold of Mark's wrists, lifting them above his head, holding them in one hand while he blazed a path down to Mark's cock with the other.

Oh, shit...

"What if I told you," Jake said, fisting Mark's cock, "that *some*one was me?"

"You?" Mark frowned, chest rising and falling hard from his heavy breathing.

"Yeah, me." Jake flicked his tongue out and licked Mark's lips. "What if I told you it was safe to fuck here? That we won't get caught? Would you do it?"

Mark thought for a few seconds. He trusted Jake, all right, but what if he was just messing about and there really *was* someone else around? Could he do it even if there was? "I don't know." His cock hardened with Jake's massaging, despite fear lingering. "Shit, man. I don't know."

Jake bit Mark's lip lightly, then said, "Your cock tells me

otherwise."

Mark's balls ached. His cock hardened further, and his arsehole tightened. "*Was* it you? And don't bullshit me either."

"It was me. I wanted to play something out. Come up behind you. Surprise you. But I coughed, realised you'd freak, and a couple of minutes later you bolted."

"Shit!"

"Forgive me?" Jake flashed his tongue out again, slipping it between the seam of Mark's lips.

Mark responded by opening his mouth, allowing that hot, wet tongue to probe inside, swirling around his and bringing on a fierce rush of desire. He struggled against the hand holding his wrists in place, but Jake held tighter and pulled his mouth away.

"Why do you need your hands free?" Jake asked, his breath skimming Mark's cheek.

"So I can touch you."

"Touch me where?"

"Everywhere."

"Everywhere…" Jake fisted Mark harder, faster, dipping his head so their brows connected. "Undress me."

He released Mark's wrists and paced backwards. The scent of Jake's aftershave still hovered close, and Mark wished Jake would move forward and kiss him again. Jake took his hand from Mark's cock—the total loss of contact had Mark lowering his hands and stepping forward so their bodies touched again.

Jake reversed another step. "Don't do anything except undress me." He reached inside his jacket pocket, brought something out, and a click sounded, followed by their space being lit by the flashlight. "See? It *was* me." Next, he took out an oblong box, bent at the waist, and put it and the flashlight on the floor.

Mark's stomach clenched in excitement. Jake stood upright, the light's glow just enough so Mark saw him a little better. He raised his hands and slipped Jake's jacket off, dropping it to the floor. With his heart beating erratically, Mark lifted the hem of Jake's t-shirt and dragged it over his lover's head. The t-shirt found a home with the jacket and, resisting the impulse to run his hands over Jake's chest, Mark popped open the buttons on the jeans that hid the cock he needed to touch.

"When you lower the jeans, kneel." Jake's voice had sounded hoarse, as though the thrill of what they were doing proved too much.

Mark knew how that felt all right, and he inhaled a deep breath to calm himself. He wanted to yank the jeans off, crush himself to Jake, and feel every damn part of him, but it seemed Jake wanted to call the shots.

What Jake wanted, Jake got—and Mark had no qualms about giving it to him, either. He shimmied the jeans over slender hips, lowering to his knees and drawing the fabric down legs that had so often gripped him around the waist as he'd fucked Jake's tight arse, legs that had shuddered as Mark sucked the cock jutting between them.

Fuck!

Mark's thoughts had him battling to remain in control. He ached, the throb so strong he held his breath until the insistent beat lessened. He released the air from his lungs and smoothed his hands up the backs of Jake's legs, the muscles taut under his palms. Cupping Jake's arse, Mark kneaded, skimming his fingertips up and down the crack. Jake's hard cock brushed Mark's chest.

Shit, this is so fucking hot.

Reaching up, Mark caressed Jake's back before returning his hands to his arse. He brought one hand around to fist Jake's erection, holding him at his base. Looking down and wetting his lips in anticipation, Mark eyed Jake. The flashlight gave enough illumination so Mark could see a glistening drop of pre-cum, and his arsehole bunched as yearning to take that hardness into his mouth gripped him. He licked away the wetness, the taste of it spreading over his tongue. He took a second to savour the moment then plunged his mouth over Jake's dick.

A barely perceptible gasp left Jake, and Mark drew upwards, creating the suction he knew his lover wanted—hard and unrelenting. He bobbed his head, taking Jake deeper every time he sucked him in. Jake buried his hands in Mark's hair, directing the pace. Mark worked faster, pulled up harder.

"Fuck, yes!" Jake hissed, clenching Mark's hair in tight fists. He gave a strangled groan, then, "Wait! Shit, wait!"

Mark eased his mouth away, looking up at Jake, who stared down at him with half-closed eyes. He slowly drew his hand up and down Jake's cock, maintaining eye contact, silently asking the question he wanted to say out loud.

"Stand up," Jake said, his words quavering. "I need… fuck, I need…"

Mark stood, still wanking Jake, still looking into his eyes. "You need what?"

"Turn around."

Mark released Jake and obeyed, waiting for Jake's next instruction. It came as a gentle push towards the pallet and the lifting of Mark's arms as Jake placed them above his head, palms pressed to the polythene. Breathing heavily in expectation, Mark listened to the shuffle of the oblong box being opened, the sound slicing through the relative quiet. He recognised the noise of a tube being taken from the box, and he smiled. Another sound came then, a small pop. Jake had dropped the tube lid?

Body heat close to Mark's back told him Jake stood near, and he closed his eyes. The cold drip of lube at the top of his arse crack had him hiking in a sharp breath of shock. Jake smoothing it down the valley with his fingertips warmed the fluid, and Mark widened his legs to give him better access. Thoughts of being fucked against the pallet, with nothing to grip except polythene… Mark wanted Jake to rush, yet at the same time he wanted to relish this moment because, fuck, they wouldn't repeat it in a hurry.

Will we?

He wasn't sure they should, but the idea of it set his cock to throbbing harder. It screamed to be touched, for Jake to take it in hand while he fucked his arse. Jake circled Mark's pucker with teasing strokes. Another dribble of lube oozed down, and Jake pushed his fingertip inside Mark. The quick burn of the intrusion fizzled out with Jake going in further, and Mark hissed out between clenched teeth.

"You feel that?" Jake asked, his voice low. "You like that?"

Mark nodded, eyes still closed, and widened his legs some more.

Jake added a second finger, moving them in and out with ease, brushing over the nub inside Mark. He sucked in air, his balls drawing up, his cock bobbing.

"Shit, that feels damn good. More." Mark opened his eyes and glanced over his shoulder.

Jake was looking down, watching his fingers moving, and the sight of him turned Mark on to the point he swore he was going to come.

"Fuck!"

Jake withdrew his fingers and pressed his body close, tilting his head to steal a kiss. Mark flashed out his tongue, and Jake did the same, their positions too awkward for their lips to meet. Jake groaned and lowered his lips to Mark's shoulder, butting the tip of his cock to Mark's arsehole. Mark nuzzled his cheek to Jake's head and waited for the stretch. It came, fast and burning, Jake pushing his cock in. Pleasure-pain seared, and Mark moaned, clenching his hands into fists.

"All of you. I want all of you," Mark said, jutting his arse out, shoving back onto Jake's cock.

That hardness he loved filled him, and Jake set up an easy rhythm, quickening along with Mark's pants. Jake gripped Mark's waist, fingertips biting into his flesh, the feel of it enticing Mark closer to the edge.

"Oh, yeah. You like that, Mark? You like my cock in your tight little ass?" Jake's skin slapped Mark's, and he thrust faster. "Fucking... tight on my... cock. Ah! Shit, I'm going to come."

Jake shunted, lancing Mark harder, reaching around to fist Mark's length. His touch and fast jolting had Mark keening, and he slammed himself back and forth, matching Jake's rhythm, aching to reach completion. He smacked the side of his fist on the boxes, hanging his head back so his torso formed a curve. Jake lightly bit Mark's shoulder, and with an animalistic grunt, he jerked Mark's cock and thrust inside him with unrelenting speed.

Mark's orgasm began to peak, tingles spreading from his balls and up his cock. His vein throbbed a second before a shot of cum sped out of him and slapped the polythene. He let out a hoarse cry, his legs spasming and his knees weakening. Wet heat filled his arse, hot and welcomed. Mark's shoulder muffled Jake's stuttered groans, and Mark's joined them, another jet leaving him, stretching his cockhole.

"Ah, fuck!" Mark closed his eyes, allowing himself to drown in the sensations spiralling through his body. After a third expulsion and more heat in his arse, he lowered his arms to fumble behind and place his hands on Jake's buttocks, encouraging his lover to slow.

Jake stopped, his breaths hot on Mark's skin. They stood still for long moments, gathering their wits and steadying their breathing.

"Shit, that was intense," Mark said, pulling away, already mourning the loss of Jake's cock inside him. He turned and pulled him close, cupping Jake's cheek and seeking out his lips.

Their kiss ended at the sound of movement in the warehouse.

Mark stared at Jake. "Shit!" he whispered, heart rate picking up speed. "Did you hear that?"

Jake's breathing faltered. He nodded and brought a finger to his lips. Quietly, he gathered his clothing in his arms and switched off the flashlight. He found Mark's hand in the darkness, and Jake led him along the narrow aisle behind the pallets. At the corner, Jake stopped and poked his head out. Giving Mark's hand a tug, he guided them to the locker room, closing the door behind them.

Mark released a breath he hadn't realised he'd held. "Holy *fuck!*"

"We're going to have to get dressed and get the hell out, quick. Where are your clothes?"

"In my locker." Mark weaved across the room, taking careful steps by memory, because he sure as shit couldn't see a damn thing in here. At his locker, he pulled out his clothes, and something came out with it, hitting the floor with a resounding crack. "Shit! Sorry!" He glanced down. His phone was face-up, the light from the screen a rectangle of brightness. Scooping it up, he put it in the bottom of his locker then dressed, his movements erratic as his earlier thoughts of being caught returned.

I can't believe someone else is here. That we fucked, risking a damn audience!

"You dressed yet?" Jake asked, his voice odd coming out of the darkness like that.

"Yeah. You?"

"Yeah. Come on. We need to go."

Mark slid his phone into his jeans pocket and walked towards where he'd left Jake. He bumped into him and almost yelled out.

Get a bloody grip!

"Okay. Let's go." He took a deep breath and followed Jake from the locker room.

They only had a few steps to take and made it to the fire exit door within seconds. Mark had disabled the alarm earlier, so opening the door didn't pose a problem.

Unless security is here for a check-up and reset the bloody thing again.

He winced. Jake pushed down the bar that kept the door closed. It swung open. No blaring alarm, no creak of the hinges. They slipped out into the cold night. Pushing the door to—it couldn't be closed from outside—Mark streaked across the car park behind Jake, the urge to laugh pushing him to clamp his lips closed. He felt alive and so damn freaked at the same time, he couldn't get to his car fast enough. He'd left it in a side street, their plan in case the very thing that was happening happened, and their cars were spotted outside the warehouse.

Once there, he fumbled in his jacket pocket for his keys. "See you at home," he said. Inside his car, he gunned the engine and sped away, releasing a shaky laugh and hoping to God it *was* security in the building. They'd left the door open, and if the place got burgled…

Shit.

He reached home in record time, mind full of what-ifs and ominous scenarios. He parked in the underground lot beneath their block of flats and breathed a sigh of relief seeing Jake's headlights cut through the semi-darkness. Mark got out of his car then locked up, waiting anxiously for Jake to do the same.

Jake strolled over. "That was a bit close, man. Too close."

"Who the hell was it?" Mark walked towards the concrete stairs, his heart thumping too hard. "I mean, it could have been anyone."

"It was Ben. I looked back as we left the car park. Saw his profile through the window. No two people have a nose like that."

Mark pushed air out through pursed lips. "Thank fuck for that!"

"Yeah, he'll spot the door, so stop worrying."

Mark led the way up the stairs. "What was he doing there, though? No security was meant to be on tonight." He rounded the landing and took another flight.

"You know what he's like. Reckon he was sitting at home, thinking about work. He never has thought that place was safe unless he's working his shift."

They entered their flat, and in the living room, Mark tossed his keys onto the table. He took off his jacket while Jake locked up. He stared at the coffee table, at the many presents on it, and knew, despite their recent mad hour or two, no present down there was going to beat the one he'd just had.

Jake came into the room and stood behind him, gathering Mark close. He linked his hands across Mark's belly. "Happy birthday, man," he whispered.

Mark smiled and stared out of the window. A million lights sparkled across the city of London. "Thanks, but…" He glanced across at the wall clock above the TV. "My birthday's over. It's yours now. Want your present?"

Jake turned Mark to face him. "You can't tell me what you've got me will beat what I gave you."

Mark lifted Jake's t-shirt for the second time. "You wanna bet?"

*****

More about Sarah Masters

Sarah Masters is a multi-published author with six pen names writing several genres. She lives with her husband, children, and two cats in an English village. She is also Head of Art for a publishing company. In another life she was an editor. Her other pen names are Natalie Dae, Geraldine O'Hara, Emmy Ellis, Charley Oweson, and she's one half of Harlem Dae.

Links

Website: http://www.emmyellisblog.blogspot.co.uk/
Facebook: http://www.facebook.com/emmy.ellis.503

Praise for Sarah Masters

"You will NOT be disappointed!! This was seriously amazing. I'm gonna read it again, and again, and again. It was THAT good!"
Amazon Review

"A perfect short story, beautifully evocative and exquisitely told."
Amazon Review

"Author Sarah Masters did a superb job of capturing the mental angst one goes through during break-up." **Amazon Review**

Francesca's Mother

By Tabitha Rayne

I couldn't help but stare.

She was perfection in her black bikini, standing in front of me in line for the waterslide. From her heels to her calves, all the way up the back of her thighs to the dip and crease of her buttocks, her legs were flawless. Olive, hair-free skin had me mesmerized. I was now glad of the long queue which previously had me shivering. With all the self assurance of a foreign exchange student, she gracefully lifted her ponytail and tied it in a knot. I swallowed hard as I caught a glimpse of thick dark hair curling under her arms. My heart leapt and I was instantly thrown back to my youth.

Francesca's mother was my guilty pleasure. I would stay for long weekends at their house and spend the whole time preoccupied by the huge maternal presence that commanded the family home with gentle force. I would find any excuse to go into the kitchen and watch her knead dough on the antique pine table, her braless breasts swinging and gently slapping together beneath a purple smock dress. She was so mighty and strong and, though I couldn't name it at the time, sensual. When she moved near me I'd inhale her scent. Underneath the rosemary and garlic, there was something else; something musky and dangerous. It at once attracted and repelled me, but I always filled my lungs with the delicious warmth, seeking that hidden perfume.

"Look at this," Francesca pulled me into her mother's bedroom one trip home from college. We sprawled on the bed reading Anais Nin and Nancy Friday books until we could gasp and giggle no more. I read the words, becoming more and more physically turned on. I'd had a few ferociously passionate encounters at college and was no stranger to sex, but I sensed these books were exploring something else too. Something more than the physical. They made me want to be with the mighty woman downstairs.

"I'm just going for a drink," I told Francesca and rolled off the bed, taking care not to show the damp spot forming in my jeans.

When I got to the kitchen, Francesca's mother was standing over a huge pot of broth on the stove. Thick meaty smells filled the room, and as she lifted her elbow to stir the great vat, a tuft of glossy black curls sprang into view. I was slightly repulsed but my mouth started watering and warmth and moisture spread between my legs. I sat on a stool and pressed my hands onto my mound, rocking my pelvis into my fists while Francesca's mother stirred the soup. I came in my jeans just as she tapped the drips off the ladle on the side of the pot.

The atmosphere was charged and I was sure I caught her eyes flit across my tiny hard nipples while she swept away wild peppery hair from her brow with her forearm. I lifted my ribcage and stared at her, daring her to look again, but she didn't. She turned back to the range and opened the oven door. Steam and the odour of fresh baked bread broke the spell and I hopped off the stool and sped back up to Francesca, at once invigorated and ashamed.

And now, at the swimming pool of all places, these feelings had returned. The queue bustled into me and I stumbled slightly into the back of the poised beauty in front. She looked haughtily round and I licked my lips involuntarily at the sight of hers. Full and raw with a dusting of fine hairs on her upper lip. Suddenly I was consumed with want for this woman. I could have grabbed her there and then. I could feel my nipples peaking as she looked at me straight in the eye.

"I'm sorry," I gasped. "It's the people behind, they keep pushing."

She slowly and languidly looked down the full length of me then turned back as the attendant signalled her to go on the slide. She grabbed the bar at the top of the entrance and flung herself into the water filled tube. My desire began to subside and I gave myself a mental shake. What was I up to?

The attendant gave me the nod and I pushed myself as hard as I could into the tunnel. I was drenched and gathered up by the flow, sliding up and down the sides of the huge tube. It was exhilarating and my lustful agitation was just easing when I collided hard into a figure jammed spread-eagled against the sides of the slide.

"What the…" I started as the woman from the queue fell heavily onto me thrusting a hand over my mouth.

"I saw the look in your eyes," her distinct voice hissed in my ear and my want came flooding back. As we writhed and twisted gathering speed, she removed her hand and kissed me hard, forcing my mouth open with her powerful sharp little tongue. It was thrilling and I reached round and grabbed her ass through her bikini bottoms.

She countered by shoving her hand in between my legs and pulled my swimsuit to the side, delving fingers inside my soaked sex. I splayed my legs open and tried to slow us down by grabbing the tube walls. She slammed her pelvis into the gap and ground her hand deeper into my pussy with the force of her mound. It felt so horny and I grabbed at her tits craning my head up and under her arm to catch another glimpse of the beautiful curls. She obliged, lifting her arm, allowing me to bury my nose into the fragrant nook. There it was. Sensual, dangerous, horny – that smell. I wallowed in it as she kneaded my clit with her thumb. I jerked and rocked as the stars that always signalled my climax swirled in my peripheral vision. My pussy began to well and she started pumping her fingers into me violently as the water gushed around us and flowed over her chest, pulling down her bikini top so that her ripe dark nipples were just a lick away. As I started coming, I engulfed one of her breasts with my hungry mouth and suckled her throbbing tit, tonguing the puckered flesh trying to take it all in. She grabbed my pussy from the inside and out, gripping my clit and g-spot together. I came, twitching and panting and gushing all over her sexy little hands. I wanted my turn, I wanted to fuck her with my fingers, my tongue, but she climbed off me, and slid away while tying her bikini back up. The slide ended abruptly and I splashed out into a deep cool pool. I swam to the surface, staring all around for my tunnel lover, but I couldn't see her anywhere.

    Later, I searched though my college things and found the books I'd quietly stolen from Francesca's mother. I spent the rest of the afternoon sprawled across my bed understanding all the things I'd missed those years before.

The Scribe

By Tabitha Rayne

I've just hitched up my skirt. I'm kneeling and the hem is at my buttocks, almost exposing them, but not quite. The familiar tingling anticipation sweeps over my flesh as I part my thighs, just a little, and lift one of the implements laid out before me. I always start with the smallest – the finest.

I hold my breath and close my eyes letting my head fall back, jaw slack, in the pose that signifies the beginning of my ritual.

I run the tip of the long fine shaft up the inside of my thigh, swirling and sweeping as I go, imagining the pattern it makes on my skin. My hand is shaking and the hairs on the back of my neck bristle in delight. If you really concentrate on your body, you can feel which nerve endings are connected. For example, if you arouse or tickle the tiny fine hairs just at the corner of your mouth, It sends a tingling sensation to the inside of your elbow – if you follow the line and sweep just there, you can trace a path all the way to the heavenly dip and peak of your sex. I defy you not to try it now. Go on, let your hand reach to the side of your mouth, go on...

The door. I hear the door open. My thighs clamp shut in shame and I'm shuffling my skirt back down when he strolls into the room.

"What's going on here then?" He sounds like he's being jokey but I'm so humiliated and ashamed at being caught that I can't read his expression. I have a flashback to the same scene when I was small, only it had been my mother who'd walked in then.

"What the hell do you think you're doing?" she'd screamed in an explosion of fury and I'd stared at my stained skin and cried.

"Nothing," I stammer gathering my pens and brushes to my bosom and scramble to standing.

"Come on." He stoops low and I surrender back onto my heels. "Show me."

He stares at me with those eyes. Those artist's eyes that scrutinise, study, absorb and analyse. He knows my body intimately, inside and out. I've posed for him a hundred times and lain down for him a thousand.

He eases the pens from my grip and lays them on the floor. His fingertips are cold as he gathers my skirt and pulls it up to my resisting fists which are balled into my lap.

"Please, let me see."

I watch the curling ink come into view as I relax my hands. Hard black scribbles both adorn and sear my flesh.

"What's this?" he asks with curiosity, not anger and I feel I might tell him.

"It's mine."

"Your what?"

"My arousal," I say. He slides his palms onto my thighs, tugging the fabric up further and sighs. I tremble, thinking he's going to chastise me for marking myself so viciously.

"It's beautiful," he says and shuffles backwards so he's on all fours staring at my work. He leans in and parts my knees, inhaling my dampening want. He reaches out and picks up one of my pens. A Rotring thick nib fountain pen. One of my favourites. "May I?" he asks tentatively and I am wide eyed at his request.

"Of course," I whisper, quivering. I lean back on my palms and spread my thighs wide. He is intense as he makes the first mark. A long sweeping scroll from knee to groin. I shudder as he stops short of my thickening pussy lips. I hold my breath and indulge in the sensation of the ink drying. That's it. That's the nirvana I'm after. It's such a subtle tiny triumph; you have to be in a very special place to perceive it. It's like being licked by a tiny angel. He does the same on the other leg, slower this time so it dries while he's still applying it, raising goose bumps in its wake and shooting a nerve tentacle of pleasure to the peak of my clitoris. The rising carries on its journey and I fill my chest with breath to meet it at the tip of my nipple before it retreats back to my pussy. He's on to a brush now. He swirls my Japanese sable bamboo onto the wet charcoal block, round and round until it's good and swollen with moisture. He bids me to unfurl my knees and lie back like a Vitruvian man.

He paints the soles of my feet, between my toes then over the arch and ankles. My whole being is centred in the tip of the cool fibres as he continues, swirling and caressing every dip and curve of my body. My stomach flutters as he makes his way over first one knee then the other, writing, drawing. I feel letters being teased onto me, then shapes and waves. I am losing myself in this slow careful ecstasy. At last the brush swoops over my mons, intertwining with my own curling fibres. My pussy is slick with desire now and I wish he would dip into me. I open my legs as wide as I can and tense my buttocks, forcing my entrance high. He obliges and sinks his face onto me, inhaling and breathing me in. He parts my thighs further with his forearms while a finger from each hand opens my plump ripe lips. He waits for a second or two, just watching my pussy twitch and contract in anticipation. I reach down and grab his hair, pulling him onto me, my bud, my cunt. He flattens his tongue down the whole length of my sex and I groan as he expertly points and darts into me then back to my clit where he swirls and laps and paints all the patterns he has made on my legs. Just as my inner muscles begin to convulse in that tell tale peaking, he stops and lifts his face away.

"You like to feel the ink drying, don't you," he says then blows gently onto me, ruffling my pelt. It is sublime. He crawls up over my body keeping my legs thrust apart with his own meaty thighs. I can see him bulging through his trousers. I know he wants me, I know I've turned him on. He pulls at his zipper and his cock falls out heavily, full with want and desire. A thick feral musk fills the room as our scents meet. I reach down to pleasure him but he grabs and pins me by the wrists over my head with one of his hands. With the other, he grabs his shaft and guides it to my opening. He lets go and just hovers there, pressing lightly until my pussy can bear the teasing no longer and I lift my hips to urge him inside. He releases his tension and sinks into my hot clutching depths and I can hear us both groaning in the distance as I become that point, that tiny point where everything begins. It is minuscule and expansive at the same time and he stretches me beyond myself as he thrusts in and out, faster and stronger until I feel raw with his ramming. He slides three of his artist's rough fingers into my mouth and mimics head until they are soaked with my saliva. He grabs my breast on the way back down and squeezes, causing me to squeal in pleasure as the shock waves travel to the desperate nub between my lips. With his fat cock buried deep inside me, he starts thrumming my clit with his three fingers, bringing me off in a flurry of heat and moisture. I breathe through each wave as they build and build until my pussy is spasming and my clit is peaking, and I'm thrashing about underneath him begging him to go on, to fuck me, give me everything. And he does. The surge comes from deep within his groin and out into me, spurting heat and wet and I clench around him not wanting to let him go.

He collapses on top of me and we pant softly together, our

hearts almost meeting through the boundary of our chests. Eventually he flops off to the side and closes his eyes, falling into a gentle twitching dose.

I sit up to look at the mess that has been made of my legs and the cloying shame of defiling myself threatens to spoil my bliss – until I see what he has drawn. On each thigh in the most exquisite design, two birds hold a delicate banner containing the most beautiful script. My breath is taken from me as I read the simple words:

I love you.

More about Tabitha Rayne

Tabitha Rayne has been told she is quirky, lovely and kinky – not necessarily in that order or by the same person. She writes erotic romance and as long as there's a love scene – she'll explore any genre.

Obsessed with sex and emotion, she loves to write stories that she hopes will tease and move you in equal measure. She also has a passion for drawing ladies in erotic situations.

Her short stories are included in anthologies from Xcite Books, Cleis Press, Burning Books Press, Ravenous Romance, HarperCollins Mischief, and House of Erotica. She has novels with Beachwalk Press and Xcite Books.

Links

Website: http://www.tabitharayne.co.uk
Twitter: http://www.twitter.com/tabithaerotica
Facebook: https://www.facebook.com/pages/Tabitha-Rayne-Author/158082444215098
Goodreads: https://www.goodreads.com/TabithaRayne
Pinterest: http://www.pinterest.com/pintabitha/

Praise for Tabitha Rayne

"Ms. Rayne lays out a feast of sexual pleasure that will please any reader." **Candy at Sensual Reads**

"Eroticism at its finest." **Sassy's Sex Toys Reviews**

"Just the feather to tickle the fancy of the reader who loves the forbidden." **Frishawn at Nocturne Romance**

Thank you for reading, we hope you enjoyed
Sexy Just Walked Into Town!

Find out more about The Brit Babes and their work at:
http://www.TheBritBabes.co.uk/
See you there!
xxx

Made in the USA
Charleston, SC
23 March 2014